To John

CW00829141

THE
YAKUZA'S COVENANT

All the best
and best wishes

MK LISTER

8. 9. 2018.

Martin the warrior

First Published in Great Britain 2018 by Mirador Publishing.

First edition: 2018

Any reference to real names and places are purely fictional and are constructs of the author. Any offence the references produce is unintentional and in no way reflects the reality of any locations or people involved.

ISBN: 978-1-912601-23-3

Mirador Publishing
10 Greenbrook Terrace
Taunton
Somerset
UK
TA1 1UT

The Yakuza's Covenant

By

MK Lister

CHAPTER 1

The smell of sweat was trailing its way through his nostrils and clinging to the back of his throat; it was mixed with an earthy stench of dust that was ground into the deeply grained wooden floor. The words *look at nothing and see everything* repeated over and over in his mind. He moved slowly forward, feeling each and every muscle tighten as his feet made contact with the ground. Another step and still nothing, the feeling of anticipation increased his heart rate as adrenalin rushed through his body. Another step, still nothing; his mouth began to dry, and his tongue to stick to the jagged edges of the chipped teeth inside. He tentatively edged his left foot forward with his toes clenching at the floor; the ball of his foot glided on the wood like a worn piece of sandpaper on a smooth timber beam. Gradually he placed almost all of his weight on his leading leg, holding back from a complete weight shift until he cleared the first door, then he slowly edged forward again; the corridor had six doors evenly distributed on both sides and all were fully opened. The light pierced through the last door on the left, illuminating the floating dust which hung in the air like a suspended spider's web ready to snare its unsuspecting prey.

He passed the second door, this time on the right hand side – two doors now and just stillness. He made his way past the third and fourth doors and reached the last pair. He was immediately aware of something different; stealthily he edged forward, closer and closer to the door with the light. The air at this point transmitted a tension, a tension he recognised as that which precedes an encounter.

His heart started to thump inside his chest, faster and faster as he fought with his body's natural instinct to turn and run. So many thoughts flooded through his mind; he knew he had to clear those thoughts to have a chance of success.

He was now at the door's edge, and before he could place his right foot on the ground the sound of a low pitch whoosh cracked the silence and scattered the glowing dust near the illuminated door. Without even realising it he had already twisted his right shoulder away from the oncoming weapon, his mind completely clear. He reacted instinctively and moved rapidly towards his attacker – his intention to take advantage of the momentum of the fast moving mass hurtling towards him. The reverse punch to the solar plexus and the open hand strike to the back of the neck sent the opponent spinning. His thoughts were now focused on the weapon; he knew this would swiftly fire back towards his head at lightning pace as his attacker regained his balance, and his glancing block was ready to divert the glistening black bokken flashing through the air, cutting the drifting dust like a fighter jet's wing cuts through a rain cloud.

With the execution of the block timed to perfection he caught his opponent off balance and swiftly released the weapon from his grasp. However, his attacker did not give up easily and quickly threw a roundhouse punch which connected with his ribs; wisely he knew that by absorbing that punch he could pull his opponent off balance and forward towards the ground to finish him with a stamping kick to the neck. The fatal blow is delivered and the attacker is disarmed.

"Yame," shouted Master Tokugawa. "Pick up your weapon and stand in line. You too, Michael."

Master Tokugawa barks out his commands.

"Everyone face the front and prepare to bow."

All twelve karateka stand to attention. Beads of sweat glisten on all of those assembled, and as the sun continues to beam in through the windows, the sweat trickles down their faces falling towards the dojo floor like pearls of incandescent light contained in a capsule of dew; not one of them dare wipe their faces for fear of punishment. The drips of perspiration explode on the wooden floor creating shiny patches dappled on the sunlit surface, but still no one remotely flinches.

Finally they are told to relax – that today's lesson for the junior class is over, and they should shower quickly before the arrival of the next class: the class to follow is for those aged over sixteen – the seniors – and Michael who stands among the ranks, often trains in both classes due to his advanced ability.

"Michael, your father has arrived," shouts Master Tokugawa.

"Can you inform him there is a letter on my desk for him to collect, the desk in my office?"

"No problem, I will let him know," replied Michael.

"Are you joining in with the sword training at the end of the seniors' class, Michael?" asked Master Tokugawa.

"Your technique has vastly improved since you started training with the seniors; there is no mistaking that you are Doug Harris's son, that's for sure."

"Yes I will be," replied Michael.

Michael headed down the corridor and out of the door at the end of the dojo; he was heading to his father to relay the message from Master Tokugawa. His father would be waiting as always in the warm up area adjacent to the dojo itself.

The Sekigahara dojo was purpose built for all the different types of martial arts that Master Tokugawa, Michael's father, and all the other instructors taught. It was named after the battle of Sekigahara which took place in 1600, clearing the way for the establishment of the Tokugawa Shogun. Renowned as the largest and most successful dojo in Tokyo, it contained many specialist training areas and numerous rooms equipped with weapons, kick bags and mook jongs. It was kitted out solely for the purpose of intense martial arts combat and self-defence instruction.

Michael needed to visit the toilet before he met with his father. He was there a short while; it was while he was in there that he heard a muffled noise coming from the dojo outside the door.

What happened next would completely change the way Michael lived the rest of his life.

The dull sounds of cracks and thuds were coming from the dojo, and these were accompanied by loud ear piercing screams. These screams, however, were not screams of pain. Michael instantly recognised the screams as screams of spirit and aggression; these were what the Japanese call a Kiai, a shout from deep inside the stomach used when attacking an opponent. On hearing this commotion from inside the toilets, Michael immediately knew that something was terribly wrong.

His chest tightened as his heart thumped against his ribcage. The sound of his beating heart made him think of the noise a leather bound drum would make if beaten rapidly with a cotton covered drum stick. The noise was so intense he could hear the pounding in his head.

This was no training session occurring in the dojo – the sounds were sounds of intense fighting and death and he knew he needed to confront it, or run.

That decision was rapidly taken away from him as the sound of screeching car tyres sped away from the drive; Michael presumed that whoever had been there had left as quickly as they had arrived. As he made his way along the corridor to the door which led to the dojo, he was racked with fear over what he would see on the other side.

There was now an eerie silence that was not normally associated with Master Tokugawa's Sekigahara dojo. It was always a place of hustle, bustle and commotion, but right now there was a stark silence.

He reached the door and slowly turned the handle. Because of the lack of oil on the lever, the handle creaked like it always had, but on this occasion that noise resonated like the sound of a car horn in a library because of the deathly quiet. Michael tentatively pushed the door until it slowly swung open. It then carried on opening under its own weight, the creaking of the stiff hinges punching through the silent air, the only sound present until the door came to an abrupt halt as its underside scraped along the dust covered floor.

Michael's jaw fell slowly downward from his bone dry mouth.

"No, no, no," he breathlessly said.

He wanted to shout but could not make a sound with his voice; his mouth was paralysed with fear. The carnage was everywhere in the room. All the instructors and karateka students were lying on the floor, their gis were gleaming white from the reflecting sun piercing its way through the windows; but the white was fractured by the bright red blood which appeared to be bursting from inside each body. No one in the dojo was moving. Master Tokugawa and everyone else in the room appeared to be dead. Michael immediately thought of his father.

Running down the corridor towards the warm up area he shouted to his father.

"Dad, Dad, are you there? Dad please answer, are you there?"

He continued to run towards the warm up area and burst through the door.

The same fate had befallen his father as had all the others in the dojo.

His father's gi was torn away from the shoulder as if there had been a vicious struggle; he was lying face down and across his back was a foot long gash. The gash resembled a painted red river meandering all the way down his back; this river of dark red blood was still running. His father's blood was oozing out of multiple wounds on his body – erupting volcanic vents spewing molten lava from various holes in the mountain side to form a lake at the bottom. The lake was the shining puddle of blood sprawled along the dojo floor.

"Please, no, no. Dad speak to me, speak to me," Michael shouted as he heaved at his father's body to turn him over. He struggled to lift him, but somehow managed to prop him up against Master Tokugawa's office desk. Surprisingly his father was still alive, and gasping for air while choking on his own blood: his gasps were echoing round the room at the speed of a heartbeat, each beat accompanied by the squeeze of air from his father's throat.

Michael leaned forward and tried to reassure his father and as he did so his father pulled him towards his mouth. Michael could sense his father's whole body tensed up, shaking uncontrollably.

His final words slowly exhaled from his mouth.

"Yakuza."

At the very point the word was spoken his father's shaking stopped. His final sound had resembled air spluttering through the bubbling water of a blocked pipe. It was his father's last gasp of life; then once again all fell silent.

"No, why? Why?" Michael's voice rang out all around the building, as he screamed the same words over and over.

He ran down the stairs and out onto the street, screaming for help, but no one came; all the houses had their shutters and blinds closed. He knocked on the doors of the houses closest to the dojo shouting as loud as he could. "Help! Someone please help! Everyone in the dojo has been killed! Please help me."

Still there was no response, not a flicker from a blind, not a twitch from a curtain, no one who lived nearby wanted to know. It was too much for Michael to take and he fell to his knees clutching his face, then overwhelmed by grief, he flopped onto his side and curled his body into a ball on the pavement in front of the dojo. Finally a passing car pulled over, whereupon a man and a young girl quickly ran over to see what was wrong.

"Can we help you?" exclaimed the driver of the car.

"What has happened?" the girl cried. "Why are you covered in blood, are you hurt?"

"No, I'm okay, but please, you must phone the police, there has been a massacre inside the dojo." Michael pointed to the dojo entrance, "In there."

The girl quickly ran towards the payphone on the other side of the street and began to phone for help.

Before she returned from the payphone Michael turned, lifted his head from his hands and slowly sat up. He quickly turned his head towards the dojo and muttered to himself,

"The letter, I must get the letter."

With the agility of a gazelle escaping from the swipe of a cheetah's hooked paw, he leapt to his feet and sprinted back to the sensei's office. He bounded up the stairs two at a time, pulling himself up with the rail at great speed. Bursting into the office he swiftly lunged towards the desk where he discovered what he was looking for – a white envelope with the words 'Doug Harris' written on the front. He had no idea what was in the letter or whether it would have any significant meaning to what had happened that day; all that concerned Michael was that he needed to take that letter with him. Ignoring the carnage all around him he grasped the envelope, concealed it inside his gi and made a sharp exit from the building.

The barrage of noise that greeted him, deafened him the same way his large steel belled alarm clock did when it woke him every morning before the school day. The sirens on the Japanese police cars were ringing mercilessly inside his head. The sound was amplified as they approached the road outside the dojo.

"Where have you been? I called the police and you disappeared," the girl from the car suspiciously questioned.

"I needed to retrieve something I had left behind," Michael explained, his hands extended in a calming gesture. "It was important to me."

At that moment the police cars screamed around the bend at the end of the street and the whole area immediately in front of the dojo was draped in a blanket of incandescent red flashing lights, accompanied by the deafening sound of stuttering sirens which individually stopped like a wheezing old man would stop after each constricted breath.

The man who accompanied the girl in the car approached the police and directed them towards the dojo. The girl with him brought the police over to Michael, who by this time was leaning up against the wall that skirted the driveway leading to the dojo. A mature and athletic looking senior police officer walked towards Michael, at the same time indicating to the girl to talk to his junior officers and share any relevant information.

"Are you the young man that witnessed what happened here?"

Michael quickly straightened his posture out of respect for this man's authority.

"I was there, sir, but I did not witness anything. It happened while I was at the toilet and then… and then… it, it, it…"

Michael began to struggle forming his words.

"It's okay, son, you're safe now, it's all over, calm yourself down," the officer reassured Michael.

In Michael's mind, after hearing his father's last words, he could only think that this was just the beginning of a terrible time for him.

"What's your full name?"

"Michael."

"What is your full name please? I know you are shaken up by this, but we need to know who you are and who the people inside were."

"Michael, Michael."

No matter how much he shouted, the officer was not going to extract anything from his only witness at this point; a shocked and very pale boy stood like a rabbit would stand while being harried by a weasel before its inevitable capture; stunned and lifeless.

"May Lin." The officer waved his colleague over from the other side of the road. "You and Jozin take the boy to the station and get him a hot drink and something to eat; he has witnessed carnage here today and is in deep shock. Try to find out who and where his parents are if you can and keep him secure. If this nasty business is the work of who I think it is, he could be the next target – he is the only witness."

"Okay, sir. Have we any idea what could be the motive for this?" May Lin enquired.

The officer twisted his lips to one side, clasped his hands together and slowly placed them on top of his closely shaven head; he began to shake his head slowly from side to side.

"Not a clue. But I would hazard a guess at gambling or drugs. Or maybe even both; I'm hoping the boy can fill in the blanks."

The two officers gently coaxed Michael into the police car and headed off to the Shinjuku district police station. Leaning back over the passenger seat May Lin consoled Michael.

"Don't worry; we will have you re-united with your parents back at the station as soon as you can help us to contact them. It would really help if you could tell us your father's or mother's address and telephone number."

Michael gazed out of the rear side window of the car; he could smell the stench of stale sweat on the cheap seat covers inside; someone had tried in vain to eliminate the smell with a lemon fragranced car cleaning product, but all it achieved was to mix the two in a pungent cocktail. Then the odour of sweat seemed to overpower the other smell and it began to galvanise his thoughts. He turned his head towards May Lin sitting in the front seat. The smell reminded him of the smell at the end of a Jiyu Kumite fighting session back at the dojo; that smell of mature sweat rekindled his thoughts of everyone ensconced in their routines earlier in the day, with no idea of the carnage that was soon to follow.

May Lin spoke reassuringly to Michael.

"What is it, Michael? What can you tell me? Please let me help."

Their car pulled up at the traffic lights and stopped with barely a sound from the engine. Michael's words broke the silence in the car.

"My father is dead."

The silence returned after this revelation – only to be dramatically broken by an ear splitting clamour– a sound as piercing as the screech of a squealing pig. It was the incessant sound of a moped horn blasting out from behind the car in which they were sitting. The moped rider's impatience at the car's inactivity following the light change from red to green prompted Jozin to leap out of the driver's seat with his police badge fervently grasped in his hand; he thrust it into the moped rider's face.

"Unless you want to be wearing this up your arsehole, I suggest you stop blasting that heap of shit's horn." The rider immediately stopped blasting his horn and sped off away from the lights waving his hand in a gesture of defiance.

Jozin apologised.

"Sorry about that. I guess the red mist came down there. Come on, let's get you to the station, Michael."

No sooner had he uttered the words, when an almighty crack rang out inside the car, then again and again.

"Jesus Christ what's happening?" screamed May Lin.

She screamed again.

"Jozin! Drive the god damn car quick! Get us out of here now." The cracks were gun shots, and the bullets ripped into the car piercing the metal body with the ease of a screw driver puncturing an empty *Coke* can. Each cracking sound was followed by a muffled thud as the bullets embedded themselves in the soft parts on the inside of the car. May Lin tugged at Jozin's arm, shouting at him to drive; he slumped to her side revealing a hole in his throat which was pulsing blood onto his shoulder.

Michael noticed the horror on May Lin's face as she registered that her colleague was dead.

He quickly observed that the red car which was speeding past them had a man leaning out of the window with a gun in his hands; his piercing glare drew Michael to him. Something averted Michael's gaze from his evil sunken eyes; it was a huge and bright tattoo of an orange tiger weaving across his arm. Michael had no time to be shocked by what was happening. With some panic he registered the car's brake lights at the end of the street – brightly illuminated and menacingly red – followed by two billowing puffs of smoke the size of small clouds gushing from the tyres.

"They're coming back. May Lin! May Lin!"

Michael shouted at the top of his voice, surprisingly now May Lin was the one in shock. "May Lin!" Michael grabbed at her arm and twisted her to face the back of the car, and her body crumpled in two like a folded broadsheet. Michael looked her in the eyes and spoke very slowly and very firmly.

"You need to drive the car or we are both going to die, right here and right now." May Lin gazed vacantly into Michael's eyes and the words slurred from her mouth.

"They will never stop."

Michael's anger took over.

"That might be true, whatever that means. But I was taught from a very early age to fight my corner and that's exactly what I'm going to do."

Michael swiftly leaned over from the back seat and pulled the door handle on the driver's side door. With a determined effort he pushed Jozin out of the car onto the roadside. Leading May Lin's hand, he placed it on the steering wheel, pushed her into the driver's seat and pleaded with her to drive. By now the other car was accelerating up the road towards them, closer and closer.

"For God's sake drive the car, May Lin. Drive, drive." Michael yelled until his inflamed face looked like it would burst at any moment.

The speeding car was within fifty yards of their rear bumper when Michael felt the car move. Their police car screeched away from the junction, leaving a cloud of dust and smoking rubber. Michael looked back at the congested intersection through the rear window of the car. The road was full of traffic stopping to attend to the body at the traffic lights. The whole area was a jumble of cars, smoke and pedestrians. As quickly as it had begun, the attack was over and Michael and May Lin could, for now, evade the people trying to kill them. They raced away from the scene until they were far enough removed to be out of sight. They began their approach to the road that would lead them to the police station and relative safety.

As other police officers met May Lin and Michael at the entrance, Inspector Bando was also returning to the station from the dojo having already been informed en route of the incident at the traffic lights. Michael helped to guide May Lin into the police station.

"She's in shock," he pleaded.

The desk sergeant gave a bewildered reply:

"Who are you? You're not the boy they brought back from the Sekigahara dojo are you?"

"Yes," Michael replied, surprised that the police sergeant needed to ask that question after all the commotion. The desk sergeant gave Michael a long disdainful stare.

"A man like you will bring trouble here."

It was bad enough for Michael to be glared at, but worse still to be looked upon as the cause of all that commotion. Michael did not bother to deliberate with the desk sergeant over any of his remarks and he was very much used to being mistaken for a full grown man. He already stood six feet five inches tall, with a matured face for someone so young; a face weathered in the same way a mountain is weathered by the attrition of wind-blown sand. He already wore that roughened look, made worse by the deep scar on his right cheekbone from a misdirected knife during his English schooldays. His large and athletic physique combined with his gravel etched looks, were deceptive, suggesting a man older than his real years. Though often seen as advantageous and enviable by children of a similar age, at times like this it could be a heavy burden to carry on such young shoulders.

The desk sergeant growled a command at Michael.

"Take a seat in Inspector Bando's office. I'll get a hot drink sent down for you."

"Why are you being so mean to me?" Michael questioned cautiously.

"Jozin was a good man and because of you he's dead," the desk sergeant retorted bluntly. Infuriated, Michael turned and faced him.

"My father was a good man, and so was my instructor and every other person who was killed in that dojo. Do you think I could have done anything to prevent that or what happened to Jozin? Your other officer and I were nearly wiped out on the way here and I have no idea why that is and you're blaming me, are you for real?"

The desk sergeant reared up and raced around the desk the way a tornado would hurl its way around a prairie field. He lunged towards Michael, arms extended and hands open like grappling irons. Before he was able to grab him, Michael had twisted to his side, moving his body towards the floor, his leg thrust back from his body. As he continued to twist his body further round, he swept his leg completely under the desk sergeant's two feet, hurling him up in the air; the desk sergeant was catapulted upwards into a foetus shaped figure and rapidly began his descent towards the floor whereupon Michael was waiting to crunch his fist into his crumpled face. The thud of the landing came first and before Michael could land his telling blow, a voice rang out in the room.

"Oy, what the hell's going on?" Inspector Bando had arrived back at the station and he quickly took control of the situation. "Get yourself home, Sergeant, before you end up with your head cracked open. I will deal with you in the morning. Go on, hurry up, get out." Inspector Bando barked his command.

"As if we haven't had enough shit to deal with this evening, then we go fighting our witnesses in the station. I can't believe what I have just seen." He pointed at Michael. "Come with me, young man." Inspector Bando spun around and dropped his head back before shouting,

"Someone bring some drinks to my office." Inspector Bando directed Michael towards his office, one hand grasping a clutch of documents which were slipping from his grip, and the other hand holding a padded black jacket.

"Here, put that on." He threw the jacket for Michael to put on over his karate gi. He then proceeded to drop his paperwork which skidded across the floor in his office, with an earth shattering clatter, like a jar of dried spaghetti scattering on a floor of terracotta tiles. The sound was irritating to Michael who was now beginning to tire after the traumas of the day, and he was beginning to feel agitated over even the slightest thing.

"Listen, Michael, we need to get as much of what you know written down while it is fresh in your mind. So please, just relax and try to co-operate. Okay?"

Michael at this point was sweeping up the dropped papers with his hands; as he placed the chaotic pile on the inspector's desk, his attention was suddenly alerted as his eyes scanned the words

'Multi Casino' scribbled almost illegibly, adjacent to the name Doug Harris. He quickly bundled the papers together and moved away from the inspector's desk.

The inspector ushered the papers to one side and slid the quickly served mug of tea across his desk, a desk that was polished to such a shine that Michael could see his face in the varnish. It was surrounded by the dazzling reflection of lights shining down inside the brightly lit room.

"Get that down you. It's a mug of sweet English tea – it will make you feel better."

Michael felt more comfortable with the inspector and replied respectfully,

"Thank you, Inspector, and I'm sorry about Jozin. It wasn't my fault."

"Forget that now. Jozin was a good man and he knew this area well. He made a bad choice getting out of that car at the lights. It cost him time and that cost him his life. The guy on the moped was doing a job – his job was to mark you out as the target for the gunmen. Jozin unintentionally handed your assailants extra minutes to allow them to get at you."

"Is Officer May Lin okay?"

"She has been very shaken by all of this, but she tells me you did well back there. You acted very maturely in a situation which would have fazed most kids your age; is that what the martial arts teach you?"

"I guess so,"

Michael responded, almost in a whisper as he desperately tried to make sense of the information he had just been given.

His thoughts were interrupted as Inspector Bando pushed his chair along the floor behind him, the screech created mimicked the high-pitch screech of the wheels of a train braking abruptly on a track. The squeal of the noise immediately focused Michael's mind, as if the inspector had intended to get his full attention, he stood up and walked to the side of the table near to where Michael was sitting and slowly plonked his backside down on the table.

"Your instructor had a tremendous reputation in the martial arts world, as did your father. For them to be wiped out like that doesn't sit right with me. I think they knew their attackers and what's more they trusted them to allow them to get that close."

The inspector was drilling his gaze deep into the back of Michael's eyes. "And I think because of that you may know who they are too."

Michael began to shake; he wanted to scream out the words he had heard his father utter in his last breath, but something stopped him.

Maybe he didn't trust the inspector that much after all; maybe he could trust no one?

"Think back to that moment at the dojo. Close your eyes and try to remember the sounds, the smells, anything you saw that was unusual," the inspector said hopefully.

Michael was well aware of the list of unusual occurrences from today: the letter, the final words of his father, the tattoo of the gunman, and he was also certain that he did not want to reveal anything to the police.

"It's all just a blur, I can't focus my mind on anything, I can't see anything but darkness, I'm sorry."

Michael may have been young, but he knew that corruption was rife in the district police. And if this was the work of the Yakuza, and Michael felt certain that it was, telling the police could seal his own fate. Moreover, he also knew that irrespective of what he did or didn't say, his fate could already be sealed.

"Come on, Michael," the inspector said, clearly resigned to the fact that his questioning was leading nowhere.

"I'll take you to a safe location myself tonight and we can arrange for your mother to come and meet you there."

"My mother is in England with her partner." Michael uttered the words and then his few youthful years showed through his tough exterior. His cold tears meandered down his cheeks and dispersed onto his parched lips; the whole day had now overwhelmed him and he yearned for rest.

The inspector raised his hand and placed it slowly on Michael's drooped head. He patted it delicately.

"I will go and get my car and take you to a safe house. May Lin will come and look after you there. I was not aware your mother was not in Japan; maybe you can shed some light on why that is after you get some rest."

The inspector handed Michael a tightly scrunched up handkerchief from his pocket.

"Dry your eyes on that. I will return in a few minutes."

As the inspector exited the room he shouted for May Lin to come over and sit with Michael.

"You're not going to be happy with me are you?" Michael said to her as she entered the room. "I am deeply sorry for your partner."

May Lin sat opposite Michael and looked over to where he was sitting. She snaked her hair around her long elegant fingers, revealing her dark red painted fingernails and the miniature white dragons tattooed on the inside of her beautifully arched thumbs. She gathered her hair quickly with a magician like flick of the wrist and whisked it into a perfect pony tail. Michael was drawn to her jet black hair glinting in the office light and couldn't help but admire the svelte curves of her athletic physique. Her fitted beige suit and white shirt caressed her figure, while her trousers swirled all the way to her feet, meeting her black high heels to complete the curved cascade.

Michael's eyes followed the heel of her shoe to the floor where the sharp tip mimicked an ink pen marking a full stop precisely onto a crisp white sheet of paper.

"Can you keep your eyes up here please? You're too young to be giving looks like that." Her words reality checked the atmosphere.

"Sorry. I don't mean to be offensive." Michael nervously squeezed out his words.

"Let's forget it. I should be thanking you for pulling us through that situation at the lights; Jozin was unpredictable: I always worried what his next move would be and that's a worrying way to be in our job."

The inspector shouted from the door,

"Let's go, we're heading out the back to the car, then on to the safe house. May Lin you will need to stay there with Michael tonight."

"Where are you going?" May Lin enquired.

"I need to head over to the other side of town; we have a lead in this case. Michael you need to phone your mother tonight. It looks like you will be heading back to England."

Michael's grimacing expression said everything.

"England? Are you serious? What's going on? Why a safe house?"

"Where else? I've just been informed that without a parent or guardian we can't keep you here; anyway it may be safer for you to be out of this country as soon as possible. But until then, the safe house is for your own protection." The inspector held his hands in the air in acceptance of defeat.

May Lin turned to put her hand on the nape of Michael's neck and guided him gently towards the door. As she withdrew her hand, a scented plume of air feathered Michael's face, leaving a mixture of coolness blended with a youthful alluring perfume.

"Grab the jacket and follow me, Michael; it may be a good idea to stick these sunglasses and cap on too. Hurry now."

The car was ready in an underground car park and they quickly exited the offices and left the police station at great speed. Within minutes they were leaving the dazzling orange lights of the town and were heading along unlit roads in the countryside.

"Michael, Michael, wake up. Wake up, we're here."

May Lin was stroking Michael's face. He noticed how much more tactile May Lin had become with him, showing unreserved compassion and on this occasion it helped to rouse him from a deep sleep; however it did not prevent the heavy burden thumping back to the front of his mind. As he moved his head lethargically from its resting place on the damp window of the car the reality of the day hit him. He had lost not only his father but also good friends and the emotional numbness he was experiencing as a result was overwhelming.

"This is the house; we need to quickly move inside. I have a holdall of clothes which we had lying around in lost property, you need to have a look through it and maybe find something your size. We have an odd giant or two frequenting the station."

As May Lin spoke those words she was looking into Michael's eyes and awaiting a reaction. Michael raised an eyebrow the way a scorpion would arch its tail when threatened by danger, but then quickly realised that May Lin was smiling. He acknowledged her smile and swiftly reciprocated, to the delight of May Lin.

The inspector drove the car slowly down the drive, away from the safe house; he kept the headlights switched off, and quickly disappeared behind the roadside hedge as he made his way onto the main road before he switched his lights on. The main beam illuminated the sky with nothing short of the amount of brightness an air raid light would produce when prepared to highlight enemy aircraft during a World War Two bombing raid. Michael looked back to hear the sound of the inspector's car accelerating away into the distance observing the peculiar uneven trace the lights made in the darkness. As the lights disappeared out of sight the area around the house fell completely black.

May Lin made her way up the wooden steps onto the deck surrounding the front of the house. As Michael followed her into the darkness an overpowering stench forced him to instinctively clench his finger and thumb over his nose.

"What's that awful smell?"

May Lin replied,

"It's the pig farm in the field behind the house. Don't worry – when you're inside and the doors are closed the smell will disappear."

The inside of the house had a homely and rustic feel to it, with an open fire nestled into a green slate inglenook, with years of baked jet black soot smoothing out the edges of the bricks at the rear of the fire. An old split bamboo rug was sprawled out across the length of the floor in front of the hearth and the lounge area had a very basic range of low set brown leather furniture facing the area of the fire. The walls leading to the small kitchen and the two bedrooms were covered with the décor that would be found in a traditional Japanese home, however the owner of this cottage had not quite completed the transformation from the original cottage.

"Whose house is this?" Michael asked.

"It belonged to the inspector's mother, and he is now halfway through converting it to a ryokan. I will set the fire to get it warmed up in here and get us some hot water for a shower," May Lin replied as she locked and bolted the door behind her before drawing the blinds.

"Yes I could do with a clean-up too."

Michael was desperate to cleanse himself of the toils and troubles of the day.

"Where is the phone? I'll need to call my mother in England and let her know I will be on a flight home tomorrow; that will cheer her up." Michael pulled his face into a twisted grimace.

"She probably won't be too unhappy when I inform her of my father's demise."

"Their relationship sounds like it was embroiled in a great deal of bitterness," May Lin replied, curiously.

"That's an understatement," Michael said.

"Let me know how it goes when I come out of the shower." May Lin then turned and headed into the bathroom closing the door behind her.

Michael was somewhat apprehensive about phoning.

He had left his home town of Sunderland to be with his father around five years ago at the age of ten. His father had informed Michael at the time that he was accepting a posting to Japan with the company he worked for in Sunderland, and this coincided with Michael's mother having an affair and consequently insisting on a divorce from him. His father often told him how he loved the North East of England, but knew he could not remain in his home town with Michael's mother co-habiting with another man, a man who Michael's father often referred to as a drunken bum.

Michael had always shared his father's passion for karate and Japanese weapons training, so when he was given the choice to either stay at home or follow his father to Japan, there would be only one outcome, much to the sadness of his mother. The opportunity to learn from the Japanese senseis in all the varieties of martial arts and weapons training was too great an attraction for him. But right now he needed to inform his mother he was returning home and he truly had no idea how she would react. He picked up the phone receiver and slowly scraped his fingers around the clear plastic dial. Each time his finger pulled back on the dial, he was mulling over what he would tell his mother, and when the last number to be dialled was spinning back around the phone, he shook with trepidation as he wondered what respect his mother would show for his father.

He waited while the ringing echoed through the receiver.

His mother answered,

"Hello."

"Mam. It's Michael."

His mother was silent for a few seconds.

"This is a pleasant surprise. And to what do I owe the pleasure?" More silence followed.

"My father's dead... and... and... I need to come home, Mam." Michael spoke the words and could barely grasp the reality of the situation and what he had just said. An intense pain rhythmically beat its way around the inside of his head; he imagined a swirl of wind spinning inside his skull, creating the sound a tornado would make as it picked sand up from the ground of a parched desert.

He was lost in his own thoughts and confused by the reality of what was happening to him. He was thrust back to reality by his mother's soft voice.

"How did it happen? How did your father die?" His mother tried to show compassion, but Michael knew it was a hollow gesture. He began to tell her, but was stopped in his tracks by the words from his mother's mouth as her soft tone swiftly changed.

"It'll have been that stupid sword fighting was it? Stupid hobby, I always said that would come to no good." Before his mother could draw breath, she continued on a tirade of insults and derogatory remarks about Michael's father.

Michael brought her to an abrupt halt.

"Mother, will you please stop talking like that about my dad? It's not the right time for it – we can talk about it tomorrow evening when I come home," Michael said abruptly.

"Blimey, you're coming home tomorrow? Why so soon?"

"Mother, I'm not yet sixteen, I can't exactly stay here can I?" Michael shouted down the phone.

"Besides, I think the people who killed my father are trying to kill me."

His mother yelled her retort, "Bloody hell. What the hell has he been up to over there? Someone killed him? I knew he was no good, why do yah think I left him?"

"Enough. Mother please; enough. I'm weary of all this already. I will be heading home to Porter Street in the morning, expect a knock at the door sometime tomorrow evening," and with those words Michael crashed the phone down on to its cradle, his hand frozen to the receiver like a raptor's claw gripping its freshly killed prey, never to let go.

The silence gave him time to gather his thoughts, but those thoughts were short-lived, as other delicate words broke the silence, they feathered their way slowly up his neck, enveloping his ears and stripping away all the tension of the phone call.

"Why don't you get yourself a hot shower and relax? I will have a nice hot drink of tea waiting for you when you are finished." May Lin's soft words calmed the tension in the room. Michael turned around, drawn in by the silkiness of May Lin's voice.

She was folded in a soft fur dressing gown that nestled just above her knee, her sallow coloured skin contrasting with the black gown she was wearing. Her soaking wet, long black hair draped over both of her shoulders, weaving down through the fur on her dressing gown like an icy mountain river carving its way through a steep dark rock face. Her eyes were reflecting the soft orange lighting in the room, giving a warm welcoming glow that transported Michael a long way from the thoughts of his phone call. His gaze once again drifted down her body, admiring every curve of her breasts, then her waist and hips, flowing all the way to her smooth petite legs.

On this occasion May Lin did not make any comment about Michael's age, as he watched her intently, but she quietly repeated her instruction.

"Please get a shower, and don't be long."

Michael looked at May Lin and was old enough to know she wanted him next to her.

"What do you fear?" Michael asked.

"It's nothing, Michael; just don't be long, please," May Lin insisted.

"Okay I won't, but then you need to tell me what is bothering you."

Once Michael had finished showering, he grabbed the clothes that May Lin had brought him and quickly got dressed. He had a quick look at his face in the mirror, and his reflection confirmed what he suspected – he had physically aged after what had happened today, and he shook his head in disbelief. He quickly brushed his hair back from his face while it was still wet and walked into the room where May Lin was waiting. He was not expecting the reception he received – She burst into uncontrollable laughter, cupping her hands up to her mouth.

"Oh my God." She sat up from the low slung chair.

"Have you seen how you look in those clothes?" She continued to laugh to the point where she was fighting back her tears. Michael was expecting something completely different when he walked through the door, but because he had been checking how his face looked in the mirror, he had forgotten to check how he looked in the borrowed clothes. Before he could lower his head to take a look at himself, a giggling May Lin grabbed him by the arm and dragged him back in front of the bathroom mirror. Michael could now see why May Lin was bent double with laughter, belly laughing at him.

"I desperately need to call at home for some clothes before we head to the airport, bloody Yakuza or not," Michael grumbled.

The clothes May Lin had brought in the bag would probably struggle to fit a man of five feet tall, let alone six feet five inches. To add insult to injury, the top was coloured with blue and white horizontal stripes, and the tight white trousers he was unflatteringly poured into, clung to every undulation on his body.

"I look like a stick of Blackpool rock," Michael said, he too was now laughing profusely.

May Lin by now was stood alongside Michael in the full length mirror, tugging at the side of his tight pants with one hand and holding herself up on his shoulder with the other.

"That's hilarious, Michael. It seems like a long time since I have had the opportunity to smile like this, not to mention laughing like this." And with those words she reached up to his face with her hand and slowly placed her forefinger on his scar. Her nail slipped down the side of it, following the line of the scar to the end, like a fairground helter-skelter, which would send a rider spiralling down the slide to the bottom.

"You're a rough diamond, Michael, but a very sexy one, and it seems, a good guy to boot."

Michael turned his head towards May Lin and as soon as she made contact with his eyes, he leaned forward to firmly touch her lips with his.

"Stop, Michael." May Lin spoke softly.

"Please don't, I would be in big trouble."

"Why? Because I'm under age?" Michael replied naively.

"No not because of that, Michael, well yes, but..." she answered hesitantly.

"But what? Is this what has been bothering you?" Michael cautiously questioned. He wanted to know if it wasn't his age, then what was it?

"For God's sake, Michael I'm meant to be protecting you and ensuring you get safe passage to the airport tomorrow, not sleeping with you. If this got out, I would be disgraced."

"So you're bothered about your reputation, is that it?" Michael gave a terse reply.

May Lin turned away and moved towards the orange flames of the fire with her head drooped forward and her arms tightly crossed.

"I like you, Michael; you have calmness about you which takes me away from this mad world I work in." May Lin continued to speak, but remained facing away from Michael.

"The way you reacted at the traffic lights," she paused,

"I know grown men who would have frozen with fear if they were put in that situation and you handled it with such composure. And the way you reacted at the station." But before she could utter another word May Lin felt a firm but reassuring hand rest on her shoulder. Michael slowly moved his hand from her shoulder and down her arm, capturing every tingling sensation of warmth in his fingertips as he touched her. His wrist twisted to follow every contour of her arm the way a silk scarf might weave its way through the air when teased from a woman's neck. He repeated this with his other hand and was now standing directly behind her, both of his arms enveloping both of hers.

He slowly nudged his cheek along the side of her neck, sensing the silky soft hair swirling from her head around her ear. He held her hands firm and kissed her scented skin. He pulled her tightly towards him and squeezed his aroused body against her perfectly shaped figure. May Lin's next few words aroused Michael to a heightened state of excitement.

"Don't stop," she urged him.

Michael twirled her around to face him as easily as you would twirl an ice cream cone to catch the ice cream before it dripped onto your hand. He was still clutching her hands tightly in his, but was gently persuaded to let go by May Lin's tender guidance. "Ease up, tough guy, I'm only delicate."

She pulled his arms around her back; he could feel every undulating curve of her svelte body. She could feel him pulling her in closer, as he kissed her firmly on her welcoming lips. He peeled away her dressing gown and laid it down on the tatami mat below her, her naked body was illuminated by the dancing orange flames from the log fire, highlighting every smooth edge of her beautiful form. He slowly guided her to the floor. She quietly giggled and sprayed the softly lit room with her smile. "Would you like me to help you with your extremely tight clothes?"

"Yes, thanks. Have I ruined the moment?" Michael asked.

"Definitely not," May Lin said reassuringly.

She took his hand and pushed it towards the inside of her legs. He gently moved his hand up to where she wanted it to be and began moving her legs apart. May Lin clung to Michael's bare back and pulled him closer to her, sinking her long nails into his skin; He was now deep inside her, revelling in the sensation his body was feeling from this intimacy. His eyes were fixed to every movement and every expression on her face as she once again smoothed the sharp flickers of the fire's flames with her soft smile. Michael moved his head close to hers and took a deep breath to indulge in every moment and relish the aroma of her hair.

His nose twitched at the smell he now encountered. It wasn't the smell of perfume. It was the smell of pig manure: Michael immediately froze. His heart missed a beat and very quickly began thumping against the inside of his chest. He whispered into May Lin's ear,

"Stay completely still and don't follow me when I look away." Michael pushed his head deep into her hair near her neck, gradually edging his lips along the skin on her collarbone towards her shoulder. This subtle manoeuvre enabled him to look towards the door, and he cautiously lifted his eyes to the left.

"What is it, Michael? You're scaring me."

"Shh." He pushed his forefinger over May Lin's mouth.

"Someone is opening the door."

Michael was now watching the door gradually open and knew he needed to move away from May Lin to have any chance of confronting whatever it was that was making its way into the room. He crept his knees forward and tentatively lifted his body away from the floor without giving away that he was aware of someone being there; a second glancing look allowed him to catch a glimpse of a silver flash of light piercing its way through a gap in the door, reminiscent of the ancient warning flash cattlemen would make by reflecting sunlight off a mirror to warn of an imminent red Indian attack. When it flashed again, bouncing the fire light back into the room, Michael recognised the approaching shape, and this instant identification set his heart racing faster still. It was the polished silvery blade of a katana.

At that very moment the door was flung open rattling the blind fixed to the back of it and clattering the door handle against the wall. In ran a masked assailant wielding the glistening weapon. Michael yelled at May Lin,

"Get out of the way!" He grabbed her arm and threw her across the room, placing himself directly in front of the oncoming attacker, who had both hands fixed around the bone handle of his katana. His arms were held above his shoulders and he was bearing down with the katana blade towards Michael's head. The katana thundered past him, just missing his head, and slashed down towards his naked body, glancing across the edge of his side, slicing a wafer thin piece of Michael's skin and flesh away with the sweep of the blade. Michael exhaled a roar of pain, but with that pain came the blood rush that surged within him, and the overpowering need to survive from within his inner self. The attacker had not missed Michael with the katana; instead Michael - like the fluid bones of a cat evading capture - had slipped his body away from the lethal edge of the blade. The katana crashed down onto the tatami mat slicing its way through May Lin's gown and splintering the tatami mat obliquely to all parts of the room.

Only now could Michael see the attacker's form; he was completely blacked out from head to toe. Michael knew from all the lessons he had endured with katana training that the attacker had over committed his body and was off balance. In an instant Michael turned his own body to follow that of the attacker's, and sensing his opportunity he crunched his knee into his assailant's solar plexus with such force that the attacker blurted saliva and air from his mouth and dropped the katana. Although in considerable pain, his attacker still twisted his body up towards Michael and unleashed a roundhouse punch square into Michael's ribs. The resulting pain was immediate and needle-like in intensity, but Michael knew this was the punch he would have to take to get his man where he wanted him. Michael used his own body and his attacker's punch to position his hooded black head square in front of his own shoulders, and with a punch that drove from way down in his left leg and erupted all the way through his hips into his right arm with an anvil crashing collision, he pounded the assailant on his nose, sending him careering towards the stone fireplace. His torso was limp and now wavering backwards with the expectant feeling that he would crash into the blazing fire, but before he finished his fall, Michael grasped the katana from the ground, swung it upwards and slashed it across his stomach with lightning ferocity, the way a fishmonger would gut a fish. This powerful and lethal blow left the attacker sliding down the burning logs of the fire with a blood curdling scream escaping from his mouth. The silence that followed could mean only one thing, if the katana blade had not killed him, then the blazing fire certainly did.

Michael swiftly turned to May Lin and shouted,

"Quickly, help me pull him off the fire," but May Lin was frozen to the spot. Michael presumed she was in shock again, just as she had been when they were together in the car at the traffic lights. Michael dragged the body away himself and shouted at May Lin once again,

"Come on, May Lin, snap out of it."

He looked straight at her this time to see what was wrong; her naked skin was still softly illuminated by the now glowing embers of the wood fire. Michael's attention was drawn to her right hand, in which she was holding a gun and she was pointing it at Michael. This time it was Michael's voice that shattered the silence as he spoke with disbelief.

"Please don't say you're in on all this."

May Lin said nothing; her bottom lip curled up and quivered, and a tear trickled down each of her cheeks, slowly edging towards her chin. Suddenly the unlocked door swung open again and the sound of the blinds clattering on the window was the only noise audible above the intermittent wind whistling through the open door blowing back and forth.

Michael fixed his gaze towards May Lin's fear filled eyes.

"Talk to me, May Lin, please, just talk to me."

She remained silent and instead tentatively walked towards the window and pulled back one side of the curtain, revealing half of the window, which faced onto the darkness outside. She moved her hand up behind the curtain, still pointing the gun at Michael; her hand found the light switch which she swiftly flicked on and off. As soon as she completed this manoeuvre, the muffled sound of a car engine could be heard starting in the distance. The sound of the car lured Michael to look out the window where car headlights were now clearly lighting up the darkness; one of the lights was pointing at an inclined angle towards the sky as it slowly disappeared into the night. Michael spoke slowly with dejection in his voice,

"Is that Inspector Bando's car?" He waited for an answer from May Lin, but her lack of reply just created more anxiety and he now really feared he was going to be shot, rather than be given any explanation. As the sound of the car engine started to fade into the distance he became even more confused. May Lin proceeded to close the curtain at the window and then collapsed to her knees in tears, placing the gun on the table beside her. Michael grabbed the dressing gown from the floor and cautiously made his way towards her; he wrapped the gown around her shoulders and lifted her onto the sofa. May Lin was still shaking when she spoke.

"You have just killed the Shogun Ashikaga's son and I have just signalled to the Inspector that Ashikaga's son has killed you," May Lin explained to Michael with a dawning fear in her voice.

Michael was completely baffled by it all.

"What? Who is Ashikaga? Why was the inspector outside? And why were you pointing a gun at me? I thought you were here to protect me. Is he the Yakuza? Is he the one who was behind the massacre at the dojo?"

"Yes, he is and I was, I was…" May Lin hung her head in shame.

"Go on please." Michael was losing his patience and shouted with anger towards May Lin, "Go on, tell me!"

"I was to shoot you if anything went wrong with…"

Michael stopped her there. "Went wrong? What do you mean went wrong?" Michael pointed towards the charred body near the fire.

"You were going to let that man cut me in two while we had sex? Here's me thinking this was something really special and all along you were plotting to assassinate me?"

May Lin was sobbing.

"You have no idea how bad these people are; how much influence and power they have. I had no choice; I just hoped that you could win through."

"I don't believe I'm hearing this, May Lin. I'm not sure whether I should thank you or knock your head off."

May Lin pulled herself to her feet and walked towards Michael.

"I don't deserve a thank you and if you wish to – as you put it – knock my head off, then that may be a blessing; when they discover what I have done here I won't have a head to knock off."

Michael took a deep breath and calmed himself down before speaking.

"These people killed my father, my sensei and many of my friends and they did that for a reason. You must know what that reason is. And why does it involve me now? It's not as if I witnessed who did it. Not that that would matter a jot anyway, as it seems most of the cops in Tokyo are bent."

May Lin moved towards Michael and gestured with open arms,

"Your father and your sensei had something that Ashikaga wanted and they obviously did not want to give that up. Ashikaga is not a man to be told no and that is why he went to that dojo with his men to wipe out the people who were standing in his way."

Michael interrupted,

"This so-called Shogun, Ashikaga, killed lads my age in that dojo. That's a nasty piece of work in anyone's book."

May Lin looked deep into his eyes and spoke slowly and deliberately.

"Michael. He either believes that you are a witness, or you have something that he wants. By killing you he will solve that one way or another. I have now betrayed him and he will discover that in the morning when I'm not at his house with your dead body. For Michael Harris's sake, you still need to get out of this country, and I, if you trust me to do it, will try to help you, in the short space of time we have left."

Michael's face had a puzzled look.

"Just remind me why you want to do that? You have just been pointing a gun at me."

"Yes. And I could have pulled the trigger, but I didn't. There's more to this,

Michael, much more, and you need to trust me. You still… You still… somehow you make me forget all this trouble when I'm with you." May Lin looked him in the eyes and smiled sadly.

Michael flopped back on the sofa and sighed.

"I'm exhausted with all this. Help me to try and understand. So this guy here is the Yakuza's son, and he was sent by the Yakuza to kill me; so why did he come armed with a katana and not a gun? And how come you had a gun, yes a gun pointing at me? And… and… and also at the same time the inspector has waited outside for your signal to say that I have been killed. Please explain, I'm all ears," he finished, unable to contain his tone of sarcasm.

May Lin moved over and sat down gently beside him on the sofa. She placed her arm around his shoulder, but he moved his shoulder away angrily. Michael was confused about the way events had transpired, and irritated with what seemed like evasive answers coming from May Lin.

May Lin looked straight into his eyes and spoke softly. "Please don't move away. You must trust me now. You really must believe me when I say I had nothing to do with what happened at the dojo and I want to help you get to safety, because I truly care about you. Ashikaga sent his son to kill you as a way of showing respect to you, and in the same way that there were no guns used at the dojo, he wanted you to be killed by the Samurai sword.

Michael retorted sarcastically, "How very honourable of him."

May Lin continued,

"Do you know the meaning of Bushido?"

Michael reluctantly replied,

"Is it a death wish?"

"Kind of," May Lin said.

"Bushido is the way of the Samurai, a way of dying – making the choice to die in defence of your lord or your name, rather than be humiliated with a meaningless death. This empowers the Samurai and in turn gives greater power to the lord or Shogun. Unfortunately for you and me, you ended up killing the Samurai; even more unfortunate for us, that Samurai sent here tonight was Ashikaga's son – Ashikaga, the so-called Shogun. I was supposed to shoot you if the Samurai failed, but you now know why I could not do that. However, because I have made that choice, I am now as much a target for Ashikaga as you are."

Michael was beginning to get the picture of what kind of man was out to get him: a man of honour in a kind of warped and perverted way. Although he had a certain respect for Ashikaga's ideology, today the Shogun had been on the wrong side of the law, and the merciless slaughter of his family and friends at the dojo was unforgiveable. Michael now had the death of someone on his conscience and not just anyone, the son of a Yakuza, the same Yakuza who was shrouding himself in all the traditions of the Shogun and the Samurai as a way of masking his criminal activity. Michael was suspicious of May Lin's intentions and knew he needed to proceed with caution around her, particularly as she worked closely with Inspector Bando.

"What about the inspector? Where does he figure in all this? I thought he was a half decent guy?" Michael asked.

"The inspector is involved with the Yakuza, because he has a young son who Ashikaga Yoshimitsu has threatened to harm, if he does not comply with his demands; however, he is working hard to break the hold Ashikaga has over him, by moving his family to a safer place," May Lin explained.

"That sounds like a weak excuse if you ask me, May Lin."

May Lin shook her head, while her whole body was shaking at the mere thought of this man.

"You have no idea how powerful this man is, Michael. He is beyond the realms of evil."

Michael consoled May Lin with a gentle touch to her tear laden cheek.

"Why don't you come back to England with me?"

May Lin replied with a forlorn look on her face,

"If only it was that simple."

Michael gingerly raised his weary and aching body from the sofa and moved towards the door, closing it to stop the blinds rattling in the wind; as he looked outside, the uneven headlights of the inspector's car faded into the distance, etching their dance of yellow light across the evening sky, presenting the shadows of trees and telegraph poles as an enormous landscape freeze in the midnight air.

"Looks like he is completely gone now and I'm so glad because I am absolutely knackered, May Lin. I need to sleep, but somehow I know you're going to insist that I can't."

May Lin looked up at Michael, compelled to stare into his eyes. She moved her hand to his cheek and gently stroked it and this time Michael did not pull away.

"I'm sorry, Michael, but this is the most valuable time. We have from now until the morning when Ashikaga will not be looking for you. We need to drive you to your house to collect whatever essentials you need, and then we must ensure you are on the early flight to London.

"Did your father keep money at the house?"

Michael ran through the home he and his dad had shared, in his mind.

"We keep emergency money with the passports in the study."

May Lin turned her head towards the bedroom.

"We need to grab our clothes and get ready, and we need to move fast. Come on. Please hurry."

May Lin walked towards the bedroom to collect her clothes, but before she did she leaned forward to pick up the katana. She clutched Michael's hand as he walked ahead of her and pushed the bone handle into his hand, "Carry this with you – you seem to know how to use it."

"I don't feel too good about that right now." Michael hung his head looking back at the dead body he had left sprawled on the ryokan floor.

"You did what you had to do. Try to forget about that now Michael and get in the car. Come on please, we need to get moving." May Lin hastened towards the car, gesturing to Michael to move.

Together they drove away from the cottage with the car headlights off until they reached the main road; the old *Datsun* was bouncing from side to side along the country lanes. Inside the car the blow heaters on the dashboard were quickly heating up and warming the cool air into the vehicle. The combination of motion and warmth was having a soporific effect on Michael and he began to drift in and out of sleep; each time he closed his eyes he drifted to happy childhood memories of football games with his father in the garden at their home. Then an unpredictable bump in the road would bring him cruelly back to reality and the pain of his loss. Slowly drifting into sleep again he was once more back at home, standing together with his father at the front of the house; this time standing on the lawn in the midday sun practising stick fights with each other. He was so tired he was falling into a very deep sleep and remembering the days when his mother was with his father at their home in Sunderland. They were clutching hands and engrossed in laughter together while Michael weaved between their legs tugging at their clothes for attention. Intermittently his parents interrupted their laughter and affectionate kisses to pursue Michael as he ran away chuckling.

"Michael, Michael, we are here. Wake up, wake up."

May Lin's voice shattered the silence and crashed him into consciousness as if the car window had been smashed with a brick, shattering the glass to the floor and spraying the glare of the street lights into his barely open eyes. The lights that were shining were those of the interior of the car, which rapidly returned Michael to his daunting real life situation. Michael was dazed and confused when he spoke.

"Is this sensible coming to my father's house? Would they not look here for me first?"

May Lin's retort was succinct.

"In Ashikaga's eyes you're already dead."

"Sorry, for a moment I had completely forgotten what had happened at the ryokan," Michael replied.

May Lin leaned over from the driver's side of the car and kissed Michael on the side of his cheek, she began speaking slowly.

"When Ashikaga finds out what happened at the ryokan, he certainly won't forget. Come on my young warrior we need to get you prepared for the airport."

Michael and May Lin headed up the steps to the door of his father's house. Michael looked up and down the lane before he got to the top of the steps – all of the street lamps had a yellow glow and the further he looked down the lane, the more the glow became distorted in the early morning mist that was draped from lamp post to lamp post, it had the appearance of festive cotton wool draped around a Christmas tree.

Michael and his father lived in a generously sized house that would not have looked out of place on a main street in London. Their home was part of a terrace of houses which sat on a busy lane, and the pathway of the lane was scattered with willow trees. The houses had large arched front windows top and bottom and huge front doors. Their door had been forced open, and with some force to be able to bust it's very sturdy lock. The damaged door was ajar.

"Looks like someone has already been here. Are you sure they won't still be in there, May Lin?"

May Lin placed the palm of her hand over Michael's huge knuckles. Her dainty fingers were dwarfed by his, and her hand was enveloped as she grasped the inside of his hand tightly and whispered,

"Proceed with caution – just in case – I would guess they were here before they attacked the dojo."

Michael slowly pushed the door. It begrudgingly squeaked its way open until eventually giving way, swinging against the wall where it juddered to a stop. May Lin switched the light on to reveal the ransacked house that was Michael's home. Drawers had been randomly pulled out and scattered across the floor; wardrobes had been emptied, then pulled away from the wall and slammed face down over their contents. Ornaments, lamps and all Michael's trophies were dumped in the middle of the floor, broken pieces of glass, porcelain and alabaster strewn across the inverted table and chairs. There was so much mess on the floor, the rug and wooden floor were barely visible.

"Whatever they are looking for they seem very determined to find it," May Lin said while observing Michael's shocked reaction.

"This house reflects how I feel right now," Michael replied.

"Come on, Michael, please don't let it get you down, you can start a new life back in England," May Lin said, reassuringly.

Michael's face contorted with a feeling of deep dismay.

"This was my life. Ashikaga has stripped me of that – even my clothes are covered in the spilt blood of his ruination. This was me right here in this house; all my valued possessions have been erased."

May Lin moved close to Michael and cupped his shaking face with her cold hands.

"Look at me, Michael." She slowly guided his face towards hers.

"If you crumble, he has won. I know I recognise the dragon spirit in you. It shines brightly inside you and you are not the kind of person who would be finished by this. Brush yourself down, put your clothes in the case and turn your back on all this. Remember those words you said to me, *'I was taught always to fight my corner'*, that's what you said."

May Lin smiled and kissed Michael on his lips. He directed his gaze straight at her and then spoke with a determined guile in his voice.

"I am not going to crumble. He obviously thinks he can finish me here; well he has to learn that Michael Harris will not cow down to his bullying tactics. I will have my case ready to go in two minutes."

May Lin dropped her hands from Michael's face to his shoulders.

"I knew I could count on you."

Michael stuffed what belongings he could into the case, including his gi from the dojo. He quickly zipped it shut and swung it up in the air with one hand as if he was carrying just a school lunch box; he strode over the mess on the floor towards the door and headed out into the street to get in the car. Before May Lin followed him she paused to pick up a torn photograph of Michael's father holding him as a small boy; she quickly tucked it inside her jacket pocket before leaving the house.

Michael was sitting in the car with his case on his lap and his arms draped over the front when May Lin opened the door. She climbed into the car and immediately looked at her watch. "Okay, we still have two hours before Ashikaga realises I have not returned with your body. He will then order his men to search the ryokan, at which point he will discover his son's body; we are approximately thirty minutes from the airport and it will take approximately thirty minutes to check in. All being well your flight to London should take off around forty-five minutes after this.

"Christ, we're cutting this fine," Michael said while looking anxiously at May Lin.

"Alright, so let's get going then," she replied.

CHAPTER 2

"Where are they?"

"We have no idea, Yoshimitsu san." Kobyashi relayed his message reluctantly. Kobyashi was Ashikaga Yoshimitsu's second-in-command, deservedly so as his martial art skills were of the highest calibre, and his katana skills made him stand out as a true traditional Samurai. He stood five feet ten inches tall with a thickset build. His head was shaven completely bald, his demeanour aggressive. He carried only one scar on his face across his left eye, a scar which was not inflicted upon him by any man, but by a dog that was set upon him by one of Ashikaga's enemies; no man had ever been close enough to scar him. He was dressed in a grey loose fitting silk suit which did not hide his rounded muscular tone; and his black shirt was open to the second button, revealing his enormous neck which betrayed no indication of any curves. From his ears, a line could be drawn vertically and completely straight down to his shoulders, shoulders that whilst concealed in his jacket, looked padded, but were certainly not. The girth of his torso was evident as he struggled to fasten his jacket buttons and his legs were bowed due to their tree trunk size. This tank of a man was devoutly loyal to Ashikaga, and the honour and way associated with Bushido. He would be the last line of defence if anyone tried to attack his Shogun.

He was altogether different from Ashikaga, who towered above him; Ashikaga was tall for a Japanese man, standing at six feet four inches with a slim athletic build. His facial features were strong, pronounced and bony; his skin was pitted from acne scars and these were interwoven with deeper scars from previous battles throughout his life. His jet black hair was brushed back from his high forehead and fastened into a tight pony tail suspended down the centre of his back. With long slender arms and legs, he had an atypical Asian physique and stood out in a crowd because of it. Although quite ministerial in his appearance, wearing a black suit of obvious superior quality, with a white roll neck jumper, ministerial he certainly was not. He was respected and feared in equal measures by his enemies, who named him the devil Yakuza because of the evil way he dealt out punishment while watching his victims with a piercing merciless glare. He called himself a Shogun, but the people who he terrified knew he was nothing more than a gangster. He would often have people tortured by his men and occasionally mutilated by their razor sharp katanas.

His main henchman, Kobyashi, was in charge of a team of twenty men, who, as part of their remit, needed to be confident in using a katana and possess a certain level of martial arts ability. They were instructed to only use a gun as a last resort; this was instilled into them by Ashikaga, he adopted this traditional Shogun doctrine whilst running his business of corruption and extortion in the city.

"I want to know why my son and May Lin have not returned? Get someone over to that ryokan and find out where that boy Michael Harris is and what has happened to May Lin and my son? And do it now." Ashikaga barked out his command with a grimacing look towards Kobyashi.

"Yes, Ashikaga san." Kobyashi bowed and clicked his fingers while simultaneously pointing at three of the men; the three men dashed towards the exit and hastily disappeared.

"I don't like this," said Ashikaga.

"May Lin would not dare to betray you," Kobyashi replied.

"I need to speak to Inspector Bando. If something has gone wrong, he will know what has happened to May Lin."

Ashikaga was milling the possibilities over in his mind.

"I will do my best to get hold of Inspector Bando to get answers," Kobyashi replied as he walked to the hallway to use the phone.

"This boy has been more than enough trouble already, but I'm convinced that he has what I want; in the meantime, we must get to him before he understands what that is."

Ashikaga held his clenched fist with his other hand and crunched his hands together in anguish.

CHAPTER 3

"Ten minutes and we will be at the airport."

May Lin was pointing to a plane taking off above the car as she approached the air terminal.

Michael looked across at May Lin and spoke in a slow concerned tone,

"Am I going to get through this?"

May Lin answered,

"I don't know, Michael, I'm guessing that Ashikaga will have no reason to suspect that you will head towards the airport; that is until he discovers what's happened at the ryokan: we just need to stay calm and remain vigilant. We will be at the airport soon, whereupon we will head to the check in desk and purchase a ticket."

"What will you do when I'm gone?"

Michael asked.

"I will head to my mother's house; she lives in a remote village near Kochi on the island of Shikoku. Ashikaga knows nothing of my mother's home so I will be safe there,"

May Lin replied with a fearful tone while looking deep into Michael's eyes.

Michael was not convinced by May Lin's reply and knew she was very much in danger. As they approached the airport car park, May Lin remained quiet and kept her gaze straight ahead: Michael gazed at her from the passenger's seat of the car, her eyes were filling up, and just like the first melting drops of spring water from suspended river icicles, the tears slowly trickled down her face, one after another, glistening in the morning light which was beaming in through the car window. May Lin pulled up at the car park where she drove immediately to the underground section, found a space, stopped the car and proceeded to wrench the handbrake on and turn the ignition off. The car was now silent and still.

"My God, Michael, we're here," May Lin announced with a surprise in her voice and a billowing gasp in her breath.

"As I may not get the chance later, May Lin, I want to take this opportunity to thank you for all you have done for me; I will never forget this,"

Michael said, while lifting his hand towards May Lin's face to wipe away a tear from her eye.

May Lin paused,

"Please don't thank me yet. Until you are on that plane taking off, in my book you're not safe."

"Really, but I thought you said he wouldn't find out about the ryokan for a while yet?"

Michael hopefully enquired.

"I don't want to tempt fate that's all," May Lin replied.

May Lin swiftly jumped out of the car and pulled Michael's case out of the boot. They headed for the check in desk via the underground escalator. As early as it was, Narita Airport was busy, and Michael and May Lin were being jostled and bumped as they headed towards a crowded escalator to travel upstairs to the first floor, the check in desk was on the second floor. The second escalator faced the opposite way and had a good view of the airport roads which brought the traffic into the airport: May Lin pointed to the desk where the tickets are purchased.

"There, Michael, get the money ready and go to that desk, she will sort your ticket for you."

"I can see,"

Michael replied, and then promptly scurried towards the desk hauling his hefty case behind him.

"A ticket to London Heathrow please."

Michael handed over the money and lifted his bag onto the conveyer belt to be dispatched.

The check in girl received his passport; she then stared at Michael and May Lin for a long while, and then proceeded to look down at the passport, before looking up again. She looked over her shoulder and shouted her colleague over to discuss something. Michael became extremely nervous.

Why was there a delay? What did they know? Was he now a wanted person? Had the body at the ryokan been discovered?

All these thoughts were rushing through his head. At this point, when May Lin turned momentarily away from the direction of the check in desk, she looked out of the airport windows and across the roads in the distance. Half a mile away she could make out two black *Mercedes Benz* cars speeding towards the airport. May Lin froze.

"Shit, it's Ashikaga's men,"

May Lin shouted with a strain in her voice.

Michael quickly turned round to look in the same direction as May Lin.

"Are you sure? Where? Show me."

May Lin was frozen to the spot and slowly lifted her arm up to point to the road that could be seen through the large window panes to the side of the check in desk. She spoke very slowly, her voice shaking with fear and apprehension.

"That's them, I know it is."

What started as a simple plan to leave Japan for London was now starting to unravel.

"Is everything alright, sir, madam?"

Asked the check in girl.

Michael gave an anxious reply,

"Yeah, yeah it's fine, is everything okay with the passport?"

"If you don't mind stepping to one side I would like you to have a word with my superior."

The check in girl instructed Michael.

May Lin leaned across Michael and revealed her badge to the girl behind the desk.

"Look, I'm a police officer, is everything in order?"

"It's just routine I believe; when a minor is travelling on his own we need to ask a few mandatory questions."

Michael moved to the side of the desk where the girl's superior was waiting. He proceeded to ask Michael a few questions.

"What is the reason for your journey, young man?"

"I am going to see my mother," Michael replied.

"And why are you travelling alone? And why is this police officer with you? Has something happened?"

The man was looking directly at Michael waiting for his reaction.

"No, nothing has happened; she is with me because she is a friend."

The two black *Mercedes* cars were now entering the airport's grounds, and the sound of their tyres screeching was attracting attention within the airport. May Lin knew she needed to speed things along if Michael was going to make that flight home.

"Is there a reason why you are stopping Michael from checking in?"

May Lin moved between the superior and Michael.

"We have been informed that the young gentleman is wanted for questioning at your station, Officer."

The manager creased a smug grin into his fat oval face.

May Lin instantly recognised that look; it was a look of pure avarice. Someone had got to him with money or the promise of it. Michael leaned forward and whispered into May Lin's ear,

"What's going on, why are they keeping me here?"

May Lin turned her back to the manager and whispered to Michael.

"The money you collected from your house, I need some. Quickly place it in my hand."

Michael looked confused.

"Why do you want the money?"

May Lin glanced over her shoulder at the manager and was greeted with the same repugnant grin. She glanced back at Michael. "He's corrupt, you can tell, we see that face time and time again, all over the district. I need to play his game and bribe him to let you through."

May Lin turned back to face the manager with the money tightly concealed in her fist, but her attention was distracted by a group of men in black suits leaping over the entrance barriers to the car park across the road. May Lin was immediately fearful for herself and Michael's safety, in a few minutes Ashikaga's men would be heading up the same escalator to the floor where her and Michael were standing only a few minutes earlier. Her shaking started again and she was beginning to seize up.

"Come on, May Lin."

Michael placed his enormous hand on May Lin's shoulder and turned her around; his hand was like something you might observe in a scrapyard, when a crane grabs the scrap car and lifts it around the yard: his huge hand dwarfing her petite shoulder. Michael calmed her again the same way he did when she froze at the traffic lights on their way to the station. His hand was now firmly grasping her collar bone.

"Give him the money, May Lin, just move your hand forward and give him the money."

There was no response from May Lin.

"Listen. May Lin, you need to give him the money now if I'm going to have any chance of getting on that plane."

The sound of shouting broke through the quiet melee at the check in desk.

"Move! Move!"

Could be heard from two floors below the area Michael and May Lin were standing in; this was the sound of Ashikaga's men pushing their way through the crowd to get to the check in desk area. Heads were turning to look over towards the commotion taking place below. People were waiting in anticipation of what would appear next at the top of the escalator, the impending chaos downstairs focused Michael's mind, he needed to make May Lin snap out of this if he was to continue on his way.

"May Lin, listen to me."

Michael spun her round with his hand and looked deep into her eyes, eyes that were racked with fear.

"I want you to give the money to this guy, then you need to get as far away from here and as quickly as possible, for your own safety: I'm telling you this because soon our painstaking journey is going to seem pointless. All that effort getting here, and for what? To be stopped from getting on the plane by some gangster's lackeys? I know you don't want that, so snap out of it, come on."

Michael raised his voice for the final few words while grasping May Lin's arms and turning her towards the manager.

"Will this do?"

May Lin spoke directly to the manager and handed him the money. Once again he dallied and increased the tension for Michael and May Lin, but with almost no warning he handed the passport back.

"You're free to go, sir."

May Lin turned and looked at Michael as if she had been woken from a coma.

"Did I freeze again?"

"Yes you did, but you also got me the okay to go to security, so once again thanks for that.

May Lin, you really need to get out of here; Ashikaga's men are going to appear at the top of that escalator at any minute."

May Lin's face was ashen and her eyes were glazed over. At the sound of the airport tannoy, she seemed to drift back to reality and was looking straight at Michael with a glint of wanting in her eyes. May Lin kissed Michael on the lips and held both of his hands in front of him,

"Good luck, sleep with one eye open and stay safe. Your best chance to get on that plane is being on your own, because these goons will not know what you look like."

And with that May Lin walked to the side of the check in area. She still had a glazed look on her face as if in a spell of fear; she stood perfectly still. Michael's attention was momentarily distracted by the heavy thumping noise made by the stamp bashing down on his passport, and then the words rang out from the check in girl at the desk,

"You're free to head to security, young man."

"I'm on my way, May…"

Michael turned round to speak with May Lin, but she was gone. He looked across the airport floor towards the windows as he began to dash towards security without delay. He could see May Lin was stood waiting at the top of the escalators; she gestured towards Michael to go and go quickly. She was waving her arm, but Michael was already moving with great haste away from the check in desk. May Lin knew that Michael's best chance of evading Ashikaga's men, was for her to distract them, and that was exactly what she did.

Ashikaga's men caught sight of her at the top of the escalator, at that very moment Michael was already checking through security. All of the staff there were more interested in the rumpus being created back at the escalators to notice anything out of the ordinary at security; so much so that all staff members moved to the back of the security desk and were peering over the balcony to look at the area below. Michael took one last glance back over his shoulder before heading through to the waiting area. May Lin was running across the floor of the airport towards the exit with six men pursuing her like a pack of wolves. Michael's urge to help her was intense, but he knew it was suicide to even try. He suppressed his urge and walked quietly on his way.

The image of May Lin running for her life like that imprinted itself in Michael's mind, the fear was stretched across her face as if being pulled from her body by the chasing mob, as she pushed every ounce of energy through her muscles to run. Her facial expression reminded him of the faces of rabbits whilst being hunted by weasels; there was that realisation of being caught.

Michael needed to turn his back and walk through to the lounge area; he did this with a tear in his eye and with a heavy feeling of failure towards May Lin. Exhausted, Michael sat in front of a screen and watched for his flight information, in one hour he was leaving Japan for London.

CHAPTER 4

"Why have they not phoned from the airport?"

Ashikaga growled his question towards his henchmen.

"We are still waiting, Ashikaga san, we have heard nothing."

Ashikaga's face swelled up and flushed with rage until his skin was the colour of chilli powder.

"What! Heard nothing, they have been at the airport for an hour now, this is a woman and a god damn boy."

Ashikaga launched his fist into the bureau so hard, the power propelled him from his chair and onto his feet. He stalked over towards the bringer of bad news and with a fiery stare in his eyes, he moved his face within inches of Katsushige's face; he spoke slowly at first.

"We sent my son and that bitch of a bent cop to kill this boy; I lose my son and she runs off to the airport with this piece of shit, I then send six of my so-called best men to find them at the airport and they can't even do that."

Ashikaga increased the volume of his shouting.

"Maybe this boy should be working for me, because he's ten times better than any of you useless idiots, get out of my sight."

Ashikaga paced up and down in front of the window of his front room while all of his men rapidly dispersed out of his way. He was seething, with no news of what was happening at the airport, he was completely out of control of the situation and he detested it.

"Someone must know something, how can we have so many people on the ground at that airport and still have no idea of what is going on?"

He yelled another command.

"Ring the information desk. Ask if there has been an incident. Get more men down there and get me an answer, someone ring our contacts in the police and find out what they know, someone must know something, anything, I need answers and I need them now!"

All of his men were obeying his every command as they scampered out of his home, looking like nothing more than mice fleeing from a pouncing cat.

CHAPTER 5

Michael was now thirty minutes away from his flight taking off for Heathrow and again he could not stop thinking of May Lin and her plight. He headed down the long corridors towards his gate and kept contemplating what they would be doing to May Lin in his mind. He felt deep regret that she had sacrificed herself as bait to send him safely on his way and here he was ambling along as if nothing had happened, in his head it just wasn't right.

He stopped at the toilet to wash his face and freshen up before arriving at the gate. He pulled up his case in front of the sinks and filled one of the basins with cold water; he looked at his reflection in the mirror and could see himself as almost a grown man. He was there because a considerate and compassionate lady had decided she was less important than him. May Lin was willing to jeopardise her safety for the safety of another who she barely knew. If this act of kindness was accomplished to make her feel good about doing the right thing, it did nothing but pull at Michael's heart with a feeling of helplessness and shame. He leaned his head forward and scooped his hands into the basin of water, splashing it over his head and instantly cooling himself as a way of washing his troubled thoughts away from his mind. He lifted his head back up from the basin, before lowering his head once more to immerse it in the water again. He raised his head from the water this time to be met with the sound of a strange voice in his ear.

"Don't move a muscle, big guy, or I'll stick this straight in your spleen."

Michael looked in the mirror as his head drew level with it and standing there beside him was a man in a cleaner's uniform. Michael glanced down towards his right hand side and observed a glistening blade pressed firmly against his body.

"I said don't move, that means eyes front until I say otherwise."

Michael did as he was told. The knife was painfully tight against his clothing and he knew if he made a sudden move this man could easily drive it into his stomach.

"We are going to walk right out of here and towards the exit that I direct you to."

The man covered the blade with a black bin liner full of rubbish and gestured with his head for Michael to move forward and head out of the toilets past Michael's case. The man was not easing up on the pressure he exerted on the blade and Michael could now feel it cutting into his skin under his clothing. They both began to walk towards the toilet's exit, leaving Michael's case behind as they slowly passed the urinals. At that very point, the echo chamber that was the empty washrooms rang out with the final call for Michael's flight over the tannoy.

"Could all passengers for flight BA663 please make their way to gate twenty-one."

This sound startled the man, causing him to relinquish his grip on Michael, which in turn allowed Michael to edge his body away from the knife. Michael threw himself towards the other side of the toilets; his feet sliding to a halt on the slippery floor as he did so. Michael agilely twisted his body around to face his attacker. He found himself with his back to the urinals. The man quickly turned to face Michael and lunged forward to stab him in the stomach. Michael glanced his body smoothly to the side of the blade and instantaneously brought his fist crashing down on the man's arm that was carrying the knife, at which point he dropped it. Due to the power of the blow to his arm, the attacker's head flopped forward. Michael immediately grabbed the man's head by his hair and thrust him forward towards the urinals, where his head thundered into the chrome pipe in the centre of the porcelain bowl with enough force to smash the urinal, pulling the whole bowl away from the wall. With a sound resembling a dagger puncturing a car tyre and releasing the pressurised air inside it, the water erupted from the broken pipe spraying the whole room. The man's head slid down the bowl of the urinal like a melting scoop of ice cream sliding from the end of a spoon. It splashed down onto the marble tiled floor and painted a glistening red swirl of monkey's blood for the ball of ice cream that was the attacker's cracked head.

"This is the final call for passenger Michael Harris travelling to London

Heathrow on BA663, please make your way to gate twenty-one immediately."

Michael grabbed his case and ran out of the toilets for his gate. He didn't look back and soon arrived at his gate where he was welcomed with a smile by the airline staff.

"Boarding pass please. You need to take your seat immediately, sir."

Michael just made it to the plane to the sound of a disgruntled hurray from the passengers as he walked down the aisle to take his seat. He took his place beside an elderly English lady who made a remark to welcome him.

"You cut it fine there, young man."

Michael looked across at the woman sat with her flight blanket wrapped around her knees and a mohair cardigan buttoned up to her neck. She wore tiny oval glasses perched on a wrinkled nose which had three sprouting hairs of a similar length to those on her eyebrows; she was peering over her glasses as a way of admonishing Michael for being late and keeping everyone waiting on the plane.

Michael saw the funny side of her comment about cutting it fine after what had just happened to him in the toilet, and he smirked to himself.

"It's no laughing matter, we have sat here fifteen minutes after our departure time, that means I will be late for the people who are collecting me in London,"

Michael looked down at this petite old woman and was quite perturbed by her presence. He had clashed with Yakuza and Samurai and escaped unscathed and this little lady who he presumed to be demure by her looks, was anything but.

"I am sorry, I wasn't laughing at my bad punctuality, it was something you said that made me think of something completely different."

As if to impatiently move on, the woman accepted Michael's apology.

"That's fine. Now let's forget it and you can tell me all about yourself."

It was at this point that Michael wished he had been rude, as she began - not to ask questions about him - but to tell Michael all about her life and what she was up to. Michael slumped into his seat with a feeling of relief and assured safeness. He remembered hearing the words,

"I have a sister…"

bellowing out from the old woman's mouth, at which point he swiftly nodded off to sleep.

He was drifting in and out of a deep dream; he dreamt of his father and his mother together yet again, his thoughts would take him to the people in the dojo and his instructor and all his friends: His mind was jumping him from one part of his life to another. May Lin now appeared in his dream. Michael was sat with her in a house watching her make a meal for him. She began to walk around the room, collecting things to bring to him. She walked towards him and spoke the words,

"Your food, sir."

Michael wanted to reach out and hold her the way he did at the ryokan, but he could not bring her close to him. She muttered the words again,

"Your food, sir, sir, your food."

Michael's eyes opened and he reared up from his seat with a startled and confused look on his face.

"It's okay."

Michael felt a reassuring hand on his shoulder.

"It's okay, sir, it's your lunch, and you have been asleep."

The air stewardess was holding Michael's shoulder and indicating towards his lunch in front of him. Finally Michael had grabbed a few hours' sleep.

"How long before we land?"

Michael asked.

"We will be in London in three hours."

The stewardess said with a comforting smile. Michael looked across at the old lady sat beside him and she looked back with a frowning expression of contempt.

"Great company you are on a flight."

Michael again apologised.

"Sorry, it's been a long day."

The old lady leaned to the side prompting Michael to do the same. She gestured with her hand for Michael to move his ear close to her mouth,

"I'm a retired nurse."

Michael nodded his head wondering why she was telling him this.

"Oh, are you?"

"They probably would have taken you off the plane if they had spotted it."
She said.

Michael was baffled by this conversation and had no idea where it was going.

"I'm sorry; I have no idea what you're talking about."

The old lady lifted her arm out from beneath her travel blanket and pointed to Michael's side.

"I placed a dressing on it, I used cotton wool that I had in my handbag and I borrowed some *Sellotape* from the air stewardess; that's why I have tape around my perfectly good glasses."

Michael looked to his side where she was gesturing. The old lady lifted the newspaper that was lodged between Michael and the arm rest; she lifted her head up to speak to Michael.

"I thought you might have been in trouble, I noticed the blood soaking through your top, so I applied the makeshift swab, the bleeding has ceased, however I suggest you go to a hospital when we land in London. I hope you don't mind, I did try to wake you, but you were out for the count."

Michael's jaw dropped; he was in awe of this very frail old lady who had administered first aid to him, and had done it without any commotion while on a plane full of passengers. Michael lifted his top to see how bad the injury was, but could only make out a bulge of red cotton wool and shiny Sellotape.

"How bad is the cut?"

Michael asked the old lady.

"You'll live, I suggest you go to hospital because I think that it may need a few stitches."

She looked up at Michael with a concerned look.

"In my humble opinion that looks like a knife wound: I hope you managed to leave the bother behind in Japan."

Michael paused before answering, the fact that he didn't comment on her remark confirmed what she suspected.

"Thank you, sorry I don't even know your name?"

Michael cracked a beaming smile as he asked the question.

"Just call me Elsa."

She replied.

Michael swung his right hand around and offered it to Elsa to shake hers.

"I'm Michael, thank you again for what you have done for me."

Elsa wrinkled her face up and her glasses edged forward to the hairy tip of her nose.

"Well you're gonna have to build your energy up mister, so start by eating that meal in front of you; you can eat mine too, I've never liked airline food, go on get it down you."

Michael didn't wait for her to change her mind and tucked in to both meals immediately.

CHAPTER 6

"Sakigawa is in Shinjuku hospital, Ashikaga san," Kobyashi revealed to Ashikaga.

The room fell silent, six of Ashikaga's best men stood before him awaiting their fate. Ashikaga dropped his head forward staring at the floor beneath him; he took a deep breath and exhaled a lingering sigh. He was humiliated by today's events, everyone in the room stood perfectly still. Ashikaga slowly raised his head.

Ashikaga's men had a nickname for him, he was known as Fujikaga after the Mount Fujiyama volcano. When he was angry his veins stood proud on his head and his face flushed to a fiery red, then like a pyroclastic explosion, his words spewed from his mouth with such ferocity - that just like a volcano - you didn't want to be near him when his verbosities blew. Ashikaga turned his attention towards the window of the room before he spoke.

"Kobyashi, which one of these imbeciles is responsible for losing this boy?"

Ashikaga slowly lurched his head towards his six men, each one receiving a split second of a piercing stare which began to sweep across the room from one man to the next, each time his eyes met with their eyes, their heads immediately bowed in shame.

Kobyashi barked out his question.

"Who was with Sakigawa at the airport?"

One man stepped forward; that man was Toshimasa, his face showed no fear; however he could not prevent or hide his hands from shaking by his side. Ashikaga clicked his fingers, and Kobyashi walked forward towards Toshimasa.

"Move to the centre of the room," Kobyashi instructed him. Kobyashi removed his tailored suit jacket and with a delicate action he folded it across the chair, taking care to have each arm folded underneath to prevent it from creasing. He executed this action with military precision. His huge physique was not concealed by his loosely fitted shirt; his forearms squeezed out of his shirt cuffs as he folded back his sleeves, each turn increasingly more difficult as the shirt doubled back over his rotund arms, arms that were the width of most men's legs. He began to roll his shoulders and shake his arms by his side as he slipped his shoes under the chair holding his jacket. He then proceeded to warm his legs by shaking them too.

While Kobyashi warmed his muscles, Toshimasa stood completely still in the centre of the room, the only movement coming from a bead of sweat traversing across the side of his temple; Toshimasa knew he was in trouble, but also knew because of his honour he would have to grin and bear it, and be respectful of the punishment he deserved for his failure. Kobyashi walked over towards the katanas on the wall and reached up to grasp his weapon, and in a flash he unsheathed it, the steel glinting in the light.

"No weapons," Ashikaga shouted across the room to Kobyashi.

"I want no more death today." Kobyashi looked across at Toshimasa with a disdainful glare while slowly re-housing the glistening blade of the katana.

Kobyashi walked to the centre of the room where Toshimasa was standing perfectly still. He stopped a body's length in front of him; there he waited. Toshimasa knew what he was required to do, but he needed to summon the energy and spirit to do it.

With a blood-curdling scream, he lunged forward with a flailing right arm to punch Kobyash. With hope more than skill, he brought his left knee thrusting up towards Kobyashi's waist with the intent of catching him off guard. Before his attack could make any contact, Kobyashi had twisted his body sideways and where a normal man would probably move backwards to defend himself, Kobyashi moved forward blocking Toshimasa's knee with his powerful right forearm, driving his elbow up and forward from this position, he landed a crippling blow to Toshimasa's throat, incapacitating him. This allowed him the split second he needed to bring his right fist swiftly to bear on Toshimasa's genitals. Before his body had the time to buckle, Kobyashi grabbed his chest with his left hand supported by his forearm and gripped his inner thigh with his right hand, driving his nails into his flesh the way a grappling hook would cling to a rock face; he then proceeded to throw him over his shoulder and landed him on his back with a bone crunching crash as he hit the floor. It was all over in seconds.

Ashikaga stood in front of his men with a stoical expression on his face.

"I do not accept failure. My father before me, his father before him and many fathers before them did not accept failure; it is scorched into the soul of our bloodline and has been for many decades. Tokugawa tried to stand in my way and I crushed him, Doug Harris, an imposter, also tried to stand in my way and I crushed him too. This mere boy got lucky; he wants to pray that we find what we are looking for, before we find him."

Everyone in the room knew instantly that this was a reprieve, all of the men standing; including Kobyashi bowed and awaited Ashikaga's next command.

"Take him out and clean him up." Ashikaga pointed towards Toshimasa, then thrust his arm out in the direction of the door instructing his men to get him out; the men scurried around Toshimasa, whereupon they dragged him across the floor towards the exit. Ashikaga roared his next command as they neared the door. "Find me May Lin! Convince her friends or family to reveal where she is and bring her back to me, I have a score to settle with that one."

CHAPTER 7

"Don't forget what I said, Michael, injuries like that can fester if you don't get them looked at."

Michael thanked Elsa for her help, picked up his case and walked towards his train at Kings Cross Station. A train journey seemed very appealing after the day he had just experienced - and on checking the timetable - he would be on his way in fifteen minutes, but first he needed to locate a phone box with the intention of letting his mother know he would soon arrive in Sunderland. A phone box cleared in front of the platform where he would catch his train; he climbed inside and lifted the receiver. He blocked his nose with his fingers to prevent the smell of urine drifting up his nostrils and began to dial his mother's number.

"Hello, it's me, I'm just about to board the train at Kings Cross, I should be just a few hours."

Michael was hoping for a happy response at the other end of the phone, but he received what he realistically expected: a terse response unfortunately was no surprise.

"Oh, it's yee. I was expecting the call to be Trevor, what do yah want?" his mother abruptly asked.

Michael overlooked the comment and quickly replied,

"Looking forward to seeing you soon, bye."

He hung up the phone before any further comments were returned from his mother. A sadness that he had not experienced since his father and mother first separated, overwhelmed him and gripped his stomach tight; going home was not going to be an experience to look forward to. At that very moment the reality of how alone he was in the world, dawned on him, the loss of his father and friends and all that was his life in Japan weighed heavy on his young mind. Maybe the slim hope that some support from his estranged mother could help with his spirit, was shattered with a few thoughtless words at the end of a phone. He now faced another battle, sadly this time he would not have his fists and feet as his weapons of defence and this exposed his vulnerability. Still somewhat dazed by his mother's reaction, he boarded the train. Michael took his seat and within minutes the train pulled out of the station.

Refreshed from his flight, his mind turned once again to May Lin and how not only did he feel worried about her, but also how he missed her too. Immediately his thoughts were distracted by the sunshine that punched its way into the train as it exited the tunnels out of the capital. The countryside of England bathed in bright sunlight lifted his spirit, seeing the green fields and the trees beginning to change colour from green to soft reds, browns and yellows, gave him a feeling of warmth and contentment.

CHAPTER 8

"Will yah pick Michael up from the station, Trevor?" Michael's mam asked her boyfriend.

"Ha'way, you're having a laugh aren't yah?" replied Trevor.

"I'm off to the club."

Michael's mother had a look of dismay on her face.

"How's he gonna get back from the station then?"

Trevor turned to gesture with his thumb held out and twitching to the side.

"He'll have to wark or hitch a lift won't he, Shirley."

Michael's mam looked over towards Trevor slowly shaking her head from side to side in reluctant acceptance of how unhelpful Trevor was being.

"Yah heartless bastard, can yah not miss the club for one night?"

"Who do yah think you're talking to? Yah better watch your lip. Anyhow, yee can't talk, you've never bothered to contact the lad for years." Trevor stood gesticulating with his forefinger while admonishing Michael's mam, he then proceeded to walk out, slammed the door and drove off spinning the wheels of his *Ford Cortina* down the street and off the estate.

Michael's mam slumped down from the arm of the sofa onto the seat; her bottom lip jittered as her emotions got the better of her and then all the tension that was twisted in her face was released. Tears burst from her eyes and rolled relentlessly down her face onto her factory overall that was still fastened across her thighs; the tears changed the colour of the light pink overall to dark pink the way the first rain to follow a long hot summer can bring colour to parched clay on a worn football pitch goalmouth. She turned to her left while rubbing her tear soaked eyes on her forearm and reached for her cigarettes. In her eyes the only sanctuary for her was a dependant inhalation of nicotine as a way of calming her nerves and allowing her to deal with the rest of the evening.

Just as she struck the match on the matchbox, her phone began ringing on the window sill; with a large suck on the filtered tip, enough to burn halfway down the cigarette, she stood up and quickly grabbed the phone.

"Hello." There was no reply at the other end of the phone, so Michael's mother repeated herself.

"Hello." The phone was still silent.

"Hello, who is it, is that yee, Michael? I can't hear yah." The line went dead. Michael's mam replaced the phone receiver and thought to herself that it was probably Michael struggling to work the payphone at the station. She took another deep puff of her cigarette and sat back down, only to hear the phone ring once more.

"Hello, is that yee, Michael?" Michael's mam asked.

"Yes it is. How did you know?" Michael replied.

"Yah were trying before weren't yah and yah couldn't get through?" Michael's mam expected an acknowledgement of this question.

"No. This is the first time I have phoned since calling from Kings Cross." This immediately made Michael nervous and prompted him to enquire,

"Did you hear anyone speak?"

"No. Listen it will probably have been my friend, so forget it." Michael's mam brushed it aside and continued to inform Michael of her situation.

"I'm in on me own and I don't have the car so ya'll need to walk from the station."

Michael did not ask where Trevor was out of respect for his mother, but he knew that he would most likely be at the club drinking.

"Don't worry, I can walk." He continued to ask about the phone calls.

"Have you had any other calls like the one earlier?"

Michael's mam sounded somewhat confused.

"What? Ey? Phone calls, no. Why are yah asking?"

"It's nothing, just forget it," Michael replied.

His mother did just that and began to lay down the law over the phone. "Yah need to understand that things are different in this house to when your father and I were together, Trevor has his ways of doing things and yah might not agree with them, however he is the man of the house and…"

Michael interrupted,

"Mam, I kind of hear what you're saying, but can it wait until I get back, my change is running out and I also just want to get back, dump this case and get my head down?"

His mother abruptly hung up the phone.

"Hello, hello, Mam? Great. Welcome home, Michael." Michael put the phone down and headed out of the station towards the town centre. He definitely knew he was home when he exited the train station; it was a typical early evening in Sunderland town centre. The screeching sound of the sea gulls echoed in the wind while they flew overhead on their way back to the coast. The instant cooling effect of the cold wind blowing up the street from the direction of the North Sea, dragging discarded crisp packets and old newspapers with it. The sound of the echoing bus brakes screeching as the bright red vehicles delivered their passengers into the bus depot at relentless speed and the dim orange glow of the street lights as they powered up to light up the roads, all were reminiscent.

Michael wished it had been a happier return to his home town, but unfortunately this was his welcoming party.

Michael headed away from the train station and approached a passer-by.

"Excuse me. Could you tell me the way to Southwick? It's been a while since I've been here and I'm a little unsure of which way to go."

The passer-by stopped and replied,

"You're not thinking of walking are yah? It's miles. Wait two minutes and I'll run yah up, am garn that way."

"Are you sure?" Michael said.

"Way aye, it's nee bother," the man replied.

Michael was overcome with a warm glow on hearing those words, first because it instantly lifted him to remember how friendly the people were and second, it cheered him the way he spoke, it immediately reminded him of his father and although his father had been in Japan for years, he kept his Sunderland accent all the years he was there.

The man quickly returned from the post box after posting two letters and walked towards the red wagon on the opposite side of the road. The wagon had the words 'Arthur's fruit and veg' blazoned along the side in huge white letters. The back doors were open revealing empty fruit boxes crushed inside each other and splayed all over the wooden floor; a floor that was polished smooth from the years of heavy loads sliding to the rear of the wagon.

"I'm Arthur by the way, jump in."

Arthur walked to the other side of the wagon as Michael climbed in the passenger door and dragged his case up beside him. Michael looked over towards Arthur.

"My name's Michael Harris by the way, pleased to meet you." Michael offered him his hand. Arthur looked at Michael with a perplexed expression as he shook his outstretched hand.

"Not Doug's son?"

"Yes, did you know him?" Michael enquired.

Arthur started the engine on the wagon, releasing a puff of smoke into the cab and an instant rattling noise as the gear stick began to shake inside the cab. Arthur pulled the wagon away from the roadside and looked to his driver side mirror before replying,

"Did I knar him? We used to train together down the gym and he also worked the doors with me."

As the wagon pulled away from the kerbside, the driver's side door flung open and Arthur quickly grabbed it and slammed it shut. Michael got an instant waft of fruit fragranced air from the boxes of apples and pears that were wedged in-between the centre console and himself.

"Aww Doug's a canny lad; he often helped me on the doors just to put his martial arts training into practice. He's a good one for watching your back. Is he over here like, how is he?" Arthur glanced over at Michael and then glanced back at the road. Before Michael had the time to answer, Arthur pointed to the boxes squashed against Michael's side.

"Help yerself to an apple or a pear if you're hungry Michael."

Michael picked a large red apple and twisted it in half in his hands as he filled with rage thinking about what happened to his father; telling the story in his head before speaking brought the bitter memories flooding back. Michael slowly uttered the words,

"My father was murdered by Japanese gangsters."

Arthur slammed on the brakes creating an almighty screeching sound inside the cab and a juddering of the doors and windows. He gripped the huge steering wheel tight and successfully fought with it to bring the wagon to a halt at the side of the road.

"What?" Arthur looked across at Michael and could see the look of sheer exhaustion and sorrow on his face.

"You're not joking are yah?"

Michael's words were accompanied by a deep sigh.

"I wish I was."

"Have the police arrested anyone for this?" Arthur asked.

Michael started to speak the words and could hardly believe what he was saying.

"The police are corrupt and the Yakuza are paying them to turn the other way, I was supposed to be killed with the other people who were murdered, but I escaped and fled the country with the help of a friend, that's why I'm back."

Arthur's jaw dropped.

"How many were killed?" he inquisitively asked.

Michael looked across at Arthur and began to shake his head.

"I just want to forget about it and get my head down, sorry. I'm just knackered, Arthur, would you mind taking me to my mam's house?"

Arthur nodded his head and immediately started the wagon moving again.

"I understand. Don't worry I'll get yah home. Hey listen, if yah want to talk to someone about it, just pop round to see me okay? Or if yah need to earn a little money to get by, we could always use a big lad like yee on the doors; if you're anything like Doug, ya'll be useful." Arthur stopped himself before he mentioned any more about Michael's father.

"Listen, here's my number, don't worry about your age, I will sort that; ring me any time and if yah find Trevor difficult, I could always find somewhere for yah to stay too."

Michael twisted his face,

"Is he that bad?"

"I've been told your mam has changed since she has been with Trevor, so all I'm saying is tread carefully."

Michael sat forward and pointed at the house straight ahead.

"Thank you for the heads up, I will be careful; this is my house straight ahead and I really appreciate the lift."

"It's not a problem." Arthur pulled the wagon up outside Michael's mam's house.

"I'm truly sorry about your father Michael, he was a good man, I hope to hear from yah soon okay, and I mean that."

"I will do Arthur, thanks again." Michael jumped down from the cab and waved as Arthur peeped the horn before pulling away in the wagon.

His mother's house was dimly lit with the sitting room curtains half open. Michael approached the old wooden gate to the garden which was twisted to one side and overgrown with weeds, on trying to close it, the rusted hinges pulled out of the wooden post and it collapsed in a heap onto what was once the lawn, but now resembled an overgrown meadow. On his walk up the garden path he stepped over two old paint tins, a rolled up sodden carpet and a rear box from a car exhaust pipe. When he arrived at the front door he peered into the front window where he could make out his mother who was slouched on the sofa. As he knocked on the front door it slowly swung open, the pungent odour of cigarette smoke drifted up his nose, instantly burning the back of his throat. It was a long way from the smell he encountered the last time he walked through that door.

Michael carried a fond memory of the sweet aroma coming from his gran's apple and blackberry crumble, with both of the fruits for the crumble coming from the well-tended garden that his father took such a pride in. Looking at it now made him question the type of person who could allow it to deteriorate as much as it had.

"Hello, Mam. It's Michael, I'm home." Michael pushed the door open further.

"Mam, hello, are you there? It's me Michael." There was still no reply to Michael's call; Michael walked into the kitchen past the sink full to the brim of pans, cutlery and cups, all of which were sat in pools of discoloured water and left over food. A greasy smell lingered over the sink. Michael laid his bag on the kitchen floor and pulled back the door leading to the sitting room, as he did so he noticed a large dent in the door with the marks of four knuckles being easily distinguishable.

"Mam, are you in there?" Michael enquired. Michael pulled back the door completely, revealing his mother slumped forward in her seat; her forearm was resting on the arm of the sofa, and in her hand was what remained of a burned out cigarette. There was three quarters of the length of the cigarette comprising of ash, suspended above the butt, with a tiny plume of drifting smoke meandering its way up to the ceiling. The smoke looked just like a suspended strand of lace draped across a ceiling light and forgotten by the wedding party in an abandoned bridal marquee. Michael took hold of the cigarette and stubbed it out in the ashtray which was overflowing with shrivelled up filter tips and blackened used matches. His mother woke suddenly.

"How long have yee been there?" Michael's mother asked in a flippant manner.

"Only one minute," replied Michael.

His mother looked him up and down,

"By God, what have yah been eating in Japan? You've shot away."

Michael turned to his mother and put his arms out to greet her with a hug while answering her question,

"This and that, you know."

Michael's mother walked straight past him before replying,

"Well there won't be any of this and that available here, yah'll get what you're given and like it. Yah will need to get a job to earn your keep as well; me and Trevor can't keep yah, so the sooner that happens the better."

Michael was expecting this welcome following the earlier telephone conversations with his mother.

"I still have a few months left going to school, I will need to finish that before I can work." Michael's mother turned to look Michael in the face, and then she spoke very slowly in a patronising voice,

"Yah sound just like your father, education brings nothing but trouble in this area, son, yah will go to the pit, gerra a job and bring money in, either that or you're out."

Michael knew he could very easily get sucked into an argument here and he really didn't want that, feeling as tired as he did, he spoke in a sombre voice.

"I'm really tired I just need to sleep."

Michael's mother swung her arm round and pointed up the stairs. "Your room's upstairs, it's in the same state that yah left it in when yah buggered off to Japan with your father."

Dejected and demoralised, Michael headed to his old room, wondering to himself whether this was a big mistake returning to his mother's house.

His mother was not joking; his bedroom was covered in old clothes, books, toys and much more. Everything was strewn across the bed and needed a firm sweeping arm to clear the way. When Michael finally cleared all the junk from on top of his mattress he was able to crawl into his bed and do what he had been longing to do for so many hours now… sleep.

CHAPTER 9

"Ashikaga san, the house on the left near the red Acer tree belongs to May Lin's mother."

Ashikaga waved his hand ahead, directing his driver to pull two blocks forward of the house.

"Park here and turn the engine off, Yoshiro, take Hamaguchi with you and head around the back, if she is in, wave us over, if she is not, remain at the side of the house for my signal and we will wait here for her to return.

Yoshiro and Hamaguchi sneaked around the side of the house and gestured to Ashikaga that the house was unoccupied, then they both crouched down by the side of the wood store and prepared to await the arrival of May Lin's mother. Both Yoshiro and Hamaguchi looked intently towards the open window of Ashikaga's car, never letting their gaze wander.

The street was a quiet suburb with approximately ten houses on either side running the full length. A bird was perched at the top of an acer tree piercing the silence with its song; its chorus was returned by another bird at the other end of the street which was trying to outdo its rival with louder and more complex notes.

Ten minutes passed with no sign of any activity, in all this time the two birds continued their vocal harmony, completely unfazed by the stalking activity taking place below them.

A large utility vehicle then appeared at the end of the street and began to collect the refuse outside each of the houses, but the clattering noise of the bins bouncing down onto the roads and the lids rattling as they fell to the ground did not deter Ashikaga's men's concentration, nor did it distract them. And as quickly as the vehicle appeared, even more quickly the silence resumed as it left. The street was left with a trail of scattered empty bins and missed rubbish rolling on the sides of the pavement.

At the very point the birds reignited their vocal ensemble, a Siamese cat began to slowly amble across the road towards May Lin's mother's house. It tottered its way up the path towards the front door, but instead of walking up the steps towards the entrance of the house, the cat walked over towards the side of the house near the wood store and sat down directly in front of Ashikaga's men. The cat was visible from the roadside and despite the waving of arms and the hurling of pebbles by Ashikaga's men, the cat would not budge from its spot.

"Just slow down before we turn into the street, Mam," May Lin instructed her mother.

"There won't be any problems at my house, May Lin, I told you, you're perfectly safe here," May Lin's mother replied.

May Lin had no reason to doubt her, after all, her mother lived a long way out in the countryside in a remote village with very little contact with the outside world.

Their old *Datsun* pick-up truck began to enter the street where she lived, at which point May Lin had no reason to be suspicious about the red *Toyota* parked close to the neighbour's house, or any reason to associate it with Ashikaga or his men, what transpired, changed all that, following her mother's observation.

"That's strange, May Lin," May Lin's mother commented.

"What is it? What's strange, Mother?" May Lin asked as she slowly turned the steering wheel to direct the car towards her mother's house.

"Tosca, my cat."

May Lin was immediately growing anxious.

"What about Tosca, Mam? Tell me, quickly, what?"

May Lin's mother pointed to the side of her house.

"That's where she gets her food at the side of the wood store."

May Lin looked over from the driver's side of the pick-up truck, "And?"

"Well, she only stands there when someone is waiting near the wood store to feed her, so there must be someone there."

May Lin immediately presumed that Ashikaga was waiting for her near the house.

Her fears were immediately confirmed, her eyes brought into focus

Ashikaga's face through the front window of the red *Toyota* parked straight ahead of her.

"Oh my God! It's him." May Lin then shouted an instruction to her mother.

"Hold on." May Lin gripped the steering wheel so tight, her knuckles turned white. She locked her leg out straight and rammed her foot firm up against the accelerator pedal. The vehicle lurched forward and whined with the noise a bull elephant makes before it charges at its enemies, before the engine fully engaged with the clutch. The tyres then began to spin on the tarmac, with a hawk-like screech and a dark grey, rubber burning plume of smoke, adding to the mayhem. Eventually enough traction was obtained on the road and the pick-up sped forward on a collision course with Ashikaga's red *Toyota*, but before Ashikaga had the time to react, the *Datsun* pick-up was upon him. Thundering into the bonnet of Ashikaga's car with a metal crumpling thud, the vehicle knocked him forward from the back seat of the car, head on into the rear of the front seat with such force he was pummelled unconscious.

"Hang on to your seat again," May Lin screamed as she slammed the gear stick into reverse. With her first attempt she missed the gear selection and the engine whined without any movement of the car. At this point she could see Ashikaga's men looking straight at her. She was now panicking and once again tried to select the reverse gear - again without success - the men were noticing that she could not pull away and were beginning to run towards May Lin and her mother in the car. May Lin was now fraught with fear and she slammed the gear stick into reverse while screaming at the top of her voice, willing the car to reverse away from Ashikaga's car. Just as his men were about to open her car door, she drove backwards at high speed all the way to the end of the street.

Spinning the *Datsun* around, she proceeded to slam her foot on the accelerator pedal, this allowed her to drive off and escape to a nearby lane, out of sight of Ashikaga and his men.

Yoshiro and Hamaguchi had watched the *Datsun* collide with the *Toyota*, but were powerless to stop it; they now ran over to the red *Toyota* where Ashikaga was sitting inside. Hamaguchi grabbed the rear door and pulled on the handle, the force of the collision crumpled the rear door enough to prevent him from opening it; with his foot jammed up against the front door, he pulled with all his might eventually releasing the car door. They both dragged the unconscious Ashikaga out of the car and laid him down on the grass verge. He awoke with a jolt, looking around in bewilderment over what had just happened. A trickle of oil mixed with water was snaking its way on the road from underneath the engine; the colourful rainbow display confirmed that the impact was severe enough to crack the sump and radiator.

"It was her driving the pick-up; I think her mother was with her too." Ashikaga spoke with a glazed look in his eyes and a gravel sound in his voice.

Both his men were totally shocked that May Lin had the audacity to drive her car at someone as revered as Ashikaga. Ashikaga was now beginning to speak coherently.

"We need to find May Lin and find her quickly; I know she will lead us to Michael Harris and to what he has that belongs to me."

Hamaguchi lifted Ashikaga forward with his arm.

"Are you okay, Ashikaga san?"

Ashikaga looked straight at Hamaguchi and thrust out his hand to grab his shirt, he spoke directly into his ear.

"That woman is trying my patience; I want her brought to me, I'm sick of not succeeding with such a simple task. Get me back to my office and get Kobyashi to meet me there."

Ashikaga threw Hamaguchi out of the way and lifted himself into the back seat of his car.

"Take Yoshiro with you and get me another car."

"Yes, Ashikaga san, we won't take long."

Hamaguchi and Yoshiro sped off on foot down the street.

Ashikaga flopped his head onto the rear headrest and proceeded to look to the sky, he lifted his hands up and cupped his forehead. He then began to slide his hands across the top of his head, breathed a heavy sigh and muttered words under his breath,

"I will get you May Lin and I will get you too Michael Harris, mark my words, and when I do, you will know pain."

CHAPTER 10

"You've been here two weeks now and yah still haven't got a job, I know yah have been to see Arthur, one of Doug's so-called pals, can he not get yah a job at the fruit and veg place?" Michael's mother stood in the kitchen making a cup of tea while lighting up her fourth cigarette of the morning.

"Will you consider packing those in? It makes everything stink in the house." Michael's retort was not welcomed by his mother. She raised her voice.

"Don't yah tell me what I can or can't do in my own house, yah should be…" Michael's mother stopped in mid-conversation as muffled words filtered through the ceiling from upstairs.

"Will yah shut your gobs down there? I've been on night shift, am trying to get some sleep."

Michael's mother continued her conversation in a whisper.

"When Trevor comes off night shift he's going to see the overman and get yah that job at Wearmouth pit and if yah don't take it then yah won't be staying here for free anymore."

Michael wanted to hate his mother for a comment like that, instead he pitied her.

"I'm off to meet my school friend Rachel on the way to school, I will see you tonight." As he squeezed past his mother to leave the house, Michael noticed a black and blue bruise on his mother's neck. He looked his mother straight in the eyes, his mother turned her head the other way and tried to distract him by walking to the other side of the kitchen.

"Does he hit you, Mam?" Michael's mother looked away and kept silent. Michael persisted,

"Does he hit you as much as he shouts at you?" Michael followed her to the other side of the kitchen and placed his hand on his mother's neck. He gently eased it to one side revealing a bruise the size of an apple. His mother brushed aside his hand and covered her neck with her work overall.

"I love him, besides he doesn't mean it."

"I'm gonna have a word with him, I'm not standing for this." Michael began to walk towards the door leading to upstairs. His mother grabbed his arm before it reached the door handle.

"Please don't, Michael, please, please, don't, yah don't know what he's capable of; go to school and finish your schooling like yah said yah wanted to do, but yah must try to get work, as this will all get worse if he doesn't see money coming in from yah."

Michael looked at his mother and then looked away.

"I'm off, I've seen these bruises since I returned from Japan, but I didn't want to believe it; I won't let it continue, Mother, that's not who I am."

"I said go." Michael's mother pointed to the door with a stoical look on her face. Michael left under duress and with a bitter taste in his mouth; he had just reached the garden gate when his mother's voice rang out from the house,

"I forgot to tell yah, there's a parcel for yah to collect at the post office."

Michael left the house and headed to meet his school friend Rachel. As he exited his street Rachel was sat waiting for him on a garden wall at the end of the block. A welcoming smile from her lifted his spirits immediately. Michael knew there was a welcoming wave coming too, and she didn't disappoint; she would never miss the opportunity of a wave, as if to communicate to Michael with a subliminal message that she cared for him as more than a friend. Her petite frame sat hunched on a low wall with her arms wrapped around her knees and the heels of her shoes gripping the top of the wall to stop her slipping off. Her dark hair was reflecting the morning sun which was rising above the North Sea in the distance. The shimmering of golden light through it resembled the ribbon of a floor gymnast being waved with a baton during a routine to create a spectacular display, and the wind blowing in from the sea made her hair alive and vibrant with life.

"Hey, you, how's the Japanese warrior?" Rachel asked. Michael's terse response was not what Rachel was expecting.

"Don't call me that, I don't like it."

"Sorry, who got out of the wrong side of the bed this morning?"

"Can we get to school please?" Michael asked.

"Are you okay, Michael? I was only joking you know, I didn't mean to upset you." Rachel looked up at Michael with a concerned expression on her face.

Michael looked across at Rachel and saw someone of his own age showing more compassion at that moment than his own mother had shown in all the time he had been home.

"You're a good friend, Rachel; I do appreciate how considerate you are being with me."

Rachel reached out her hand to touch Michael's while they were walking together, and their walking pace instantly slowed to a stop. Rachel turned Michael towards her with her hand by pulling it in to her side. She pressed herself tightly up against Michael and was looking straight into his piercing blue eyes. Michael let go of Rachel's hand and moved both his arms around Rachel's tiny waist, where he could feel the firmness of her body and the coldness of her jumper, as it draped down from her petite breasts onto her hips; sitting neatly over the waist band of her tight fitting black skirt.

Rachel smiled at Michael.

"Don't let what you witnessed at your mam's upset you; I'm sure all will be well with your mother and her boyfriend."

"You're a perceptive one aren't you?"

"Call it a woman's intuition."

Michael pulled away from Rachel's body; he lifted his forefinger up to his lips and then proceeded to place it gently onto Rachel's lips.

"It's okay to kiss me if you want, Michael, I know my mother is a doctor and a bit posh and all, but she likes you, I like you too."

Michael winked at Rachel and gave a reassuring smile. "I like you too, Rachel, posh or not; I'm just not straight in the head at the moment, I can't stop thinking about my dad and my friends in Japan, my father's body is still out there and I really have no idea what has happened to it; and that truly concerns me."

Rachel placed her arms around Michael again, but this time Michael gritted his teeth and flinched with pain.

"What is it, Michael?"

"It's nothing, just a stomach ache," Michael replied.

Rachel moved to hold Michael's hand; this was followed by a sincere look and very reassuring words.

"My mother will take a look at it for you."

"Thanks again, Rachel, but it's nothing really, I'm off to Arthur's gym tonight and I'm sure I can work the pain away there. There is a martial arts club training at the back of the gym; I have my gi with me and I'm hoping to join in with their training."

Rachel stared at Michael with a puzzled look.

"And a gi is what?"

"Rather than try to explain I will show you after school," Michael replied. He was trying to distract Rachel from the subject of his injury. Her next words confirmed that he had succeeded in doing so.

"Watch yourself down there, the guys in that gym are all into steroids and they have all kinds going on when they work as bouncers at the local night clubs."

Michael stopped himself from explaining that he was going there to get a job on the night club doors and instead just reiterated his intention to train at the gym.

"I'm going to get fit that's all."

The mere fact that he refrained from imparting information about his potential employment as a night club bouncer, confirmed to him that he had a soft spot for Rachel and he enjoyed being with her.

"What's your first lesson, Rachel?" Michael enquired.

"I'm off to English first," Rachel replied.

Michael began running across the yard to the school,

"Okay, have a good day, I will catch up soon."

Rachel tried to attract his attention before he got too far away.

"How about coming round to my house for tea on Saturday, Michael?"

Michael shouted back with his hand cupped against his mouth while running further away from Rachel,

"I'm going to the match with Bill from school, I think."

Rachel shouted back,

"They're away this weekend."

Michael reluctantly conceded.

"Are you sure?" But before she could answer, Michael agreed to her request.

"Alright, what time do you want me?"

Rachel now knew she had got what she wanted.

"See you at five at my house." She looked over at Michael as he walked through the main entrance of the school and caught his eye.

"Don't be late."

Michael looked back and nodded his head in acceptance.

CHAPTER 11

"Your tea is on the table with your meal, Trevor, would yah like a dessert after that hun?"

Trevor sat on the doorstep rubbing his eyes to clear the coal dust from them; this had accumulated at each corner while he was asleep. Trevor was a tall man with a muscular physique who carried very little weight upon his frame, his hair had a natural tightly scrunched curl to it, and with his pit boots and flat cap, he was all of a six foot pitman. A pitman with coal etched contours upon his face from the constant years of working the face at the pit. His fingernails were virtually non-existent from the weekly grind of working in the plumes of 'black gold' dust that covered anything in its path, including the men that fought daily with the equipment to bring the precious coal to the surface. Trevor was a heavy drinker and smoker, this was his way of releasing the pressures of working in such a harsh environment, and it contributed to the weathering of his face in such a way that made his good looking features become pitted. This gave him the appearance of always looking sun tanned, like a fisherman would look following years of trawler fishing in the cold North Sea.

Trevor finished his cigarette and walked inside to sit at the table, whereupon he clutched his mug of tea in his left hand and picked up his fork in his right, he took a sip of his tea and then promptly slammed it down on the table.

"Have yah made that tea in a pot?" Trevor asked sharply.

"Yes I have, hun, is it okay?" Michael's mother asked tentatively.

Trevor pushed the mug into the middle of the kitchen table and looked up towards Michael's mother with an indignant scowl.

"Yah know that tea is stewed, Shirley, it tastes lousy, make a new pot now and hurry yerself up." Trevor was pointing at Shirley's face and looking at her to see her reaction.

She looked back and answered quickly,

"I will do it right away, hun. Is your meal okay?"

Trevor lifted his head up from his plate and rolled his eyes slowly around to where Michael's mother was standing, his scowl relayed the message, but he backed it up with a demoralising comment.

"It's average; don't forget I'm off nights tonight, so I will want my tea on the table when I come in."

Trevor stood up and placed his arm on Shirley's shoulder, he then proceeded to twist her away from the kitchen sink so she was facing him.

"Has that useless son of yours got a job yet?" The fear welled up in Michael's mother's eyes, as she nervously spoke.

"He hasn't as yet, but he is trying."

Trevor picked up his khaki coloured haversack, stuffed his sandwiches and flask inside and headed towards the door.

"So the pit's not good enough for him is it not? We'll see about that." With those words he left the house with a slam of the door and a clatter of the blinds hanging on the back of it. The blinds continued to swing from side to side for the next few seconds until they slowly scraped their way to a halt. Michael's mother was entranced by the noise and the swaying of the blinds, but as the motion of the blinds ceased, she burst into tears, her legs weakened and she slumped to the floor in a heap. The whole idea of Trevor being in the house while Michael was there in the coming days filled her with dread.

CHAPTER 12

"Bill, didn't you say that we were going to the match on Saturday?" Michael shouted, as he and his school friend Bill met up to head home after their last lesson.

Bill looked at Michael through his National Health glasses, held together with a pink cloth plaster wrapped around the bridge.

"Your minds still away in Japan, it's next Saturday that the home game is, we're away this Saturday. Are yah sure yah can remember which strip we play in?"

"Ha ha, very funny, even when I was away I always looked out for the lads."

Michael remembered Bill from his early primary school days with many fond memories, and just as they were walking home together across the playground now, he did the same back then too.

They would often stay out playing football until they couldn't see the ball in front of them.

"Are yah up for a kick about tonight then?" Bill enquired.

"I'm busy tonight, I'm off to Arthur's gym and I'm going to pop in the karate club at the back of the gym for a session; I have been told they also have a sword specialist who teaches there."

Bill and Michael were just exiting the school gates – continuing their conversation -when they heard a voice shout out from behind the wall to the side of the school gates.

"Eww, nip lover! Yee and specky four eyes are gonna get a good kickin for being swats."

Michael slowly turned around to look at the person who hurled the abuse; he then looked across at his friend Bill.

"What did he say? I really didn't understand much of that." Bill looked up at Michael shaking his head.

"Yah really need to brush up on your local dialect and lose that posh twang. The gist of it is, Grappa doesn't like yah coz yah love Japanese, he doesn't like me coz I'm half blind and he hates anyone who remotely tries for a decent education at school."

Michael burst out laughing at the way Bill described the comments in such a nonchalant manner.

"Awe nor," Bill exclaimed.

Michael was still laughing at this point and had completely missed the fact that Grappa and his five mates were walking ever closer to where he and Bill were stood; they continued with their onslaught of abuse.

By now all of this aggressive rhetoric and gesticulating by Grappa and his pals was attracting a large crowd of school children of all ages, who had now formed a ring of bodies around the stand-off. Grappa was now stood three feet away from Michael and Bill; Grappa's pals were grouped just behind him. One of his pals shouted from behind Grappa,

"Go on, kick him in."

Michael looked over towards the boy doing the shouting and immediately stopped laughing.

"I'm pleased yah decided to take it serious, come on let's just run, I've already had my glasses smashed once by this lot, I really don't want another clout on the nose," Bill said nervously while looking around for his easiest exit away from the confrontation.

"You stay right where you are, Bill." Michael pointed to the ground at Bill's feet.

"Are yah for real? Come on, Michael, we need to run now or we're in deep…" Bill was cut off in mid-conversation by Grappa's voice.

"Yah should listen to yah specky mate there and run, ugly boy."

Michael still didn't flinch; the crowd was now four deep, forming a clear circle of around forty feet in diameter, surrounding all concerned. Each time Grappa and his gang edged forward, everyone in the circle moved the same distance. The whole spectacle resembled a shoal of fish swimming in the sea, trying its best to confuse a pursuing predator by splitting its formation into pockets of holes.

The crowd groaned after the last comment made by Grappa, because

Michael didn't budge and that could mean only one thing – there would be a ruck very soon, and like Romans baying for blood in an amphitheatre, the schoolyard crowd were goading the gladiators to attack the Christians.

The crowd that accumulated was now attracting a lot of attention, not only from the school children, but the teachers too. Rachel also heard the commotion; she began to run over to where this was taking place as soon as she observed the physical education teacher running towards the schoolyard from the school field.

Michael instinctively knew there was an attack of some kind coming from Grappa, and so did the crowd as their chanting became louder and louder. "Scrap, scrap, scrap, scrap, scrap," they all shouted in unison. The noise was deafening and the tension was unbearable. Bill was starting to shake and strangely, so was Grappa - Michael was still and calm.

Just as the barracking reached a crescendo, Grappa unleashed a flailing fist swinging towards Michael's head, he doubled up this by swinging his rider boot forward in an attempt to catch Michael between his legs with a rising kick. It was obvious by Grappa's reaction that he was taken completely by surprise by Michael's response.

Instead of trying to move backward or sideways to avoid the fist and boot from Grappa's assault, Michael reared up on his toes with a very pronounced arching posture, pulling his frame away from the attack. He then moved his body with the grace and poise of a praying mantis, but the power of a bear and thrust forward at great pace. The observing crowd barely noticed the cleverly concealed fist travelling at three times the speed of Grappa's attack, towards Grappa's face: What they did observe was the splash of blood that followed the very loud crack. Grappa was no slouch and at over six foot himself and very thickset around his shoulders and neck, he knew that something very fast, very powerful and very painful had just knocked him completely off his feet. Due to the force, he was lifted upward from the ground, with his body completely horizontal, he landed with a dull thud on the tarmac of the school yard. Michael stealthily moved forward to finish him off on the ground, just at the moment he was to drop his heel down onto Grappa's face, he was halted by a deep voice from the other side of the school yard.

"That's enough, you boys! That's enough, break this fight up immediately." The P.E. teacher was now inside the circle made by the crowd.

Michael stood above Grappa and was glaring into his eyes.

"If I hear of you bullying, Bill again, I will finish you next time, do you understand?" Grappa was concussed by the blow and slowly nodded his head which was cupped with his bloodied hands. Before the teacher got to the centre of the commotion, Michael offered his hand out to Grappa to lift him to his feet, which Grappa duly accepted.

The teacher broke through the crowd and now confronted all the boys involved in the fracas.

"All of you seven lads report to the Head's office in the morning, but right now, get yourselves home, and everyone else here, just clear off to your homes, there is nothing to see here." The teacher clapped his hands.

"Come on, clear off now I said." The crowd dispersed. Michael and Bill turned around to continue their walk across the school yard and there straight in front of them stood Rachel. She stood with her arms folded and an indignant look on her face.

"I bet you think you're a real tough guy don't you? Well I'm afraid that kind of macho bollocks won't impress the likes of me, and if you had bothered to ask, you would have discovered that Grappa and I have been over for more than two weeks." And with those words she stormed off in the opposite direction across the school field towards the bus stop.

Michael turned to look at Bill who was stood in the exact same position as he was at the beginning of the commotion, his haversack clutched in his left hand and trailing on the ground, his oversized school blazer sleeves concealing his hands and pulling down on his shoulders, which matched his extra-large trousers which crumpled over his shoes at the front and frayed at the bottom from his continual stepping on them with his heels. His glasses were perched on the very end of his nose and the Elastoplast was hanging in front of the lens on his right eye. Michael looked at Bill in complete disbelief.

"And you were saying run, how far were you expecting to get looking like that?"

Bill started laughing.

"I'm an expert when it comes to running away from, Grappa and his crew, unfortunately for me, they always catch me."

Michael also began laughing.

"Cheerfulness in the face of adversity, I like that, Bill." Michael walked over to Bill and put his arm around his shoulder.

"Come on, mate, let's get going."

Bill shrugged his shoulders and began walking.

"I suppose that whole episode has spoilt your chances with Rachel?"

"I like, Rachel, don't get me wrong, however, I have a lot of things on my plate at the moment, so maybe missing Saturday tea isn't such a bad thing: at least now it explains the whole scenario behind the Grappa confrontation. I thought it was a bit odd for him to call us swats, you and I don't really fit that bill," Michael replied.

Bill began to walk in the direction of his house.

"Yeah, I think you're right about that. Hey, don't forget to call at the post office on your way to the gym, Michael, and Michael…"

Michael abruptly replied,

"What?"

"Thank yah for today, no one has ever stood up for me like that."

"See you tomorrow, Bill."

CHAPTER 13

Michael arrived at Arthur's gym and immediately walked towards the back where the dojo was; he was forty-five minutes early and was the first person to arrive. As he pushed open the swinging fire door, he entered the hall. There was an unmistakable smell of sweat blended with ground in dust that could only be akin to a dojo. The dojo had a wooden floor which was stippled with patches of light sneaking through the half-drawn curtains at the windows; as the door swung closed behind Michael, the noise echoed all the way to the top of the extremely high and very much water damaged ceiling in the hall. The closing door stopped creaking and an eerie silence blanketed the room.

The memory of the dojo in Japan came flooding back, the whole aura in the room took Michael back to the sounds of his instructor teaching him with his father stood beside him, at that moment he was back in the dojo in Japan remembering good times. Then the flashback that he didn't want to see crept into his mind, the whole horrid event played out through his head and made him break into a sweat inside the palms of his hands. He began to fill with rage, remembering that the man who killed his father was still out there and was not being held to account for his crime.

"Now then, young Harris. How are yah?"

Michael was pulled back from his thoughts with the entrance of Arthur from the gym next door.

"Oh. Hello, Arthur. It's good to see you again," Michael replied.

"You're keen aren't yah?" Arthur said.

Michael looked across at Arthur and smiled.

"I've been to the post office to collect this parcel and because it's on the way to your gym, I thought I would come straight along."

Arthur approached Michael and placed his arm on his shoulder.

"I heard about what actually happened out there in Japan, so I understand how tough it will be for yah to put your karate suit on and start training again. I will leave yah to have some time on your own for that, however, I'm just in the office at the back of the gym if yah need me. Oh, and I've got yah your badge and a suit for the weekend; yah will be on the doors with me. Did yah say yah were gym training after your karate?"

"Yes I was hoping to."

Arthur creased a huge grin into his face. "Count it as done. And now that you're working the doors, there's no charge in the dojo or the gym either."

Michael looked astounded. "Really? Thanks, Arthur."

Arthur headed out of the room. "Don't mention it, I will leave yah to open yah parcel and sort yerself out for training."

Michael walked into the changing room and sat on the bench. He pulled the parcel close towards himself. The parcel was over five feet long a foot wide and around six inches deep; he slowly peeled back the sticky brown parcel tape to open one end of the box. Whatever it was inside was wrapped in more cardboard, and he was now able to pull the cardboard wrapped package completely out from the box. The brown tape pulled away from the end to reveal a plastic sheet, again covered with tape. On peeling back this tape the glistening blade of a Japanese katana protruded from the package and began to reflect the sunlight shining through the dojo windows. As he pulled further, the whole blade, followed by the carved bone handle revealed itself from the box. It was the very sword that Ashikaga's son used to attack Michael at the ryokan.

Immediately Michael experienced a warm sensation which promulgated through every hair on his body, before culminating at the tips of his fingers and toes; at the thought of May Lin being alive. It must have been sent by her because she was the only one who carried it away from the ryokan that day. This was soon confirmed, as a letter that was taped to the handle of the sword, dislodged itself and zig-zagged its way downwards as it slowly fell to the floor. Michael picked it up to read it.

'Dear Michael,

I hope all is well with you, it may be that by the time you receive this sword Ashikaga will have captured me; I say this because I have already had a very close encounter with him and his men, luckily on that occasion I escaped to another hideout where I am sending this letter from. I am trying to make contact with Inspector Bando and the district police here; however it is very difficult to find anyone I can trust or who is not being paid by the Yakuza. Contacting Inspector Bando seems silly after what we experienced at the ryokan, but I am trying my best to find someone to stand against Ashikaga, and I won't give up until I do.

I did manage to arrange your father's burial: a very close friend helped me with this and is also assisting me to stay hidden. Hopefully one day when justice is done here, you can come back to Japan and show your respects to your father without feeling that your life is at risk.

Finally, stay alert over there, whatever it was that Ashikaga wanted from you must have been very important to him; the fact that he lost his son trying to retrieve it, means that if he thinks you still have it, you could certainly still be in grave danger.

Enjoy your training with the katana and stay safe.

Missing you more than you would ever know.

May Lin. xx.'

Michael sat silent for a moment and then slowly raised the letter up to his nose; he could smell May Lin's scent on the paper. The night at the ryokan played over in his mind and allowed him to drift back to that evening and the memory of being so close to May Lin. He continued to think about her while he unpacked his sports holdall. He took out his gi to get dressed for training, and as he lifted his gi jacket from his bag, a white envelope fell from the inside and landed softly on the floor in front of him: the name 'Doug Harris' was on the front of the letter.

He had completely forgotten about the letter which he had collected from his instructor's desk on the day of the massacre.

He leaned forward to retrieve it, but before he could touch the envelope a gust of wind blew the letter two feet further forward from where he was standing, the dust on the changing room floor swirled around resembling something like a dust bowl in a desert, lifting the dust into a mini whirlwind. The dust in the room flashed past the sun beaming in through the windows and deposited itself over on the other side of the room. The hairs stood up on the back of Michael's neck, but this time it was not a pleasurable experience, and as he looked down at his arms, starting at his wrists, all the hairs stood erect, travelling all the way back up each arm to his elbows where they stopped with each hair standing firm like trees in a forest, following a pounding by a storm. The air which surrounded the area where Michael was standing had an eerie feel to it as it swished and swirled around his body. The door to the changing room crashed shut, returning his thoughts to the old room he was standing in and focusing his mind on the reality of why he was there.

"Are you in there, Michael?"

Michael walked to pick up the envelope and before he replied he placed the letter from May Lin in his back pocket.

"Who is it?"

"It's Rachel."

"If you have come to…"

"I've come to say sorry." Rachel cut Michael short.

"Oh, have you?" Michael tentatively enquired.

Rachel walked over and sat on the bench near Michael and gestured with her hand for him to sit down.

"I have been told about what happened with Grappa, I'm sorry for thinking that was down to you, it was my misunderstanding of the whole situation and for that I am very sorry. Can we start over again?" Michael sat down next to Rachel and looked towards the floor before he spoke.

"I like you a lot, Rachel; it's just that at this moment in time I have a huge number of things going on in my head, which you may find difficult to deal with and actually I'm not sure I want to share all those things with you."

Rachel put her hand on Michael's hand and gripped it tight.

"That's fine, Michael, I know you are having a tough time of it at the moment and I will be here if you need me; sometimes telling someone is better than bottling it up. A problem shared is..."

Michael now cut Rachel short, "Is a problem halved, I know."

"What's in the envelope, Michael?" Rachel enquired.

"I'm not sure what it is or whether I should be showing you," Michael replied.

Rachel looked at Michael with a smirk on her face.

"Come on, try me."

Michael held the envelope between two hands,

"Okay then, we will both look together."

"The tension's killing me," Rachel said.

Michael shook his head.

"See, you're not taking it serious."

Rachel put her arm around Michael and kissed him on the cheek.

"I'm messing with you, please, just open it."

Michael ripped open the envelope and pulled out a very old and very tatty yellow document with a gilt edge, it was accompanied by three pieces of white paper. The yellow document was etched in black ink with some words in red ink at the bottom of the page and all the letters were in Japanese. Rachel held the three white pieces of paper while Michael held the yellow document.

"That yellow document looks very old, a kind of valuable old, as if it has been handed down to people over a lot of years," Rachel said. Michael turned to Rachel with a dismayed look on his face.

"And when have you seen old valuable documents in your short lifetime?"

Rachel smiled and looked back at Michael with a degree of smugness in her facial expression.

"My mother has valuable old papers and books on medicine, handed down from her father and her father's father, who were all practicing medicine many years ago."

Michael slowly nodded his head with a submissive look on his face.

"You're not just a pretty face are you?"

Rachel dismissed his comment by shaking her head, but knew that she would impress Michael when she spoke about the letter.

"These white documents seem to be an English explanation for that yellow document, a lot of it is convoluted rhetoric about ownership, land rights and what seem to be descendants of high ranking Japanese lords. It appears to offer the owner some kind of protected right to something, but I'm not sure what. However I do know somebody who will be able to tell you, because he is not quite as pretty as me."

"Sorry, it was meant as a compliment," Michael hastily replied.

"And how come you have such in depth knowledge of Japan?"

Rachel stood up to leave without answering.

"Listen, if you're my friend again, why not come over for tea on Saturday and I will ask my mother if she can introduce you to my Uncle Zak, he is a professor of Asian history at Durham University. Yes, you guessed it; he is the one who taught me about Japan. He will be able to tell you what that letter means and maybe if it has any value."

Michael quickly accepted Rachel's invitation with a youthful excitement in his voice.

"Thank you very much, Rachel, I will come on Saturday. What about pretty boy, Grappa?" Michael asked.

Rachel replied while waving her hand as she exited the changing room.

"Too good looking for me, I prefer the rugged, not so pretty type. See you Saturday."

Michael didn't know what to make of that comment, but soon forgot it as he carefully folded the letter back into the envelope and continued to prepare for his training.

CHAPTER 14

"Come in, Kobyashi; please tell me you have good news for me?"

"Yes, Ashikaga san, we have found May Lin," Kobyashi replied.

Ashikaga jumped up from behind his desk and waved his hand at him,

"Bring her in here now."

Kobyashi rushed out of Ashikaga's office to fetch May Lin. Ashikaga walked over towards his office window and tugged on the sliding doors to let some fresh air into the room. He walked over towards his shiny ebony desk, loosened his jacket buttons and sat on the front of his desk holding his left fist in his right hand as he waited for Kobyashi to bring May Lin into his office.

Kobyashi walked into the room flanked by Hamaguchi and Yoshiro; they were both tightly gripping a bedraggled May Lin by her arms as they marched her over to the centre of Ashikaga's varnished wooden floor and threw her down in a heap at his feet. Her beautiful black hair was matted with dry blood and draped over her slumped head which dangled towards the floor; her posture was that of a tired dog beaten by its callous owner until it was completely subjugated and with no desire to stand. Her bare feet and legs were jet black with dirt. One of her arms was supported by the other. On her supported arm her hand had yellow and black bruising at the tips of all her fingers and from the way she held her arm, it was obviously giving her great pain. The few remaining clothes that covered her were all torn and stained with blood and dirt.

Ashikaga remained sitting on the edge of his desk.

"Have my boys been a little rough with you?" he said with a piercing glare towards May Lin.

"Well... that will be pleasant compared to what I am going to do with you.

You and your fugitive boy killed my son, and I am going to kill you if you do not tell me where the letter is that you and your boy stole from Master Tokugawa's dojo." Ashikaga raised his voice following no response from May Lin.

"Do you hear me, whore?"

May Lin's body flinched. Ashikaga moved closer to May Lin and stood over her, looking down at her crumpled torso. He lifted her right arm up and twisted it over until her palm faced towards the ceiling. Her dirt engrained hand was grazed all the way back to her wrist. Ashikaga pulled a handkerchief from his pocket and began to roll it into a ball in his hand; he spat on it and slowly rubbed the handkerchief up and down her hand. May Lin was whimpering with the pain, but Ashikaga continued until he uncovered what he was searching for.

"The tattoos on your hand are white dragons, this means you work for me, you have not only betrayed me by working against me, but you have also killed one of my family." Ashikaga continued to twist May Lin's arm as far round as he could, until her body became so contorted that her normal shape was unrecognisable. She was grimacing with pain and let out a muffled yelp that she could barely muster the energy to utter.

"You would be dead now if it wasn't for the fact that you are my best chance to get at that boy," Ashikaga said.

May Lin was looking up towards Ashikaga with the hope that he would take pity on her and show a modicum of compassion.

Instead he lifted his leg up until his thigh was in line with his waist and then he thrust his foot forward and pounded it into her neck whilst keeping a tight grip on her wrist and continuing to twist her hand round to inflict maximum pain. May Lin was close to passing out with the pain and sobbed uncontrollably. Ashikaga continued to push his foot hard against her throat and was finding great pleasure from inflicting pain on her: she was now close to choking to death. Ashikaga pulled his foot away from her throat and she gasped for air.

"Tell me Michael Harris's address in England and I might stop." There was no response from May Lin and she collapsed in a heap on the floor as her eyes gazed in obscurity at the ceiling; Ashikaga pushed her limp body over with his foot. She flopped forward and her chin bounced off the wooden floor.

"Get her out of my sight."

Hamaguchi and Yoshiro rushed over and lifted May Lin up from the floor.

Ashikaga waved his hand in the air like a referee giving a decision at a karate tournament.

"Keep her alive out the back... she will speak," Ashikaga said assuredly.

"And if she doesn't give us what we need, she will most definitely be useful as bait at some point."

CHAPTER 15

"Come on in, Michael. How was the training session?" Michael stood in front of Arthur's desk with his holdall slung across his shoulder; the bone handle of the katana was protruding from the holdall.

"Yeah, it was okay, could do with a touch more sparring time, but the guy doing sword training was very good."

"You mean Tomo?" Arthur replied.

"That's him, yeah," Michael said.

Arthur walked over to Michael and pulled Michael's katana so far out of his bag.

"Ya'll need a scabbard for that thing otherwise ya'll ruin the blade. Oh and don't bring it with yah when you're working the doors or ya'll have the bizzies chasing us."

Michael looked at Arthur and smiled reassuringly.

"I know you don't mean that."

Arthur pushed an envelope towards Michael on the table.

"Yah wouldn't believe what people have brought to work on the doors in the past. There's an advance of money for yah and the rest will follow once yah have worked the weekend."

"Thank you for this, Arthur, I won't forget it," Michael said.

Arthur sat forward in his seat.

"Doug Harris was like family around this gym and on the doors, a very popular chap and a tough cookie to boot, the least I can do is give his son a leg up. See yah on Friday seven sharp."

CHAPTER 16

Michael made his way back to his mother's house after taking a short cut through the colliery yard, making sure to avoid the ever present security guard who welcomed the opportunity to catch anyone sneaking through, but before he reached his mother's garden gate he was distracted by the upstairs window of his mother's room at the front of the house.

The bright red curtains were blowing in the wind through a broken window; it was certainly noticeable, illuminated by the early evening sun, people who were passing were turning their heads to look up at the conspicuous display that fluttered through the broken pane of glass. As he walked through the garden gate a voice shouted from behind him.

"He's beat her again, it's becoming ridiculous, that lass is always black and blue; I know she sets her lip up, but she doesn't deserve that."

Michael stopped dead in his tracks and turned to face whoever it was that uttered the words.

Standing on the other side of the garden fence was the old man from the house next door. He was wearing a set of chequered pyjamas covered with a black donkey jacket, a pair of pit boots with the laces undone and he was donning a flat cap. The smoke from the cigarette that was stuck to his bottom lip was drifting upwards towards the broken street light he was standing beneath, creating a cloudy haze around his face. Michael looked at him, looked back at the window then looked at him once more.

"Deserve what?"

The man could see the venom in Michael's eyes and began shuffling back along the path towards his own garden, knowing that he may have just earned his neighbour a good hiding.

"Now keep me out of this, I don't want any trouble," the neighbour shouted as he retreated behind his own garden gate.

Michael stared at the man momentarily until he heard a groan from the upstairs window where the break in the glass was. Michael ran towards the house and thrust his shoulder on the door while simultaneously yanking down on the handle. He rushed upstairs clearing the stairs two at a time; he ran across the landing and pushed his mother's bedroom door open. The quilt from the double bed was bundled up in the corner of the room near to where the broken window was. The pole supporting the curtain was only attached at one side with the other side perched on the cosmetic laden dresser. On the window ledge near the broken window there were large pieces of pottery from a vase which had obviously been hurled through the window. The shade on the ceiling light was crooked and hanging precariously from the bulb above it; the lamp from the bedside table was laid upon the bed with the cable strewn behind it, and the plug missing from the end. The room had a smell of foist which came from the mould growing its way through the woodchip wallpaper. The room looked like it had been turned over by a thief searching for something of value. Shoes, clothes and even drawers were scattered all over the floor.

"Mother, where are you?" Michael apprehensively called out.

A dull groan emanated from the scrunched up quilt cover in the corner. Michael leapt across the bed and hauled the quilt cover off the floor; his action was met by a low sounding yelp from underneath. Michael's mother was on her back on the floor; her eyes were black where her tears had washed her mascara down her face, her t-shirt was ripped up one side revealing her breast, and an unfastened silky black bra was entwined around her forearm. A coagulated blood patch sealed the corner of her mouth making it difficult for her to move her jaw to speak. A graze ran from her left eye to her ear; stuck to her skin in between was a half torn eyelid with eyelashes still attached. Both of her eyes were closed from the dried blood sticking them together.

"I know he did this, where is he?" Michael growled with anger.

Michael's mother reached out her left hand revealing three broken nails and grasped firmly onto Michael's right hand, she forced the words from her mouth, obviously in great pain each time she took a breath to speak.

"No, I know what yah want to do and I forbid it, I love him, Michael."

Michael's face was flushed red with ire.

"What? I don't believe I'm hearing this, how can you love someone who treats you like this? Why do you stay with him?"

His mother's grip tightened around his wrist, and she struggled to speak once again.

"Don't think yah can come back into my home after all these years and question how I live my life, yah don't understand love, so don't yah dare question mine."

Michael stared down at the pitiful mess that was his mother lying beneath him and was completely perplexed at how any person could stay in a relationship that could leave someone looking like this.

"Mother you need help, I'm calling the police." Michael peeled his mother's hand from his wrist and stood up to walk out the door. Michael's mother grabbed the side of the mattress on the bed and pulled herself upright, wincing with pain at each small movement she made.

"It's my fault, I can't stop arguing and shouting back, it's not him it's me, I won't prosecute him."

Michael halted at the bedroom door with his back to his mother; he remained facing away from her while he spoke fervently.

"I can't believe I'm hearing this, Mother, nobody is allowed to do this to someone they live with because they have an argument, this is the seventies, not the Victorian era, you can't beat a woman to a pulp and expect to get away with it, I'm phoning for an ambulance and then I'm off to find Trevor at the club; if you won't have the police sort it, then I'll sort it." Before his mother could take a breath to reply Michael was in the sitting room arranging for an ambulance, he then set off to find Trevor at the club and slammed the door behind him on his exit from his mother's house.

CHAPTER 17

Michael arrived at the working men's club to deal out justice to Trevor. He had never been inside a working men's club and had no idea what to expect, he was instantly enlightened when he walked through the entrance, the immediate stench of cigarette smoke hit the back of his throat, it had drifted towards him from the cloud of smoke that hung in the air near the open doors at the back of the club. Michael began to walk towards those doors where the sound of voices filtered through the smoky haze and up the corridor. He was stopped in his tracks by a voice shouting from behind a counter near the entrance.

"Woah, mister, are yah a member?"

Michael turned to his left to see an old man in what looked to be a converted cupboard with a sliding door and a ledge perched in front of him - a similar set up to a serving hatch in a takeaway restaurant.

"No, I'm not here to drink or partake in anything; I'm here to find Trevor Arnott."

The old man twisted his face in disbelief and spoke in a slow condescending manner.

"I don't care who yah have come to see, yah either need to be a member or yah need to find a member to sign yah in, otherwise you're going nowhere."

Michael was ready to barge his way along the corridor ignoring the doorman, but just as he was pondering his next move, a man called out from behind him.

"I'll sign him in." The father of Michael's best friend Bill was standing near the entrance.

"I bet yah don't have ten pence either do yah?"

Michael shook his head. "You're right, I don't."

Bill's father flicked ten pence to the doorman who duly caught it and dropped it into an old ashtray by his side. Michael acknowledged Bill's father with a relieved nod of his head.

"Thank you for that, Mr Wilson."

The doorman waved his hand to allow Michael to pass, but before Michael walked on, Bill's father ushered Michael to a quiet corner of the club corridor and whispered in his ear.

"Yah seem upset, Michael; you're not in trouble are yah?"

"No, I'm looking for Trevor Arnott," and before Bill's father could say another word, Michael was marching down the corridor to the main part of the club. Michael got to the end of the corridor and flung the double doors open. The noise in the room came from around fifty men sliding dominos around shiny topped tables, hitting snooker balls on the heavy slate snooker table, shuffling cards and clicking draughts. The room had no curtains open and the only natural light poured its way through two skylights in the ceiling like a torch with new batteries turned on for the first time in a blacked out forest. The smoke was illuminated by the skylights and trailed from almost every man's hand holding a cigarette; and in every other hand was a pint of beer, the noise resembled rush hour in a busy train station. As the doors where Michael entered clattered against the frames inside the room, it all went silent and everyone stopped what they were doing and stared at Michael, apart from one table in the corner where the seated men continued to slide dominos around its shiny top.

Michael was somewhat unnerved by all the eyes glaring at him, but nevertheless his pent-up rage over what had happened to his mother transfixed his thoughts.

"Where is Trevor Arnott?" Michael demanded. The last set of dominos gradually stopped sliding around the table in the corner and a man sat at a seat with his back to Michael, slid his chair around to face him.

"What do yah want, ugly boy?" Trevor said, with a mocking tone to impress his pals.

This curt remark was accompanied by taunting laughter from other men in the room. The laughter slowly ceased and the room fell to a deathly silence, everyone was now watching to see how Michael would react to this intimidating comment. Michael took a slow deep breath and directed his gaze towards Trevor's eyes, his mind flashed back to the image of his mother lying on the floor covered in blood and bruises, and a surge of adrenalin fuelled rage flooded through his body. Michael lunged forward and began striding towards where Trevor was sat. He was losing the battle to contain his fury and his only thought now was to get close to him and inflict pain in reprisal for what he had done to his mother. Michael was moving closer and closer until he got to within three feet of Trevor. What he didn't expect was the two snooker cues that were swung around to his waist, crashing the wind out of his stomach. His left arm attempted to block one of the cues, but the speed of the swing carried it through his block into his abdomen, swiftly followed by the second cue which he did not see at all, the blow buckled him over, leaving him gasping for breath. The two men at the snooker table had halted Michael with a surprise double blow, the attack slowed Michael up and made him drop to his knees, and all the men in the club proceeded to laugh. Michael could hear the laughter ringing around the room, he knew if he could steal a minute before Trevor moved he would be able to catch his breath, compose himself and close in on Trevor. The laughter started to fade and Michael was close to recovering. Trevor stood up with his pint glass in his hand.

"Who do yah think yah are, boy? Coming into my club asking for me, you're just like your disobedient mother; yah don't know your place, boy, so I'm going to show yah your place." Trevor raised his glass high in the air with the intention of smashing it straight down onto Michael's head. What Trevor didn't know was Michael was now feigning his injury and was waiting for Trevor to attack him. Everyone was silent in the club waiting to see Trevor make his move and humiliate the boy. Michael was patiently waiting to stop his attack and unleash a crushing blow to Trevor's face; Trevor was about to swing his arm with the glass when a voice rang out from the door.

"Unless you two want to be spending a night in the cells, this better stop right now. Come on you lot, get back to your darts and your dominos, otherwise your dinners will be getting cold."

Behind Michael stood a uniformed policeman. Trevor immediately sat back down, still glaring at Michael and feeling that he had scored a crushing moral victory over him; he collected his dominos and continued with his game. The policeman pointed at Michael.

"You need to go outside, there's someone waiting for you out there."

Michael straightened himself up and moved slowly away from Trevor and the men with the snooker cues. He was bitterly disappointed in himself for not capitalising on the opportunity to avenge his mother. Michael felt that this whole escapade did nothing to make the belligerent Trevor feel any remorse or regret for what he had done. Michael headed out of the club to find out who the policeman intended him to meet. Standing in the doorway was Bill and his father.

"I hope yah don't mind, Michael, my father rang me from the club and by then he had already phoned the police."

Michael looked at Bill and wanted to tell him to mind his own business, but he knew that Bill was just looking out for him.

"Thanks, Bill, you're a good friend," Michael conceded.

The policeman walked up behind Michael.

"Come on you chaps; I think you should be making your way home." The policeman placed his arm on Michael's shoulder.

"Are you sure you're okay? The barmaid in the club informs me two men hit you with snooker cues, do I need to have a word with them?"

Michael looked resolutely at the policeman. "I don't need you to speak with anyone, thank you."

"Fine, have it your way, let's have no repeat of today though, eh?" The policeman headed towards the exit and left the club. Michael followed with Bill and his father, but could not help thinking that things would have been different if people had not interfered.

Michael felt thwarted by Trevor and wanted to be angry towards Bill and Bill's father, but his friendship with Bill was too important to him to jeopardise.

Bill was quickly reacquainted with Michael when he returned to his school in Sunderland following his time in Japan, at a time when other people ignored him, Bill was a supportive friend. Michael's bond with bill was very special because of that.

"I was worried that yah might miss the match next Saturday if yah got into trouble," Bill said in a concerned voice.

Michael smiled and walked out of the club with Bill.

"I'll be there, Bill, you can count on it. Oh, and thanks for intervening tonight, who knows what might have happened in there?" Michael disguised his true feelings of dissatisfaction at not dealing with Trevor whilst smiling at Bill.

Bill patted Michael on the back and spoke reassuringly,

"Yah can tell me all about it on the way home."

Bill and his father walked all the way back to Michael's mother's house and were pleased that they had been able to help him today; but they failed in their attempt to persuade him to stay with them at their house following their arrival.

"Haway, Michael, why don't yah come to our house?" Bill's father said.

"No really I will be fine, I just need to know if my mother is here, I suspect not," Michael said sadly, knowing what a mess she looked when he left her.

Bill's father had a worried look on his face. "If your mother is in hospital, do yah really want to be staying here on your own?"

"Look, you have both done more than enough and I have no issues with staying on my own," Michael said sternly.

Bill was still concerned.

"It's not the staying alone part that worries me, it's when Trevor returns tonight, what then? If he is capable of doing that to your mother, who knows what he is capable of?"

Michael looked directly into Bill's father's eyes with the same determination that allowed him to escape the Yakuza in Japan.

"This man is a tough man when he is with his mates and he is a tough man when he is beating up my defenceless mother, but I guarantee you he won't come home tonight, because he knows that I will be waiting for him. When he wakes up in the morning on someone's sofa, he will know that he will have to face the day wondering when I will catch up to him and inflict the same pain on him that he inflicted on my mother."

Bill's father turned to Bill and flicked his thumb in the direction of home. He looked at Michael and spoke in a conciliatory tone.

"Just be careful, Michael, I have no doubt yah can handle yerself, but Trevor can call on his so-called mates and that makes the odds uneven and dangerous. Let us know how your mother is when yah hear and take care tonight. Are yah sure I can't change your mind about staying with us?"

Michael waved his hand at Bill and his father.

"See you tomorrow, now go on get yourselves home."

Even though Michael knew his mother was in a bad way when he called the ambulance, he was not expecting an empty house when he returned; this made him feel even more angered that his plans to avenge his mother were scuppered. And now he was spending a night alone sleeping – as May Lin put it – with one eye open.

CHAPTER 18

It was that thought of sleeping with one eye open that re-ignited the memory of May Lin and it was the image of her lying naked next to the fire in the ryokan that helped Michael forget tonight's events and start to unwind. He discovered that his mother was comfortable in hospital, but she was sleeping and therefore could not speak with him on the phone. Michael began to feel very much alone; staying at Bill's house was a very attractive proposition right now.

Climbing in to his single bed in a small single room at the back of the house prompted him to reflect on what he had been through in the last few weeks and his thoughts drifted to his father and friends he lost in Japan. He thought of May Lin and wondered if she was safe and whether he would ever see her again. Michael prided himself on being tough and not showing weakness, but because he was on his own, unsure of his future and worried about his past catching up with him, it was all too much; he rubbed his eyes in a vain attempt to stop himself from crying, the emotion of all that had happened to him in the past weeks, rolled down his cheeks and onto his hands as warm salty tears, each tear carried the hurt and anguish of the last few days and reminded him that he was a young man carrying the burdens of a grown man's life. His tears slowly dried on his face and he had a comforting feeling of drifting off to sleep. He had only dozed for an hour when the sound of the neighbour's dog barking woke Michael from his shallow sleep. The alarm clock was illuminated by the full moon beaming through the window in Michael's room. His immediate thoughts were to get up and get his clothes on.

Would Trevor really try to return to his home tonight after what had happened? Michael thought.

The front and back door were bolted, but Michael was taking no chances; the dog continued to bark. Michael made his way to the front of the house; he proceeded to enter his mother's bedroom, quietly dropped onto all fours and crawled towards the edge of his mother's bed. Here the broken window reflected different shades of orange from the street light flickering outside his mother's bedroom; the scattered shards of glass on the floor stood as a reminder of the mayhem that had taken place in her room. Michael eased himself up towards the window to peer out, and by this time his mouth was beginning to dry in anticipation of what he would encounter. Before he got close enough to see out of the window, he heard the noise of the door handle being pulled down. He was expecting to hear the sound of a key turning in the lock, but that sound did not transpire. Michael's mind was racing.

Why would Trevor try the door handle without using his key to enter the house?

Michael needed to see who was below the bedroom window trying to enter the door. He edged forward and peered down from the broken window and as he did so the person standing at the door looked up and caught Michael's eye. He was dressed in black with his face covered with a balaclava. On seeing Michael he immediately turned to run away from the house and as he did so another person in dark clothing ran from behind the coal house at the bottom of the garden to join him. The two men frantically ran away, hurdling the garden fence as they did so. Michael about turned and sped across the bedroom to the landing, he quickly bounded down the staircase clearing two stairs at a time. He lunged forward grabbing the handle of the back door - his hand shaking as he unlocked it - leapt outside and gave chase. When he reached the bottom of the garden at the gate, the two intruders were disappearing into the distance. Michael halted fifty yards from his house looking down the street in the direction of the men, they were now long gone, and he was gasping for breath. He turned to walk back to the house, his greatest concern was that irrespective of whom these people were, they could return and there may be more of them next time. He knew now that he would have to remain vigilant at all times, and if Trevor was being audacious enough to send his mates around to threaten him, how far would Trevor go? Michael turned around to enter the house and heard the phone ring; he quickly ran inside, locked the door behind him and grabbed the phone. His immediate fear was that this was the hospital phoning with bad news about his mother, but to his surprise and cheer he heard Rachel's sweet voice.

"Hi, Michael, you took a while to answer that, where were you?" Rachel said curiously.

"Sorry, I was otherwise occupied, nothing exciting really," Michael said calmly. As Rachel continued to speak he could feel the receiver on the phone shaking as he held it to his ear.

"I was just checking that you were still okay to come to our house for tea on Saturday?"

Michael had an image of a lovely, warm, welcoming home in his mind and this instantly lifted his spirits before he replied.

"Rachel, I can't wait, I'm really looking forward to it. I'm pleased you caught me because I was nodding off."

Rachel's happiness was immediately apparent as she replied,

"Thanks for that, Michael, I'm looking forward to it too. I should see you at school tomorrow for a chat. Have you any plans for Friday night?"

Michael hesitated to respond, knowing that he did not want to divulge any information about his job on the door.

"Er emm er… I'm off training again till quite late."

Rachel spoke confidently after Michael's jittery reply.

"Well don't come back all black and blue will you?"

"I promise I won't, Rachel," Michael said.

Rachel said her goodbyes and Michael placed the receiver back on the phone which rested on the window sill.

As he pulled the curtain back across the window, next door's dog began barking again. Immediately Michael's heart began to race. Michael walked to the back door and cautiously twisted the Venetian blinds open; he peered out the window expecting to see Trevor or more suspicious men in balaclavas, but instead he had a bird's eye view of a drunken man being sick on the path beyond the garden. The next door neighbour's Jack Russell was two feet in front of the drunk, barking at him. The man seemed oblivious to the tirade exploding from the dog's jaws and continued to prop himself up with one hand on the nearby garage wall, while he heaved his dinner all over the floor and his own shoes. The dog's barking appeared to become faster and more intense, but the man was still unfazed. The dog's barking then suddenly stopped as a taxi slowly pulled in to the street with its headlights beaming towards the drunk. The beam from the headlights illuminated the steam rising from the sick on the ground; it weaved its way up from the ground like the steam that rises from a huge pile of cow muck in a field on a crisp frosty morning. It was at this point that Michael could not contain his laughter. The dog walked closer to the man's feet and began to lick the sick on the ground, its excitement exaggerated by the rapid wagging of its tail as it continued with its feast.

Michael knew this was a good time to head off to bed, with a humorous image that would cheer him all the way.

CHAPTER 19

"Are yah sure this new lad is going to turn up tonight, we're gonna need him, we've a busy night ahead?" Arthur wrapped his arm around the nightclub owner's back and spoke reassuringly.

"He will be here, Frank, don't fret, this lad is a sound lad, just like his father Doug was." Frank looked doubtfully at Arthur.

"His father pissed off to Japan and left his mother, Arthur, that's not sound is it?"

Arthur's repost was swift and succinct.

"If that had been yee, yah would have left too."

"I suppose you're right, Michael's mother is a strange one to work out," Frank said.

Arthur put his right arm around Frank's shoulder and held the side of his forearm with his left hand. He proceeded to spin Frank one hundred and eighty degrees from the direction he was facing and indicated to Frank to look straight up the high street to the top of the hill. There striding over the horizon into full view was Michael. He was wearing a pair of grey slacks, a crisp white shirt with a red and white tie and an old beige leather jacket. His shoes were glinting as they reflected the passing car headlights with each step he made down the bank. Dusk was closing in and Michael was passing each street light as the lamps started their evening ritual of lighting the lanes in an incandescent amber glow.

"Blimey, Arthur, he's a big lad, you've come up trumps there," Frank said as he patted Arthur on the back.

Arthur turned to face Frank with a self-satisfied smirk on his face.

"Yes he is big, Frank, but more importantly when yah work the doors, he's lightning quick too."

Frank walked back towards the club entrance with his hand waving in the air.

"I don't need to hear that, Arthur, he's here to look after my punters, not to hit them."

Arthur looked towards Frank and replied, "The only problem with that is your punters try to hit us first."

Frank quickly replied,

"I'm not listening, Arthur."

Michael arrived at the club and overheard the end of the conversation.

"What's he not listening to?"

"Forget it, Michael, yah don't need to worry yerself with any of that, come on through and meet the other guys," Arthur said.

Following Michael's introductions and a run down on the evening's activities with Arthur, the club started to fill with patrons and Michael was now adopting his position with Arthur at the entrance to the club.

Two hours had passed and Michael was already thinking that this job was a breeze, standing at the main doors watching attractive ladies come and go in the nightclub and the large majority of the men were very friendly too and appeared to respect all the door men; all Michael was tasked to do was to walk inside, receive an acknowledgement from Arthur working at the bar, then return to the main doors to accompany his colleague Jason who was working with him: it was easy.

Thirty minutes later, the mood changed, and in particular Jason's mood changed. Jason was ten years older than Michael, a rugby player and built like an ox, with, as Arthur explained to Michael, a temper to match. Jason cracked his knuckles and grunted the words,

"Watch out, this is where yah earn yah money."

Michael nervously enquired,

"Earn your money with what?" but before Jason could answer Michael could immediately see what he was concerned with.

"You don't need to answer that, I can see them." Michael answered his own question before Jason had the chance to reply, as he glanced up the street. Michael naively remarked on the situation,

"We can take these can't we?"

Jason gave Michael a look a father would give his child after he had just kicked sand in his face at the beach.

"Don't be fucking stupid, go and tell Arthur and Tony to get to the main entrance quick, tell him the Hetton gypsies are here and to get some lads to cover the other entrance."

Michael did as he was told and quickly squeezed his way through the club revellers to the bar where Tony and Arthur were standing. Michael relayed the message with trepidation in his voice, and Arthur and Tony followed Michael with urgency to the main entrance. Arthur, Tony and Michael arrived at the main entrance of the club. It was a warm evening and all the club goers were dressed in t-shirts and summer dresses, but the seven gypsies were walking down the lane towards the club entrance in boots, jeans and t-shirts, with some wearing donkey jackets and some wearing parkas. They swayed as they continued towards the doors where Michael was standing with his three colleagues. Their nonchalant swagger had a threating air of arrogance about it that portrayed a message that they had no fear of bouncers, on any door. As they got closer to the entrance, the smell of strong booze drifted through the air, making it clear to everyone stood between them and the entrance to the club, that they had obviously been drinking heavily and would need to be prevented from entering. Their faces all had a weathered look like that of fishermen who had served twenty-five years resisting the attrition of the cold water and winds of the North Sea. Michael looked down from the steps of the club entrance and observed the scars on their faces; these were entwined between the clearly homemade tattoos that were used to mask the marks left from previous fights. The two oldest men were stood at the front of the group and were obviously brothers; they were proudly displaying their thick black curly hair with lashings of *Brylcreem*. As Michael looked around the group, he noticed that they all sported *Brylcreem* laden hair, whether curly or straight. And they all had the same wrinkled dirt engrained hands, which Michael surmised was from the constant outdoor living. Michael found himself staring at their unusual manner of acting jittery and on edge while they were standing in front of the doors to the club; jittery or not, Michael knew he was facing battled hardened men who liked nothing more than a scrap.

"What the fuck are yee staring at, yee fucking ugly twat?" The older of the two brothers directed that aspersion at Michael. Michael moved a step forward readying himself for trouble, but Arthur intervened.

"Come on, Gerry, let's not start any bother, it would be good for all concerned if you just moved along and visited a late night pub down the road."

Michael realised that Arthur actually knew this lot; this obviously was not the first visit the gypsies had made to the club. That mixed broken Irish accent rang out again, this time from Gerry's brother.

"Why won't yee fucking let us in? We're not pissed, ye'er just picking on us cos we're travellers."

Arthur continued with his calming manner, trying his best to diffuse the situation.

"Listen, lads, the last time yah were in here about a year ago, yah smashed the bar up and put two of the bar staff in hospital, that was a costly mistake by the owner and he won't let it happen again."

A voice piped up from the back of the group.

"Dee fucking deserved it, dee refused to serve us and it wasn't even last orders."

Arthur spoke again.

"They refused to serve yah, not because it was last orders, it was because yah were all inebriated."

The same man piped up again with a baffled look on his face.

"Because we were what?"

Arthur tried his best not to sound patronising as he spoke with a childlike slowness.

"Because yah were all fucking pissed."

Jason's tolerance and patience was far less than Arthur's as he quickly added to Arthur's message,

"And yah all fucking stunk, like yah do now."

No sooner had Jason finished his sentence, when Gerry ran straight towards him and landed a massive swinging punch onto his jaw. It took Jason completely by surprise and rocked him sideways, his legs buckled and he collapsed against the door frame of the club entrance.

A cry of,

"Nail dees bastards," echoed from the back of the gang and all seven of them hurled themselves towards the entrance, with the intention of taking out as many bouncers as they could on their way to breaching the club doors. Michael observed Arthur and Tony turn to grab Jason to lift him back to his feet; they did this like they were pushing a jaded rugby prop back into the scrum. This appeared to work as Jason lowered his head as if preparing to scrum down, and launching himself like a battering ram, he powered forward landing his huge head square onto the nose of one of the gang, knocking him off his feet and into the middle of the road.

Michael knew it would not be long before he was set upon by one of the group and he wasn't disappointed, as Gerry and his brother made a beeline for Michael, probably thinking that he was the weakest line of defence, being so young and inexperienced. Gerry was the closest to Michael and ran towards him with his arm flailing in anticipation of pounding his fist into Michael's face; he also had his boot made ready to kick Michael between the legs. When he was within striking distance, Michael deceptively lured Gerry close to him to draw his swinging punch, this ensured that Gerry would telegraph his punch and allow Michael to easily block it. Gerry's momentum carried him forward and his swinging leg was now travelling towards Michael's groin, but before it made contact, Michael thrust a side edged kick against the knee of Gerry's swinging leg, buckling his leg backwards at the knee cap and smashing his leg. As his body halted and collapsed forward, Michael unleashed a spinning reverse kick, crunching the side of his heel into Gerry's head, knocking it violently to one side the way a wooden ball would knock a coconut from a shy. Gerry was completely out of action. While this was happening Gerry's brother was already committed to running at Michael to join the affray. When he observed how Michael neutralised his brother so clinically, he tried to stop his attack, but unfortunately for Gerry's brother, Michael was already thinking about which way he would dispense with him. Michael noticed that Gerry's brother had pulled a piece of lead pipe from his donkey jacket and was wielding this towards Michael like a woodcutter's axe; because Gerry's brother was within striking distance, it was too late for him to turn back. Michael turned away from his attacker and dropped down to the ground while simultaneously swinging his foot around into a low rear foot sweep. This move lifted Gerry's brother completely into the air, at which point he dropped the lead pipe from his grasp. Michael turned to stand upright again in enough time to observe Gerry's brother crashing onto the floor on his back, whereupon Michael brought the heel of his foot down from head height to smash into Gerry's brother's face.

The bone crunching noise made the remaining gang look to see who it was being beaten; the gypsy gang were all devastated to see their two leaders knocked out cold on the kerb side.

Arthur shouted to Michael as he observed the heads turning towards him,

"Are yah okay, kidda?"

Michael turned his head to face Arthur and acknowledged his condition with a raised thumb. Just as he lifted his thumb, his eyes were doused in blackness for around two seconds, this was quickly followed by a burning sensation in his eye and a feeling that his eyeball was about to pop out. As his sight returned and he swiftly regained consciousness, he realised that one of the gang had first of all, landed a heavy blow to the side of his head, and secondly managed to jump on his back and gouge his eye with his thumb while gripping the hair on his head with his other hand.

Michael could hear his attacker screaming into his ear,

"I'll kill yee for hurting my brothers, I'll kill yee."

Michael knew this guy was serious and if he didn't get him off his back soon, he would most definitely lose his eye. The feeling of a man's thumb inside his eye socket lodged behind his eye ball, was not something he wanted to endure for much longer. Michael pulled on the attacker's hand with both of his hands while continuously spinning his body around in a circle to disorientate him; he finally extracted his thumb from his eye socket and twisted the attacker's hand until his elbow joint was in line with his own shoulder. Michael then used the locked joint of his elbow as a lever and forced his arm beyond the point of resistance until it snapped. Michael knew he could now keep the pressure on this joint to inflict maximum pain as he spun his attacker around the side of his body and off his back, sending him thumping onto the pavement. Michael fell with the full weight of his body from four feet in the air and thundered down onto the man's face with his elbow to smash into his mouth. The scream his attacker belched out was a whimpering shriek of excruciating pain. Immediately after this finishing blow, everything fell silent, apart from the sound of a few final punches that Arthur and the other door men dispatched, until the two gypsies they were dealing with followed the other two running up the street.

Michael looked down at his attacker beneath him; his attacker let out an almighty scream, he was obviously in desperate pain from his injuries, and this was followed by more groans and moans from the two gypsy brothers who were still laid prostrate on the pavement.

"Yee've smashed me fuckin knee, yee ugly bastard," Gerry angrily shouted at Michael.

Michael pushed up from the ground with his elbow which was still embedded in his final attacker's face; his movement was met with a dog-like yelp from the man beneath him. As Michael got to his feet he looked across to where Gerry and his brother were laid – he was somewhat shocked at the state he had left his attackers in.

As if to remind Michael of the silence, a blue crisp packet caught his eye, as it slowly blew its way from one side of the street to the other, meandering along; it was carried by a gentle breeze that seemed to slowly roll down the street, passing over the remaining prone gypsies' heads and flopping their greased hair from one side of their heads to the other. As Michael watched the crisp packet tumbling to its final destination - clinched around the crisscross section of a wire fence - his attention was drawn to two shadowy figures stood watching at the end of the street. The orange street lamp cast its light from behind the two men making it difficult to pick out their faces, fortunately Michael recognised their silhouettes. This was unmistakably the same two men who tried to break in to his house. Michael was suspicious that Trevor and his mates were up to no good again and this stirred Michael's thoughts to believe that they may even be behind the gypsy attack on the club. Michael stood looking towards the two men in a blinkered daze, oblivious to what carnage he had unleashed on the men that were strewn on the floor in front of him.

"Are yah okay, Michael?" Arthur asked.

"Sorry what did you say?" Michael replied.

"I said are yah okay?" Arthur asked again as he walked to where Michael was standing. Michael had a look of great consternation on his face and was struggling to clear his mind of the two people standing at the end of the street; but as he turned back from talking to Arthur to look up the street, the two shadowy figures were gone.

"Jesus, Michael, what the hell have yah done with these three?" Arthur said curtly.

"Jason."

"Aye, Arthur," Jason replied.

"Yah better go inside and phone for an ambulance and hurry up."

Arthur pointed to the entrance to direct Jason to go inside, but instead Jason walked over to where Arthur was stood near to the three worse for wear gypsies. "Bloody hell, don't let the gaffer see this mess or he'll take the door off us," Jason exclaimed.

Arthur's retort was a terse one.

"You're not listening are yah? That's why I said go and ring for an ambulance now, to get these lot out the way sharpish."

Jason walked past Michael on his way to the entrance looking him straight in the eye.

"You're a fucking liability on the door, you're not meant to half kill the bastards."

"Says you who put the nut on them," Michael responded.

"Yeah, but I'm not smashing blokes' joints like that." Jason pointed at Gerry and his accomplice before walking past.

Arthur again pointed towards the entrance and spoke in a resolute tone.

"Just drop it will yah? And, Jason get a move on and phone an ambulance right now."

Arthur turned towards Michael who still looked jaded.

"Listen, I know it's been a tough few weeks for yah with yah mother and father and all, so get yerself home and try and sort yah head out. We can catch up when you're next at training."

"Thanks, Arthur." Michael turned to walk off and looked back at Arthur somewhat sheepishly.

"I'm sorry if I've let you down, Arthur, I lost control I think."

Arthur put his hand on Michael's shoulder.

"Listen, marra, if I had been through what yah have at your age, I think I would have ended up locked up, so don't beat yerself up about it, just get yerself home and leave this to us."

"Cheers, Arthur." Michael grabbed his jacket and headed to the bus to make his way home.

CHAPTER 20

"What time is this young gentleman arriving, Rachel?" Rachel's mother enquired.

"I asked him to come for five, and he said he would do his best, but Saturday was visiting day to see his mother at hospital," Rachel replied.

"That's good, let me know when he arrives and I can introduce him to your father and your uncle. Nothing serious with the mother I hope?" Rachel's mother said in an understanding, but inquisitive manner.

Rachel held her hands to her face and tipped her head back, before speaking in a concerned manner.

"Mother, promise me you won't embarrass me by asking him about his mother, and please, try not to be so stuck up will you?"

"Oh don't be so silly, I don't go on like that at all," Rachel's mother replied.

Michael was making his way to Rachel's house straight from the other side of town where he had been visiting his mother; she was still confined to bed and looking very poorly in hospital. When he arrived at Rachel's house he stood outside contemplating whether he should knock on the door or whether he should just head home to bed, he felt tired, and seeing his mother in such a state particularly worried him. He arrived at Rachel's house and was standing still at the front door; he was staring at Rachel's bedroom window. At the very moment he was to turn around and head off, Rachel caught sight of him from her bedroom window and promptly waved: Michael immediately felt a warmness inside as he waved back and witnessed Rachel's lovely welcoming smile. Rachel came running down from upstairs, pulled open the door and invited Michael inside.

"Hello, oh I'm so pleased you've come, come in and take your coat off and I'll introduce you to everyone."

Rachel always had an adept ability for making Michael feel very relaxed in an unnerving situation, unfortunately on this occasion Rachel's next words made Michael very nervous about meeting everyone.

"Oh my God, that's some bruise on your face, Michael," Rachel exclaimed with shock. Michael had completely forgotten about the punch that had landed on his face in the fight with the gypsies, and with his only contact being with his bedridden, sleeping mother, no one had seen him to mention it.

Michael answered in a somewhat misleading manner,

"It was John, I mean Jim, at the sword training, er I mean the karate last night."

Rachel stood in front of Michael and looked up towards his face, she was unsure of Michael's intent to deceive her.

"What is it, Michael? Why are you not telling me the truth, did Trevor do this?" It was easier for Michael to just answer yes to that question and move on, but instead he kept quiet, but Rachel persisted.

"I can ask my mam if we should phone the police."

Michael had a determined look in his eyes.

"No, Rachel, please can we leave it? It happened at training last night and there is nothing to worry about."

Rachel looked doubtful, but agreed to drop it.

"So be it, come on then I will introduce you to my family; oh, I forgot to ask you, did you remember your Japanese document?"

Michael placed his hand in his jacket pocket and waved the envelope at Rachel,

"I didn't forget."

"Uncle Zak will be pleased; he is very intrigued after the description I gave him of the document," Rachel proudly announced.

Michael made it through most of the introductions that evening without too much embarrassment, and once tea was over Michael followed Uncle Zak through to the study. Michael and Rachel watched with great interest as Uncle Zak lifted a very old, tan coloured leather briefcase from beneath the desk. It was wide enough to carry a number of tomes inside, and it did just that. Uncle Zak pulled out six huge books from the case like a magician pulling rabbits from a top hat. Rachel's mother and father headed into the kitchen to clear up after tea, the mother instructed Rachel not to keep her uncle too long because he had a long journey home that night. Uncle Zak sat at the large oval desk in the study, the desk looked like it had been in the family for a lot of years and it was thick with layers of beeswax, it had a shine an officers' mess would be proud of. Uncle Zak placed himself at the head of the table, he was a tubby man, with a thick, wiry black beard; his face seemed too small for his head with squinty little eyes framed within huge circular black rimmed glasses and a turned up nose that would look better perched on a dachshund. He sat upright with his huge bulbous belly squeezed up against the edge of the table, flanked by his fat arms that were stretching his tatty olive green shirt to the limit of its stitching. His mouth was almost invisible due to the amount of hair growing around his lips, on closer inspection it was possible to distinguish the nicotine stained part of his beard where his pipe had bellowed out smoke.

"Come on then, let's have a look at this Japanese document that Rachel's been talking about," Uncle Zak said with his arm stretched across the table towards Michael.

Michael offered it to Uncle Zak.

"I hope you're not disappointed, it could be nothing."

Uncle Zak grasped hold of the envelope with his hand; Michael could not help but notice that his fingers looked like big fat sausages before they are ready to burst in a hot frying pan. Uncle Zak immediately opened the envelope and placed the document on the table; he lifted a huge magnifying glass from his briefcase and began to fastidiously inspect the very ancient piece of paper in front of him.

"Mm... Interesting, yes very interesting," Uncle Zak muttered. "Very, very interesting indeed."

Michael and Rachel looked at each other and smiled while twisting their faces in appreciation of how odd Uncle Zak sounded. He then began to flick his way through his books, a few pages of one book then a few pages of another, then back to the first book and all the while meticulously scrutinising the document with great fervour.

"Rachel tells me that you think people in Japan may want this document from you," Uncle Zak enquired.

Michael hesitated before answering looking at Rachel then Uncle Zak then Rachel again, not really sure how much Uncle Zak knew about what had happened in Japan.

"Er well er... yes I suppose you could say that."

"Mm... they may have good reason," Uncle Zak proclaimed.

Rachel walked round the table, stood at Uncle Zak's side and stared inquisitively at the document.

"Why is that, Uncle Zak, what's so important?"

Uncle Zak pushed his chair back from the table allowing his billowing belly to flop forward to his thighs; he eased his glasses down his nose with his chubby fingers and proceeded to clench his hands together across his chest. He took a deep breath and peered over his glasses.

"What's so important, as you put it, is that this document is probably around five hundred and seventy years old, give or take a few years."

Rachel looked at Michael in astonishment as she replied to Uncle Zak.

"Really, so is it very valuable?"

Uncle Zak pulled the document up to his magnifying glass to examine it again.

"To you or me it's not that valuable; however to an ancestor of the feudal lord that sanctioned this, it's priceless."

Michael looked bewildered.

"Could you explain what you mean by that?"

Uncle Zak turned the document to face Michael and pointed to it.

"This ancient piece of paper is a covenant scripted by a Shogun known as Yoshimitsu, and he hailed from a group of Shogun known as Ashikaga, during the Muromachi period." Uncle Zak rose from his chair clasped his hands behind his back and began to march around the table, looking more like an officer from Sandhurst than a professor from Durham.

"I would imagine that this meagre slip of paper has had much blood spilt over it down the centuries. It gives its owner, by decree, the ownership of a substantial piece of land in Tokyo, written here as Edo and essentially governing rights to a vast enclave that cannot be touched without the control of this document. Not until the name and the seal are changed from that which is written now, can the covenant and consequently the land be taken."

Rachel followed Uncle Zak around the table.

"So whose name and seal are on there now?"

"The last name and seal on this covenant was placed here at the bottom in 1600, the name of Tokugawa Ieyasu was the last name written and the seal is from the battle of Sekigahara." Uncle Zak turned to look at Michael with great satisfaction after his investigation and conclusive diagnosis; but Michael was gone. Rachel looked directly to the spot where Michael had been sitting and the chair was empty. The door to the garden was ajar and the curtains near to it were swaying from side to side from the draught blowing into the room.

"Michael, Michael, where are you?" Rachel yelled as she ran through the door and into the garden. Michael was sat hunched forward on a garden bench with his head in his hands. Rachel moved to his side.

"Are you okay, Michael? What is it? Why did those names spook you like that?"

Michael twisted his head to the side and the evening moonlight illuminated his bruised eye. He looked Rachel up and down and observed a schoolgirl out of uniform looking like a young woman; elegant, sexy and much more mature than he felt at that moment. Michael was shaking his head when he spoke.

"This whole thing is driving me crazy, I can't think straight when I hear about this stuff from Japan. It takes me back to…"

Rachel placed her hand on Michael's shoulder in an attempt to console him, this stopped him speaking. She silkily slipped it from one shoulder to the next and back again, she moved to sit beside him on the bench by stepping across him; by doing so she blocked out the moon which cast her hour glass shape as a silhouette in front of Michael's face, but before she could step past him, Michael placed his hand on her waist and pulled her in between his legs. Both her hands dropped to each of his shoulders and she was looking down at Michael beneath her: she gradually let her body slide closer inside Michael's legs, succumbing to his firm grip, while slowly lowering her head to place her lips close enough to feel his breath. Michael took a breath to speak, but before he could, Rachel sealed her lips against his and kissed him long and slowly; she pulled Michael's other hand onto her waist and proceeded to caress his head with her fingertips. She continued to kiss him, writhing her svelte frame in and out of the area near his crotch, she guided Michael's face close to her breasts, and then continued to kiss him more and more passionately around his neck.

"Are you two lovebirds coming back in? I'm off home now," Uncle Zak shouted from the study.

"We're on our way," Rachel stopped to quickly shout to her Uncle Zak, and then continued to kiss Michael. Rachel tenderly clutched Michael's hands and pulled them to his front, she smoothly brought her kissing to a halt and lifted her head up, leaving her hair draped across Michael's face.

"I think we should go inside and say thanks and goodbye to Uncle Zak, but before we do, what were you about to say?"

Michael turned his head to one side and pulled Rachel's stomach in to the side of his face with his arms wrapped around her bottom, he spoke slowly while staring towards the now misty moon in the distance.

"Our Japanese instructor's name was Tokugawa, and the man who killed him and my father, was Ashikaga Yoshimitsu. A dangerous Yakuza, seemingly, from what your uncle has told us, wanting to avenge his ancestor's honour while continuing to promulgate his criminal empire."

"How come their names are still the same after so many years?" Rachel asked.

Michael continued speaking without moving his head from Rachel's stomach.

"Our instructor often discussed with us that he was a direct descendant from the Tokugawa Shogun and would often entertain high ranking Japanese dignitaries and military leaders at his home. His blood line obviously carried a well-respected history and the Japanese place great value on that; unfortunately for him a name that had survived centuries was wiped out by an avaricious criminal within minutes."

Rachel pulled herself away from Michael and lifted his head to face her before speaking with bewilderment.

"Let me try to understand this, men are killing each other over an old piece of paper which gives them a right to land that their ancestors fought over five hundred and seventy years ago?"

Before Michael could answer a voice rang out from the door to the study.

"The Japanese are a proud, some might say obsessive race when it comes to history and tradition, and will overlook indiscretions if it allows them to be a greater nation and maintain their honour, however that mentality can often translate to a ruthless disregard for others, for individual gain. And if this man Ashikaga is a Yakuza, then it is likely that his honour has been corrupted in search of that personal gain." Uncle Zak stepped out into the moonlit garden.

"I must head off home, Rachel, good to meet you, Michael, that's an interesting piece of history you have there and it needs safe keeping, I have left it on the table. Don't forget, if I can be of further help, please get in touch."

Michael stood up from the garden bench offering his hand to Uncle Zak.

"Thank you, Uncle Zak, good to meet you too."

Following Uncle Zak's departure, Rachel's parents excused themselves and headed off to bed, but before doing so offered the use of their sofa to Michael if he wished to stay the night.

"My mother and father must like you if they think you are worthy of their leather Chesterfield," Rachel stated surprisingly.

"I should really get back; I need to visit my mother in hospital tomorrow," Michael replied.

Rachel slipped her fingers in between Michael's fingers and led him to the sofa.

"Sit down while I go to get a blanket for you, I won't let you stay in a house on your own when you can stay here with me, besides, I would like to continue where we left off in the garden."

Michael enjoyed that look in Rachel's eye and immediately recollected the same look in May Lin's eyes from the night at the ryokan. Rachel left to retrieve a blanket from upstairs and Michael continued to think about May Lin until his thoughts distracted him with the sound of May Lin's voice speaking over and over again in his head,

Sleep with one eye open, Michael... whatever you have Ashikaga must really want it.

Michael knew this covenant; this very piece of paper which his father collected from Master Tokugawa was the cause of all the bloodshed. Master Tokugawa must have known that Ashikaga would try to win it back and in keeping with tradition it could only happen after a victorious battle, where the victor would sign his name and place a seal on the document at the scene of the battle. Michael now knew that his father was chosen to give the covenant safe keeping if anything befell Master Tokugawa; this would prevent Ashikaga claiming back that sacred piece of land from Master Tokugawa. Instead Michael inadvertently ended up with the very document that had brought about this mayhem.

"Here we go a lovely thick blanket and some pillows for the sofa," Rachel said, while constructing a bed on the leather Chesterfield.

"Are you sure your mam and dad are okay about me staying tonight?" Michael asked, with his anxiety quickly dissipating, and leaving his tormented thoughts buried in the darkest corner of his mind.

"Michael, I'm sixteen, will you stop worrying about my mam and dad, they both trust me," Rachel answered firmly.

Rachel pulled out a record from the shelf on the sideboard and carefully placed it on the record player.

"I hope you like T Rex, this is my favourite album at the moment." The crackle of the dust on the needle was the only noise in the room at that moment, until the sound of Marc Bolan singing

"Get it on," rang out from the record player. Rachel danced her way over to where Michael was sat on the makeshift bed, looking more like one of the girls from Pans People than a schoolgirl from Michael's class. Michael looked deep into Rachel's eyes and smiled. He moved to sit on top of the blanket on the sofa, but before he could manage to sit down, Rachel had pulled back the blanket suggesting to Michael to get under it: as he did so Rachel kicked her shoes from her feet and jumped in beside him, and before he could utter a word, Rachel was kissing him once again.

"Relax, Michael, you're so tense and there's no need to be, my mam and dad won't intrude."

Michael did just that and flopped back on the sofa, this was the signal Rachel was waiting for, and she immediately climbed over Michael and straddled him, before he could react she covered both her and him in the blanket. She draped her hair over his face as she kissed him firmly on the lips. Michael did not hesitate with his response, kissing her on the lips and the neck. He began moving his hands down both sides of her tautly arched back towards her buttocks, which were clenched over the bulge in his jeans. Before he could make another move Rachel refrained from kissing him and pushed herself upright, she then proceeded to wrap her arms around herself clutching at the edges of her dark red polar neck jumper; with a smooth, seamless action, she slipped her jumper over her head and draped it over the sofa. Michael looked up towards her opening his mouth to speak, but before he could utter a word, her finger landed on his lips to silence him.

"Not a word, mister, I'm not finished yet."

Rachel's pert breasts were then revealed from inside her bra as she lifted the catch with one hand behind her back while continuing to keep her other hand over his mouth. He slowly slipped his hands from her buttocks onto the warm silky smooth skin on her waist, then he ran his hands up her body past her aroused breasts onto her shoulders; he gently slid his hands down onto her breasts, his touch was met with a soft groan and a shallow intake of breath.

"Let me take your t-shirt off," Rachel said with a determined look in her eyes. She pushed her buttocks down from the bulge in his jeans and sat on his thighs. Pulling up his t-shirt, she lifted it over his head and dropped it to the floor. Michael placed his hands on his belt and zip and began to undo his jeans, but before he could move his zip, Rachel edged forward and sat over the bulge in his trousers once more.

"I don't want to go that far yet, Michael, is that okay?" Rachel asked tentatively.

Michael at that very moment remembered how young he was and that his experience with May Lin was out of the ordinary and was also still very much in his thoughts.

"No that's fine, Rachel; you set the pace, that's the way it should be."

"Thank you, Michael, that doesn't mean you can't keep your hands warm," Rachel whispered in Michael's ear as she placed his hands on her breasts again, before sliding down beside him to cuddle in to his bare chest. She once again pulled the blanket over the both of them and moved to kiss him, but as she did so, something caught his eye. A line of dappled light traversed its way across the sitting room wall behind the sofa and slowly came to a halt directly in front of him; this was the light cast by a door opening. Michael immediately thought back to the ryokan and the attacker that attempted to kill him while he lay with May Lin, the feeling this time was different, this was a worry that Rachel's father was going to discover him with his half naked daughter, on his cherished leather Chesterfield, inside his house.

Rachel stopped kissing Michael and whispered under the blanket,

"Why is your heart pounding and why have you stopped kissing me?"

"I think one of your parents has come in the room. How should we react? Should we just make out that we are asleep?" Michael asked quietly with his head still under the blankets.

"Really, I can't believe that my mam or dad would do that," Rachel convincingly exclaimed with a whisper. Michael tensed up at this point and tried to get Rachel to forget about what she believed, and deal with the reality of the situation.

"Are we lying still or getting up? Because whoever it is, is getting extremely close, I can sense them behind me."

Rachel laid her head on the pillow and pushed Michael's head onto the pillow too, intimating to him to pretend he was asleep, which he promptly adhered to. They were both lying perfectly still with their eyes shut and the sound of their hearts thumping inside of their mouths, the way a bass drum would sound when rhythmically pounded with a drum stick. Michael now sensed the person was stood directly behind him and he knew he had to stay perfectly still.

Michael was expecting a voice to break the silence but nothing happened. At this point Michael could feel the draught from the open door wafting across his bare back which was protruding from the blanket draped over him and Rachel. The sensation was similar to the feeling you experience during a game of hide and seek when you have the best place to hide, but no matter how close people get they still can't find you. Michael instinctively knew that something was different; a sensation of movement near to the skin on his back, and then a cold wet sensation tightened the muscles either side of his spine as it touched him. Michael opened both his eyes and prodded Rachel with his finger to open hers.

"Someone has just poked me in the back," Michael whispered with trepidation.

"What? You must be mistaken," Rachel muttered in disbelief. "There is no one behind you; I'm looking straight over your shoulder."

Michael knew that someone was there and was now at the stage where he just needed to face up to Rachel's parents, if they were to discover the two of them lying together on the sofa.

Michael threw back the blanket and twisted round to confront Rachel's parents. As he did this, he was greeted with a barrage of barking from the now startled pet Alsatian that was as shocked to see him as he was to see it. The sound of the barking was deafening.

"Zimba! Be quiet, stop that, Zimba," Rachel shouted as she tried her utmost to calm the family dog. Unfortunately for Michael, Zimba thought that Michael was an intruder and bounded towards him angrily barking louder and louder.

"He will be fine, Michael, he couldn't hurt a fly," Rachel said reassuringly.

"I'm sorry, Rachel I'm not convinced, not only does your dog have a hellish loud bark, it is also flaring its nostrils and baring its teeth towards me." Michael grimaced as he gesticulated towards the dog.

Rachel's father was now out of bed and standing on the upstairs landing.

"Is everything okay down there, Rachel? Do you need me to come down to sort Zimba?"

"No, Dad, it's fine," Rachel replied as she immediately grabbed hold of Zimba's collar to prevent the dog from moving closer to Michael. She gently tapped Zimba on the nose and instructed him to be quiet.

"Silence."

The dog immediately stopped barking and moved to Rachel's side, following this it turned towards Michael who was sat on the edge of the sofa. The dog proceeded to place its head in between Michael's legs and planted its cold wet nose squarely in the middle of his crotch, at which point it began sniffing. Rachel looked towards Michael with a coy smile on her face and began laughing.

"Good job you didn't have your wicked way with me or the dog may have had your balls."

Michael jumped to his feet with an indignant scowl on his face.

"Don't even joke about that, dogs can be very unpredictable."

At that very moment the father's voice could be heard from behind the door.

"Is everything alright with Zimba, Rachel?"

Rachel quickly pulled her top on and turned to the door, whereupon her father appeared in his pyjama bottoms and a vest.

"He's fine, Dad, there's no need to worry." Rachel was answering her father and expected him to be looking at her while she was speaking; however her father's eyes were transfixed on Michael's crotch. Both Michael and Rachel immediately followed suit in staring between Michael's legs, but before another word could be uttered, Rachel's father shouted for Zimba to follow him and communicated immediate instructions to Michael.

"I think it's time for you to be heading home, Michael, goodnight," and with those succinctly put words Rachel's father headed off to bed.

Rachel and Michael looked at each other in amazement and burst out laughing, desperately trying to conceal the sound of their laughter with their hands over their mouths. Rachel pointed towards Michael's crotch while struggling to breathe due to tumultuous laughing.

"My father thinks that wet patch on your trousers is…"

Before Rachel could finish speaking, Michael who by now was bent double with laughter, interjected.

"I know what he was thinking; he also most probably thinks I'm nothing but trouble." Rachel looked at Michael with tears of laughter rolling down her cheeks.

"Don't be so paranoid, Michael; he will see the funny side when I explain it to him tomorrow."

Michael spoke in a defeated tone. "You're more confident than I would ever be with my parents, I think I should do like your father suggested and head off home."

"Are you sure, Michael?" Rachel asked.

Michael was already standing with the house door open and his jacket draped over his shoulder. "Goodnight, Rachel, thanks for a great evening and I hope we can see each other again soon." Following a kiss goodnight Michael headed back home clutching the document inside his jacket pocket.

CHAPTER 21

Michael remembered match day as a day he looked forward to, mainly because he would spend time alone with his father outside of the disciplined arena of the martial arts; but also because the excitement of cheering your team with another fifty thousand like-minded fans became engrained in your psyche. This match day would still enable Michael to experience the excitement, but unfortunately he knew it would be tinged with sadness, with his father not being there, he knew he would experience mixed emotions with his first visit to Roker Park in over five years, but he was still thrilled to be going.

His first port of call for the day was to visit his mother in hospital before meeting up with his best friend Bill.

Michael leapt off the slow trundling bus and headed up to the main entrance of the hospital, the smell of overcooked scrambled eggs drifted along the corridor as the kitchen staff cleared away the stale uneaten breakfasts from the wards; not the most pleasant of aromas to greet his walk through the doors at the entrance. Michael's mother was supposed to be on ward nine. There was no sign of her, this prompted Michael to ask a nurse.

"Could you tell me where Shirley Harris is please?" Michael asked.

The nurse started to look for her paperwork, then ceased looking and pointed to the end of the corridor.

"No need to look for that one, are yah her son?" the nurse enquired.

"Yes I am," Michael replied.

"That's a shame; yah seem like a nice guy," the nurse said acidly.

Michael flushed with embarrassment.

"Sorry, has she been difficult?"

The nurse indicated to Michael to follow her to the end of the ward.

"To say the least, she is in a solitary ward, because she keeps upsetting the other patients and the staff." The nurse stopped at the single room at the end of the ward and opened the door.

"Yah have a visitor, Shirley, aren't yah the lucky one?"

Michael thanked the nurse and walked over to sit at the side of the bed, he placed a brown bag on the bedside table.

"Yah can take those back, I don't care for grapes. Anyway what do yah want?" Michael's mother asked with deep anger in her voice.

"I see hospital hasn't improved your manners," Michael bitterly retorted.

Michael's mam looked at Michael with a sneer on her face.

"I'm only in this horrible place, with these horrible injuries, having to eat the horrible food they serve here, because of one person, and that's yee."

Michael walked to the side of the bed and picked up the water jug, the thought ran through his head to pour the water straight over his mother's head, instead he poured her a glass of water and placed it on the bedside table. He then picked up his grapes and walked to the end of the bed, preparing himself to leave.

"Where does all this hatred come from, Mother? Why do you hate me like this?"

Michael's mother rolled her head from one side of the pillow to the other, following Michael around the room to the end of the bed, she began a protracted tirade, speaking the way a teacher would speak while admonishing a naughty schoolboy.

"Because you're just like yah father, yah think yah something special with yah martial arts and yah bouncing on the doors, and that macho hard man rubbish. I had just started to get my life back together with Trevor after yah father ran off with that Asian tart May Lin from his work place in Japan, so don't stand there laying the blame at…"

Michael stopped his mother's rant.

"Did you say May Lin?"

Michael's mother continued.

"Yah heard me, May Lin, that's the woman who he left me for and yah came back here and bullied my Trevor out of my house…"

Michael was shocked by his mother's words and shouted at her,

"Will you stop? I don't want to hear anymore!"

Michael's mother stared at Michael with her eyebrows raised and a look of disbelief on her face.

"Have I touched a nerve, Michael, is that a surprise to hear that he left me for someone else? Well now yah know what kind of a man he was."

"Oh and it had nothing to do with you, did it, Mother? It was his fault entirely," Michael replied with the first thing that entered his head, because inside he was seething over the comment she made about May Lin. Michael was totally confused by that remark.

His mother continued,

"Face it, Michael, your father was a big-headed, two-faced, bastard."

Michael picked up the bag of grapes and hurled them across the room at his mother while shouting at the top of his voice,

"Will you shut up?"

"Don't yah dare shout at me like that, who do yah think yah are? If I could get out of this bed I would come across your face with my hand, boy." Michael's mother showed her fist to Michael.

Michael clenched his fist with rage and moved closer to his mother, glaring into her eyes.

"You are a bitter and twisted person and if my father or I are responsible for that, then I am truly sorry, however something inside me makes me think a lot of that bitterness is you and maybe that's why my father left you."

Michael continued to glare at his mother without averting his gaze, his mother's bottom lip started to tremble and her facial expression shifted from portraying aggression to portraying sadness, the way a child's face reacts after it has been told off for disobeying its parent. Her eyes filled with tears and like a plugged sink overflowing with water while the taps are still running, the tears burst from her eyes and poured down her face, dripping onto her pyjamas.

Michael's mother spoke for the first time with sincerity and calmness.

"I loved yah father, Michael, and it hurt me deeply when he left, he was my world, and when he moved away, he took from me all that was good in my life, but he didn't stop there, he took my son too."

Michael's tension released from his clenched fist as he started to speak. "Why did you let him take me?"

"Yah idolised your dad, Michael, yah loved the martial arts and yah wanted to go with him, I knew I would be making yah unhappy by stopping yah from being with your father; so I let yah, I let yah…"

Michael leaned over the bed and grabbed his mother's shoulders; he pulled her in close to his chest, she was sobbing uncontrollably.

"I never knew about this, Mother, I'm sorry that we left you this way. You're right I did idolise my dad and I did love the martial arts and still do, but I never intended to hurt you," Michael said in a concerned voice.

"Yah really don't have any idea how much I fell apart when the both of yah left do yah?" Michael's mother said while rubbing the tears from her eyes with her pyjama sleeves.

"Michael, I have taken beating after beating from Trevor, I have been in and out of this hospital more times than I have had hot dinners, yet in your head, yah think you're stupid for taking it all, well the truth of the matter is, I can't face another man walking out on me, and for that reason I keep having Trevor back, no matter how bad he treats me."

Michael stood up and moved away from the bed shaking his head.

"You don't have to take that, Mother, there will be someone else who will be with you for all the right reasons, you just need to be patient."

Michael's mother sat up in the bed and pulled a tissue from the box on the bedside table, she slowly wiped her eyes.

"Thank yah for seeing something in me worth staying for, I am a bitter, resentful person, because I feel I have been wronged, but maybe this time I can make a fresh start, I will be back home this afternoon, so that should make me happier. Yah get off to the match with Bill and enjoy yerself and I will see yah when yah get back."

Michael placed his hand on his mother's cheek and gave a reassuring smile.

"I will; Bill and I will both probably come back after the match."

CHAPTER 22

Michael turned the corner into Bill's street and there he was sitting on his gate at the end of his garden, red and white hat, red and white scarf and red and white football shirt.

"Bout time, marra, where have yah been?" Bill asked.

"Sorry I'm a tad late; I've been to the hospital to see my mother," Michael replied.

"How's she doing?" Bill enquired.

Michael looked down at Bill whilst holding his hand out with the palm facing down, tilting his hand from side to side.

"So so. Let's just say my visit ended better than it started, and the good news is that she is getting out this afternoon."

Bill nodded his head.

"Oh well that's good then."

Bill began walking backwards at this point and looked Michael directly in the eyes.

"Let's discuss more important things now, how did yah get on with Rachel the other night, did yah feel her tits?"

Michael kept walking and by now the pair of them were half a mile from Roker Park.

"Even if I did I'm not going to discuss it with you."

Bill began laughing.

"Ah, that must be a yes then." Michael again kept walking; Bill stopped and waved at Michael.

"Woah, where are yah going?"

Michael looked bemused.

"To the ground where do you think?"

Bill pointed towards the pub on his left.

"Hang on, Michael, there's over an hour to go before kick-off, you're gonna buy me a pint from your door wages before we go to the ground?"

Michael looked Bill up and down and flashed an insolent smile.

"Bill you need to be eighteen years of age, you're not even sixteen yet and you look about fourteen, you're not going to get served in there."

Bill's smile grew like a smug Cheshire cat.

"I know that, they call me Billy not silly, I'm not going to get served, yee are, and I'm going to wait outside in the beer garden for yah to bring me a pint of Bitter."

Michael was aghast with the audacity of Bill's premeditated plan.

"You have really thought this through haven't you? And what if I don't get served?"

"What? You're sixteen next week, you're six feet five inches tall, built like a brick shithouse and yah look about thirty, they wouldn't dare refuse yah," Bill exclaimed.

Michael had to admire his flagrant nerve.

"You're a cheeky git you, but because you're my best mate, I'll go and get us a pint each, but don't blame me if we get pulled by the bizzies."

Bill walked to the rear of the pub to the beer garden at the back, as he turned the corner to enter the garden, it seemed like every football supporter that was there turned and stared at Bill, but just as quickly as they stopped to stare, they immediately turned away from him and continued drinking and talking. Bill breathed a sigh of relief and as he turned to look for Michael, there he was sauntering out of the pub door with two pints of bitter and two perfectly proportioned heads on top of the pint glasses. He entered the pub two minutes ago with some trepidation, but he exited with a sense of achievement.

"There yah are, marra, a pint from my wages and a ham stotty to go with it," Michael proudly proclaimed.

Bill's face slowly grew a beaming smile like a cat that just got the cream.

"Listen to yee with your marra and your stotty, we will mak a mackem of yah yet, soon yah won't be able to tell that yah spent all those years in Japan." Bill raised his glass towards Michael's.

"Cheers, marra, my best mate."

Michael clicked his glass against Bill's and reciprocated the gesture.

"Cheers to you too, you sentimental softy."

As Michael and Bill supped their beers the sound of the Bay City Rollers resonated through the open windows of the pub and reverberated around the beer garden; this particular song prompted two girls to dance and sing along to the tune. The music initiated a response from the lads standing in the beer garden, they cleverly transformed the song into a Sunderland football chant to the same tune, until both the inside and outside of the pub were singing the same lyrics. The chanting became louder and louder, and by the time Michael and Bill finished their pint and stotty, the whole pub was singing along. Michael gestured towards Bill to head off to the match.

"Come on let's soak some atmosphere up at the ground."

Bill drank his beer and followed behind Michael as they began their walk towards the stadium, joining in with the passing crowds who were chanting other football songs as they neared Roker Park. The noise from within the ground was growing in intensity, the Roker roar was getting louder and louder as they were nearing the turnstiles. Michael reached inside his jacket for his ticket, and as he pulled his ticket out he also revealed the covenant which was folded around it.

"What's that?" Bill enquired.

"It's an important document relating to my father's death," Michael reluctantly replied as he handed his ticket over at the turnstile.

A confused expression appeared on Bill's face.

"Why have yah got it with yah at the match?" Michael and Bill were bunched together in a bustling crowd near to the entrance aisle to their seats.

"Because it's valuable, and I trust no one enough to leave it with."

"My life is so simple and straightforward compared to yours, Michael, come on, put that away and let's go and enjoy the match." Bill lifted his scarf up from around his neck and stretched it out above his head, and then roared a chant as loud as he could,

"We're gonna beat the Baggies, haway the lads, haway the lads, haway the lads, haway."

Michael and Bill both squeezed their way into the Fullwell end of the ground and took their place in among the fifty thousand fans, where the only noise to be heard was that mighty Roker roar. The sound of the fans singing spread from one side of the ground to the other until the whole ground became a throng of roaring football fans.

Following kick off, huge numbers of late arriving fans continued to pour into the ground, both Michael and Bill began to feel more and more squashed as increasing numbers of people filtered in at the rear of the stand. The Fullwell end of the ground as with all other areas was a sea of red and white bodies cemented together in a conglomeration of heads, arms and shoulders. Each time there was an exciting piece of action on the pitch an undulating ripple of fans leaned forward to catch a glimpse of the action, and when the action subsided the ripple of fans swayed back to its original position the way a wave would sweep up the seashore onto a sandy beach, then pull its way back to the sea whence it came. Just at the very moment when everyone settled themselves back to their original standing position, Sunderland scored a goal. The crowd erupted with roars of delight and the Fullwell end where Michael and Bill were standing, bounced around for a few seconds, and then all the jubilant fans surged forward. As this happened Bill was squashed close against the leaning bar in front of him with Michael alongside him. People to both sides of Bill and Michael were jumping up and down and falling onto one another in the crowd. Michael observed a small boy being knocked over onto the steps below in all the excitement - with an outstretched arm - he was able to pick him from the ground with one hand and deliver him safely to his father.

"I think the lads behind him got a little too excited, thanks for passing him back," the boy's father said.

Michael strained to pull his other arm in the air from down by his side and waved his hand at the boy's father.

"That's fine as long as he's okay?"

Bill looked up from the bar where he was standing with a beaming smile on his face.

"I love it when we score a goal and I'm in the standing end, a good time to score too with five minutes before half time on the clock; are yah going to the toilet before the rush, Michael?"

Michael twisted his body around to face the exit.

"Good idea, I'm busting to go, come on let's head up before half time and the crush."

Bill and Michael squeezed their way through the now settled crowd, out towards the toilets; they walked along with a handful of fans that also decided to beat the crush. Michael and Bill both ran towards the toilet doors and entered the toilet they chose with only one other person. The toilets were porcelain latrines, each standing approximately four feet high with chrome drain covers nestling at the bottom of the trough, each one of these drain covers was covered in pine fragranced urinal blocks which were used to mask the pungent aroma of a constant waterfall of urine. Michael and Bill were both relieving themselves when another man entered the toilet, passing the only other person on his way out. This man was standing at the latrine in between Bill and Michael. As he was placing his hands down by his side, Michael noticed something unusual – there was no sound coming from the urinal, the sound which always accompanies a pee was non-existent. This attracted Michael's attention and made him turn to the side and take a long look at this person, at which point he caught a swift glimpse of the man's hand, this coincided with Bill washing his hands and walking towards the exit.

"I'll wait outside for yah, Michael and we can get back before the half ends." Bill walked towards the exit and waited near the door. Michael could not look away from the man's hand and could feel the blood draining away from his face as he was overcome with fear; peering out from the man's black coat sleeve was a tattoo of a white dragon, stretching from his wrist down to the knuckles on his hand. The very same white dragon that was tattooed on May Lin's hand, was on the hand of a man stood three feet away from him. Michael averted his gaze and turned to stare at the wall above the latrine in front of him while he slowly pulled up his trouser zip. On the wall in front of him was a crackled mirror which reflected the image of an Asian man walking into the doorway of the toilet and standing across the opening, he was standing in such a way as to suggest he was standing guard in case someone walked in. The man with the white dragon tattoo reached inside of his long black trench coat with his right hand and slowly moved his arm upward. Michael knew something was amiss and knew he would need to react soon or he could be in danger. Michael decided not to move his head to the right to look at the man; instead he remained still, allowing the two men to believe they still had the element of surprise over him; he knew he was at risk of surrendering his advantage if he did not take action immediately. Any opportunity to think through a plan of defence was eliminated when a flash of steel caught the corner of Michael's eye, this man standing next to him slowly began pulling a katana out from inside his coat.

Michael calmly lifted his right leg until his boot was waist high and before the man could finish lifting the katana from his coat, Michael stamped his foot into the side of his knee, buckling the man's leg so much that he fell to the ground and crashed into the porcelain toilet, dropping the katana to the ground; Michael quickly followed the man, as he desperately tried to push himself out of the urinal with his piss soaked hand in a vain attempt to grab the gleaming white handled katana from the damp concrete floor. Michael stepped forward swinging his left leg towards the tattooed man's face, he brutally pounded his boot into his nose, splattering blood over the white porcelain sinks and their accompanying mirrors. Before he had the chance to watch the man slide down the blood stained urinal to the ground, the man at the toilet entrance was lunging at him with a katana above his head, ready to slice down upon Michael's skull.

Michael swerved his body backwards in an audacious attempt to grasp the katana which lay behind him on the toilet floor, thus preventing the other attacker's sword slicing into Michael's head. Michael was clutching at the katana handle on the floor, he swung the blade up from the ground in time to clatter it into the downward cutting blade of his attacker; the noise that rang out from the toilet resembled the sound of a blacksmith's hammer as it crashed down onto an anvil. The swordsman anticipated this and directed another katana blow towards Michael's abdomen. Michael quickly realised this attacker was a challenging adversary, as he wielded this katana with devastating accuracy and speed. Michael again brought the blade around to his side to stop the lethal attack, but again his attacker changed direction and delivered another katana blow from the opposite side, which Michael could barely stop, due to its ferocity. The clashing of the sharpened steel blades echoed an ear piercing sound so loud it was hurting Michael's ears. Michael knew he was finished if he did not change his way of engaging in battle with this man. He recalled his training and began to attack when his opponent expected him to defend; each blow was now met by an attack from Michael. Michael lunged forward again pushing his attacker closer to the exit, but just as he dared to believe he had the upper hand, he over extended his body, leaving himself off balance. His attacker swung his foot in a circular motion, connecting with Michael's lower leg, sweeping him off his feet and sending him crashing backwards into the toilet wall. The attacker ran over and pushed the edge of his blade against Michael's katana, which Michael inadvertently held near his own throat; Michael was desperately trying to defend himself.

"I know you have a document on you that belongs to Ashikaga," the attacker said with a determined look in his eyes.

Michael squeezed his words out from behind the katana he was holding in front of his chest. His katana was the only thing preventing his attacker's katana from slicing his throat open.

"I don't know what you're talking about," Michael strained to say.

The attacker pushed harder with the katana until Michael could barely breathe.

"Don't play games with me, I know you have it with you because your squealing mother told me, now you can either hand it over or I will take it off your dead body when I run you through with this blade."

Michael could feel himself boiling inside with rage; he feared that this man had extracted information about him from his mother, he dared not think what the result of that might be. He called on all his strength from deep within, and then inch by inch he forced the blade away from his chest and pushed back on the katana that was pinning him down. His attacker's eyes glared with a fiendish look, knowing that he had struck a chord with the mention of his mother. Michael pushed and pushed against the katana until he had enough distance between him and his attacker to allow him to land a front kick straight into his groin. The attacker cowered back towards the exit in pain, but quickly manoeuvred his katana to be ready for Michael's next attack; he clutched it with two hands by his side and readied himself. Before either of them made a move, a shadow cast across the floor of the toilets and a voice filtered through the cold dank atmosphere inside,

"Are yah alright in here, Michael? What the hell's going on?" Bill said with a concerned voice. Bill was stood in the doorway behind Michael's attacker.

Michael screamed as loud as he could towards Bill,

"No, Bill, get out!"

Before Michael could finish his words, the attacker thrust his katana to his rear, piercing straight into Bill's stomach.

Michael screamed again,

"No!" The echo of Michael's voice rebounded around the enclosed concrete walls like a ricocheting bullet fired in a prison cell.

Bill slumped to the ground in a heap; his head flopped slowly to one side and thudded onto the concrete floor. His attacker calmly removed the katana from Bill's stomach and charged at Michael. This time Michael was ready, and he blocked the wielding swordsman with the katana he had retrieved from the floor, and swung his blade down from above his head and across the front of his attacker's stomach, slicing through the black trench coat he was wearing and into his flesh. The attacker looked down in disbelief at the blood immediately oozing from his abdomen.

"How dare you cut me?" the man said in an indignant tone.

"I am a master of the katana and you are a worthless boy."

Michael did not take his eyes off his opponent, instead he lifted his katana ready to attack; Michael spoke with a gravel tone.

"Fuck you, I'm a better master of the katana and for what you have done to my friend you are going to fucking pay." As soon as Michael finished speaking, he charged at the attacker, feinting to the left and the right and then landing another crashing blow, this time into his opponent's shoulder. The sight of the katana crunching into his bone made his opponent rapidly lose the will to fight and he stood completely still, shocked by the speed of the attack. Michael pushed him further back towards the exit, blow after blow rained down on the attacker's body, weakening him more and more. Finally Michael moved his katana to his side and struck him square in the face with a punch that sent him spinning out of the exit and tumbling down the concrete steps; he had fallen to a halt on the tarmac below. Michael knew he had him beaten and moved in closer to finish him off, but before he could get near, the attacker summoned enough energy to raise himself up on his knees, he collected his katana that had fallen in front of him, pulling it towards him with his blood soaked hands. Grasping at the now bloodied blade, he positioned it to face the centre of his stomach, while looking directly at Michael.

"Ashikaga will kill you for this and then he will kill May Lin."

Michael took one step towards him, but before he could move another step, his attacker lifted his arms up into the air while tightly gripping the katana. With a clinical action he pushed his katana straight into his own stomach and lifelessly slumped forward towards the ground with the blade protruding from his back.

Michael's immediate thoughts were to attend to Bill; he turned without hesitation and ran up the steps into the toilets where Bill was lying in a pool of blood.

"Bill, can you hear me? Hang in there, man, Bill can you hear me? Don't fall asleep, talk to me." Michael pulled him into his side and yelled as loud as he could,

"Help me please, someone help me, we need an ambulance."

The half time whistle had just sounded in the ground and soon the toilet would be packed with people. Michael willed this to happen quickly so he could get help for Bill.

"Did we win?" Bill whispered.

Michael lifted Bill further up from the ground removed his own jacket and pushed it over the wound.

"It's only half time, marra, hang in there, Bill; someone will be here to help real soon." Bill gripped Michael's arm and stared into his eyes.

"Is it bad, Michael? Cos it hurts like hell."

Michael pushed down on the coat to stop the bleeding.

"You're gonna make it, Bill, don't think about anything else."

"What the bloody hell has happened here?"

Michael looked back to the exit as men started piling into the toilet with complete shock on their faces.

"Someone call an ambulance please and quickly," Michael shouted.

One of the men ran to get help.

"It's a bit late for an ambulance for that bloke outside, what the hell has gone on in here?" one of the men asked.

"We were attacked with swords by that man outside and that man over in the corner." Michael pointed to the corner where he presumed the other attacker would be lying, but the man was gone.

CHAPTER 23

"Excuse me, Ashikaga san, I have some news from England," Sakigawa informed Ashikaga.

"Gentlemen, I must bring this meeting to a close, we will talk again soon. I am hoping this news will have an influence on our plans for the casino, gentlemen. As Yakuza, we will not be prevented from pursuing our objectives, now please excuse me." Ashikaga stepped away from the table and as he did so his action prompted an equivalent response from the others involved in the meeting, he slowly bowed and then headed for the exit, before the people assembled could reciprocate.

"Is it good news, Sakigawa? Do they have what I want?" Ashikaga asked with an assured confidence.

Sakigawa lowered his head, directing his words towards the ground.

"They do not, Ashikaga san… and Hasegawa is dead."

Ashikaga clenched his hands tightly into a fist and twisted his face as if his mouth was wrestling with a sour fruit.

"Where is, Nishimoto now?"

"He is on the run from the English police; he has informed me that he will be lying low before he tries to return to Japan," Sakigawa nervously answered.

Ashikaga showed no remorse over Hasegawa; since losing his son the lives of his men were scant in comparison.

"If he rings again, tell him not to bother returning unless he wants his head served on a plate to his mother."

Sakigawa bowed and headed out of the room.

"Yes, Ashikaga san, I will relay your message."

Ashikaga looked towards Sakigawa with a subjugating stare.

"Where is, Kobyashi? I want to speak with him."

"He is with, May Lin, Ashikaga san," Sakigawa cautiously replied.

Ashikaga's face flushed red with anger as he shouted at Sakigawa,

"She is the cause of all this, that deceitful little bitch, get Kobyashi to bring her to me."

Sakigawa scurried away without delay to bring Kobyashi.

Ashikaga walked over to his desk and sat on his chair, he spun the chair around until he was facing out onto his garden, and he lifted both of his hands from his lap and covered his face, leaving only his nose and mouth protruding. He blasted out a roar of anger, with his arms shaking as the tension gripped his whole body. Ashikaga's patience was stretched to the limit; he knew he had to deliver on his word to appease the other Yakuza and he once again had been thwarted by Michael Harris. This boy from England held the one thing that could allow Ashikaga Yoshimitsu to be the most powerful and wealthy Yakuza in the whole of Tokyo. Ashikaga's avarice drove his desire to get what he wanted and he needed that ancient covenant from Michael Harris, and for him, not having it, was not an option. Sakigawa knocked on the door.

"Kobyashi and May Lin are here, Ashikaga san."

Ashikaga took a deep breath and puffed his chest out, showing a weary frustration at how difficult it was to get this covenant from a boy. He yelled at Sakigawa,

"Send them in."

Kobyashi entered the room, dragging a dishevelled and bruised May Lin behind him; she was so weak she could not stand. Kobyashi held her up by the arm, with her flaccid torso drooped down the side of his leg and onto the floor, his grip of her arm was so tight her mouth was open like a yelping dog ready to scream, but she was so weak she could not make a noise. Ashikaga waved his arm and clicked his fingers.

"Bring her to my desk." Ashikaga sat down in his seat as Kobyashi dragged her over to where he was sitting and pushed her onto the desk. Her body landed face down with her stomach and hips pressed firmly against the top of Ashikaga's old oak desk. Her scuffed legs dangled over the side with the toes of her dirt engrained feet just touching the floor. Her black hair completely covered her face as she lay lifeless in front of him. Ashikaga leaned forward from his chair and reached out to touch May Lin's head; he gripped her hair and yanked on it the way you would yank on a stubborn weed when you pulled it from the soil. Her face revealed the bruising around her eyes and cheekbones from the numerous beatings she had been subjected to.

"It seems that you could be of use to me after all, so I was right not to throw you to my dogs. Your English boyfriend has somehow evaded my pusillanimous men yet again and neither of them has relieved him of the covenant that belongs to me." Ashikaga dropped May Lin's head and it thudded onto the desk. He stood up from his seat and walked around his desk towards the rear of May Lin's body.

"You see… traitor scum like you really shouldn't get a second chance, you are dishonourable to your employers and dishonourable to your nation, and for that alone you do not deserve to live and that may be your fate once I'm done with you."

Ashikaga paused before speaking again.

"Unless you prove yourself useful to me." Ashikaga was now stood behind May Lin as she lay motionless on the desk. He lifted up her skirt to reveal her bruised buttocks and her stained pants. He pulled her pants to one side, grabbed the flesh on one of her buttocks and wrenched it up to reveal her vagina. He then violently thrust his fingers inside her vagina.

"Authority gives you power you see and with that power I can do what I want." He dug his nails into her vagina's wall until she spurted out a yelp of pain.

Kobyashi was so shocked he turned away until Ashikaga was finished.

"If you want to use this filthy gash between your legs again, then you better make contact with that boyfriend of yours and get him to come and see you, and if you're not convincing…" Ashikaga once again tightened his grip; this again was met with a painful yelp from May Lin, "…I will cut this out and leave you to bleed to death, do you understand?" There was no reply, so Ashikaga squeezed again. "I said do you understand?"

Kobyashi walked forward.

"Ashikaga san, she is unconscious."

Ashikaga pulled his hand from between May Lin's legs with a disdainful look on his face and then proceeded to push her off his desk, whereupon she flopped onto the floor.

"Get her out of my sight and get her something to eat, we need her to make a phone call, so we need her conscious."

"Yes, Ashikaga san," Kobyashi acknowledged as he lifted May Lin over his shoulder and carried her out of the room.

CHAPTER 24

"Can I come with him, he's my best friend?" Michael asked.

"Were yah the one that was with him?" the ambulance driver enquired.

"Yes I was," Michael replied with remorseful guilt.

"Okay, jump in with the medics in the back."

Michael struggled to recognise Bill on the stretcher in the back of the ambulance. His face was barely visible with the oxygen mask clamped across his mouth and his face drained of colour, due to the amount of blood he had lost. The first medic looked over at Michael who sat opposite Bill.

"Did yah fasten the jacket over the wound?"

"I did," Michael replied.

"Well yah may have saved his life and with a bit of luck, whatever it was that caused the wound may have missed his vital organs."

The second medic peered over towards Michael with a look of disgust.

"I heard it was a Samurai sword that did this, is that down to yee?"

Michael hung his head in shame.

"I guess you could say that…"

The first medic interrupted Michael.

"Look, let's not start apportioning blame right now, this guy lying here is this guy's friend and no matter how he got into this mess, he also tried to save him."

Again the second medic continued to stare at Michael.

"Well I would make yerself scarce when we arrive at hospital if I was yee. His parents will not be impressed with you."

Michael sat staring at Bill lying on the stretcher fighting for his life. As he stared, his thoughts were of other people and how he had brought suffering to them: May Lin, his mother and now Bill. His thoughts then returned to his mother who was home from hospital after being discharged and the anguish he burdened her with by returning home, his thoughts then flashed back to the fight in the toilets at Roker Park, he then repeated the words the attacker said over and over in his head.

Your squealing mother told me, your squealing mother told me. His thoughts were interrupted when the ambulance came to an abrupt halt and began to reverse, but that did not stop him shouting out,

"My mother!"

The ambulance then stopped again and soon after the rear doors burst open to reveal the ambulance driver and Bill's father and mother, they were standing at the accident and emergency entrance to the hospital. Bill's mother was glaring at Michael with an accusing look on her face.

"I might have known yee were involved in this, get away from my son." Bill's mother observed her son being carried out of the ambulance linked to an oxygen mask and engulfed in blood stained bandages like a soldier being dragged from a battlefield. She wailed and began to cry.

"Oh my beautiful little boy, what have yah done to him? Yee and your family bring nothing but bother to this town, keep away from me and my family, do you hear me? Keep away."

Michael stood forlorn and dejected.

"I tried to help him, Mrs Richardson, I did my best."

Bill's mother lunged forward towards Michael and he knew what was coming next, but did not try to stop her, with a flailing swing Bill's mother slapped Michael flat across the face; the sound was loud enough to make the ambulance driver flinch with shock. The slap was followed by more wailing and crying from Bill's mother as she accompanied the stretcher into the hospital.

Bill's father turned to Michael before following her.

"I think it's best if yah don't contact Bill, Michael, our Bill worships the ground yah walk on and look what he gets in return, I don't even want to ask how he got in this state."

Michael tried to interject,

"If you could give me a minute I could…"

Bill's father stopped him.

"I think it's best if yah just leave." Bill's father turned his back on Michael and followed his wife into the hospital.

Michael was left watching his best friend disappear into the bright lights of the hospital entrance, not knowing whether he would be alive the next morning.

His moment of solitude and calm was very quickly shattered by the sound of a police siren in the distance and the distinct blue flashing light illuminating what was now a dusky evening sky. His urge now was to get back to his house to make sure his mother was safe. He glanced towards the bottom of the street and observed the police car turning in towards the entrance to the hospital. He immediately looked to his side where the bins were kept at the rear entrance; he dashed towards them leapt onto one of the bins and cleared the fence before the police caught sight of him. He ran towards his house as fast as his legs could carry him. Again his mind flashed back to the fight in the football ground toilets and what the attacker said about his mother.

As he neared the bottom of the street leading to his house he could once again see blue flashing lights flickering in and out of the alleyways between his neighbourhood and the surrounding streets. The bright blue lights intermittently illuminated the roads and gardens nearby, it was apparent that crowds had gathered outside Michael's house to discover what was going on. These crowds cast shadows onto the surrounding house walls each time the blue lights flashed in front of them, the dancing images created a lure to Michael, giving him the urge to walk towards the lights and his house. As he approached it became evident that not only were the blue lights from police cars, but an ambulance was also in attendance. His urge to walk became a fear to walk and a necessity to run. He began piecing all the events together in his mind: the Japanese attackers, the covenant, his mother giving his location away and the ambulance outside his house. Now the only noise he could hear were his shoes pounding the road and his breathing as he desperately sucked in air in an attempt to run faster towards his house. He was close to the crowds outside the house now and they were all turning around to see who was running behind them. He slowed down before he got to the crowd; he pushed his way through, much to the annoyance of the engrossed onlookers, until he was confronted by a policeman.

"Sorry, sir, you can't go in there, this whole area has been cordoned off from the public."

Michael noticed the policeman looking curiously at Michael's face and deliberating over his next move, the policeman was just about to speak, but Michael spoke first,

"I live here, Officer, that's my mother's house."

The words seemed to paralyse the policeman's thoughts, rendering him useless. Michael continued nonchalantly walking past the crowd and through his garden gate towards the door to his house. The policeman finally controlled his shock and shouted to the group of police standing beside the ambulance,

"Sarge, I think you may want to stop that man, I believe that's Michael Harris."

The sergeant looked up and peered over his colleague's shoulder towards the tall man entering the house.

"Jesus… Officer Wilson, why the hell didn't you stop him?" The sergeant turned and ran towards the door to the house; Michael was now inside the house and walking towards the living room. He pushed the door and it swung open with a hinge rusting creek; he stepped inside to find two police officers standing in the corner smoking a cigarette with a halo of smoke draped around their heads. Their faces were illuminated by the subtle down light hanging from the ceiling. Michael looked across the other side of the room; he could make out a body lying flat on its back, his eyes scanned up from the legs towards the midriff and then up towards the shoulders. The head was missing. Michael warily turned his head to his right and stared into the corner of the room, away from the body, and there immediately in front of him was the blood soaked severed head of his mother. His knees buckled and he fell to the floor.

"For fuck's sake, get him out of there." The sergeant's voice rang out from the back door.

The two officers nipped the ends of their cigarettes and quickly slipped them into their pockets.

"We thought he was one of the forensics team, Sarge," one of the officers exclaimed in embarrassment. The two officers quickly grabbed each of Michael's shoulders and began to drag him out of the room.

The sergeant's voiced bellowed again,

"How the hell did he get past the cordon?"

Michael was in a daze, as the two police officers pulled upon his shoulders. Michael grabbed hold of a hand of each of the officers and twisted them both into a lock that produced so much discomfort that they both cried out with pain. Michael proceeded to pull down on their wrists and hurtled them towards the living room wall, they collided with the sideboard, creating an almighty crunch, leaving ornaments and lamps strewn upon the floor. The sergeant was now standing in the doorway just in time to see the floundering officers with a posture that resembled school children who had just been pushed over in the school yard by a smaller child.

"Can you two wait outside and I will deal with this?" the experienced sergeant tersely instructed his men. The sergeant carried a blanket to the body and covered it; he then collected the severed head with another blanket and placed it near the shoulders, the whole body was now completely covered.

"Michael, I'm sorry you had to see that, forensics asked us not to move the body and to be fair to the two young officers, they were just following orders."

Michael's eyes were glazed over with shock and when he spoke his voice changed little in tone.

"My mother was right; I've brought this on her by returning home, I've involved my best friend too." Michael spoke while staring at the body.

The sergeant edged towards Michael and placed his hand slowly onto his shoulder. "Your next door neighbour walked in on this and phoned it in to us…Listen." The sergeant tried to calm Michael with his understanding tone.

"You do realise that I have to do my job and take you down to the station don't you? I am sorry to say that, son, but we need to know what's going on here, we can't have people running around killing people with Samurai swords, this is bloody Sunderland not a crazy Kung Fu film," the sergeant exclaimed in disbelief. The sergeant heard sniffling as Michael started crying.

"I was just beginning to make things better between my mother and me and now she's dead, just like my father, and for what?"

The sergeant spoke in a calming but inquisitive tone,

"That's what we all don't understand, what's this all about, Michael, have you done this?"

Michael was in too much shock to answer and just shook his head.

"Where's the weapon that did this, Michael?"

Michael shook his head again.

"I didn't kill my mother, Sergeant."

The sergeant placed a firm hand on Michael's shoulder,

"We will need to get to the bottom of this and that's why I will need you to come to the station and clear this up: hopefully you can do that without any more violence directed towards my officers."

Michael looked towards the sergeant and rubbed his sleeve across his eyes to dry his tears.

"I needed to see my mother and they were trying to drag me out of the room."

The sergeant moved to the side of him and placed his hand on Michael's arm.

"I will give you ten minutes, Michael, you can pay your last respects, then I'm going to trust you to walk out and come with me to the station."

Michael nodded his head in agreement. The sergeant walked out closing the door behind him.

Michael could hear the muffled conversations taking place outside between the police, but the sergeant was keeping his word and no one entered the house.

Michael took the opportunity to say goodbye to his mother, he kneeled down facing her.

"I am deeply sorry for all of this, Mother, I hope you can see your way to forgiving me, as I did not intentionally bring this trouble to your door." Michael paused to think of his final words… The silence broke with the ringing of the telephone on the dining table at the rear of the living room. The noise seemed to intensify as it kept ringing louder and louder. Michael moved towards it holding his hand above the receiver, hoping that it might ring off before he picked it up and therefore not requiring him to speak to someone who was most probably ringing to speak to his mother. It continued to ring, so he tentatively lifted the receiver and placed it to his ear.

"Hello, who's speaking please?" Michael politely asked.

"Is that, Michael?" the caller enquired.

"Yes it is," Michael replied, pausing before he spoke again.

"Who is that?"

The caller spoke in a slow velvet tone,

"It's, May Lin."

Michael was instantly cheered by the sound of her voice.

"Oh, May Lin you really don't know how good it is to hear your voice, I thought something might have happened to you."

May Lin continued,

"No, I'm perfectly fine, I'm just missing you so much, Michael, I could really do with seeing you."

"How do you mean…? Are you coming… to England?" Michael said hesitantly.

"I can't, Michael, I have so much going on with helping my mother, I can't really leave her," May Lin answered.

For that small moment, Michael had completely forgotten what was happening to him and drifted off into a world of warmth with May Lin lying next to him, until May Lin mentioned the word mother, and he was abruptly reminded of his current situation. Michael started speaking,

"I ca…"

May Lin interrupted him.

"Michael, it would be truly fantastic if you could make it back to Japan to visit me, I miss you so much."

Michael was warmed by those last words.

"My mother…" Michael changed the direction of his conversation again. "Really, May Lin, I don't have the money to travel back to Japan, even though nothing would make me more happy right now." Michael still could not bring himself to mention his mother.

Speaking in a hurried tone, May Lin reassured Michael,

"I'm sure you will be able to visit me, Michael if you want to, because I'm willing to send money to you to help with the cost of the journey, so if you do want to come, then you can."

Michael was overwhelmed by this.

"You would do that for me, May Lin?"

"If it means I get to see you, of course."

"Would I not be putting us both in grave danger with the Yakuza by being back in the country?"

At this point May Lin felt the sharp edge of a katana squeeze tightly against her neck.

"No, Michael that has all died down now, we would both be fine."

"Then I would love to come back."

Ashikaga put his hand over the mouthpiece of the phone and instructed May Lin,

"Tell him that you will post the money for the ticket and enclose a number to ring you when he is at Heathrow Airport a fortnight from now."

May Lin nervously delivered Ashikaga's instructions.

"I am going to post you the money." May Lin's voice was shaking, and this prompted another push of the blade on her throat.

Michael sounded his concern.

"Are you okay, May Lin?"

May Lin took a deep breath and composed herself.

"When you receive the money there will be a note inside, the note will have a number written on it, the next flight to Narita will be from Heathrow Airport in a fortnight's time, once you have your ticket, phone me from the airport and I will make arrangements to collect you when you arrive here in Japan. Now I must go, because my mother needs me, Michael, she's not well."

"What's wrong with her?"

Ashikaga grabbed the phone from May Lin and placed it on the receiver.

"Hello, hello, May Lin are you there?" Michael wanted to ask May Lin so much more, but instead was left listening to the dialling tone. Michael was overcome with a pressing feeling of frustration. He mulled over the conversation with May Lin in his mind.

May Lin rings and asks me to visit her, and I can't even explain to her that I'm likely to be locked up.

Michael found a pen and wrote, a fortnight, Heathrow, Narita, on the inside of his arm, he then pulled his sleeve over it, and placed the receiver down on the phone. Michael walked back to where his mother was lying. His shoes stuck to the floor from his mother's blood that had soaked into the carpet like a spilt glass of red wine. He looked down at his feet and once again was overcome with rage as he saw his feet surrounded by his mother's life that had drained away from her body.

"Goodbye, Mam, I know you never approved of my martial arts and could never understand what it meant to me, so I guess you won't approve of what I am going to do, but I will get revenge for this, for you, for my father and all the friends that I have lost, I will have my day. Miss you, Mam and though you may be surprised to hear this, I always loved you too."

Michael slowly turned away and walked towards the back door. As he opened the door to exit the house, the sergeant and all the other police officers were waiting outside, as Michael began walking down the garden path, all the police officers lifted their helmets from their heads and placed them on their chests. The sergeant guided Michael to the awaiting police car and asked him to get in. Michael looked across at the sergeant.

"Will they look after my mother, Sarge?"

The sergeant nodded, acknowledging Michael's request.

"I will see to it personally, Michael."

CHAPTER 25

"You were so convincing on the phone you almost had me believing you, if it wasn't for the fact that I knew you were a duplicitous little whore. Get her a drink for her efforts."

"Yes, Ashikaga san." Sakigawa bowed as he dragged May Lin from the room.

May Lin certainly took heart from her conversation with Michael, but her feelings were tinged with remorse as she knew she was helping Ashikaga to set a trap for Michael. Following May Lin's removal from the room Ashikaga called Kobyashi over to his desk. He doled out his instructions to Kobyashi with devious guile.

"When we send the money to Michael's house, make sure we have a letter in the envelope from May Lin asking Michael to bring the covenant with him, make sure it sounds convincing, it would be sensible to tell Michael that this document is needed to help May Lin's mother. Force May Lin – when Michael phones – to mention that her mother is not well and the document can help with raising money for treatment; this will remove any suspicion he has for any ulterior motive." Kobyashi did not move and stared at Ashikaga with a look of trepidation. Ashikaga looked back at Kobyashi with annoyance.

"What? Why are you looking at me like that? Have you any better ideas?"

Kobyashi's retort was not intended to undermine Ashikaga, but it did.

"This guy may be young, but in my short time in dealing with him, he's no fool, I think he will smell a rat."

Ashikaga banged his fist down on the desk.

"Listen to me, he probably has every intention of coming after me anyhow, as you succinctly put it, he's no fool, however, if we can distract him with this deception surrounding May Lin, then maybe, just maybe we can get the covenant back, we can move forward with the land acquisitions and get rid of him for good, yes, do you agree?"

Kobyashi rolled his thickset shoulders in a way only he could do and accepted Ashikaga's plan with a reluctant nod of the head. Ashikaga sat at his desk and waved his hand.

"Go ahead, get her to comply, we need to get this moving and fast."

Kobyashi disappeared from the room, leaving Ashikaga to contemplate his next move. Ashikaga was growing weary of this whole debacle, keeping May Lin in his home against her will did not please him and he did not enjoy the attention from the police, each visit cost him financially with payments being made to buy their silence. He could also detect a growing resentment from his men and particularly from Kobyashi; this was entrenched by the loss of his own son and Kobyashi's good friend Hasegawa. He also knew Kobyashi was unimpressed with his treatment of Nishimoto, not letting him return home in Kobyashi's eyes was a betrayal. As the man the other Yakuza looked up to, Ashikaga needed to show he was in control, that he was ruthless, and that he ruled by fear. The other Yakuza needed to see this from their leader to give them inspiration and the confidence to believe in him as their leader. He knew that delivering on the covenant and all that transpired after, would elevate him to a status nothing short of a Shogun, but he also knew there was a diffuse boundary between being at the top of one's game and being at the bottom of the river wearing a pair of concrete boots.

CHAPTER 26

"Okay, Michael, I'm going to leave you in this room and Detective Superintendent Bob Marsh is going to have a chat with you, I've explained to him as much as I know from what you have told me, so he has some understanding of the events today, however I think he will want you to elaborate on them, okay?" the sergeant reassured Michael.

"Thanks, Sergeant, I will try to make things clear, but you all must believe me that I did not kill my mam or the man at the stadium."

The sergeant walked towards the door of the interrogation room while nodding his head.

"I know, son, I know; just tell the DSI the truth and I'm sure you will be back home before you know it." The look that the sergeant gave Michael as he walked past the desk was not an assured look; this look succeeded in making Michael nervous of what was to come.

The sergeant closed the door behind him, leaving Michael sat behind an old oak desk with an array of files and paper folders scattered from one side to the next. The desk was flanked with two paint flaking grey cabinets with photo frames of police officers in group poses, adorning the tops. The whole room had an eerie familiarity about it and as Michael glanced towards the ceiling he then realised why. The lamp shade hanging down cast the same light over the room as the lamp shade did in Inspector Bando's room in Japan. Michael's mind began to drift back to that very room at the Tokyo police station where he first had feelings for May Lin, the images of her hair and her lingering scent in the room.

"Penny for your thoughts." Michael was immediately brought back to the here and now by the words that crashed into his vivid memories.

"Sorry, I was miles away," Michael postulated.

"That's alright, young man; I will have you right here where I want you in next to no time," DSI Marsh said with an array of smugness.

Michael looked over towards the DSI and trailed him with a lingering stare from one side of the room to the other. The DSI made his way to the back of the office where a weathered oak table stood. He poured himself a black coffee and returned to the desk where Michael was sat, without offering Michael a drink. He then threw a brown folder onto the desk in front of Michael with the name 'Michael Harris' written on the front, in red biro.

"I suggest you don't try to stare me out, sunshine, you're already looking at a stretch for the murder of that poor guy at the stadium, so getting on the wrong side of me is not a good idea."

Michael was shell-shocked with the words he was hearing from DSI Marsh; the sergeant had lulled Michael into a false sense of security. This man was talking in a completely different tone to the sergeant.

"I have already explained to the people before you that I did not kill the man at the stadium, just like I did not kill my mam, I was defending myself from two attackers at the stadium who were trying to kill me with katanas; the man who you found dead actually killed himself."

The DSI opened his notes to take a look, and then looked into Michael's eyes.

"What's a katana?"

"It's a sword, a Samurai sword."

"Then name it a sword."

The DSI sat down opposite Michael; he picked up Michael's folder and slowly perused the pages in front of him.

"He committed hari kari is that right?" The DSI was reading from the notes in the file and looking up at Michael.

"It's called seppulco," Michael replied in a trite manner.

The DSI slammed his mug onto the desk propelling half of his cup of coffee two feet into the air splashing all of the files that were laid upon the desk.

"Don't get fucking smart with me, boy, he didn't commit seppulco or hari kari or whatever you call it, because you murdered him with a sword, didn't you?" The DSI continued with his rant. "You're one of these crazy Kung Fu fuckers aren't you and you thought it would be good to kill someone with a sword at a football match to get revenge for them chopping your mother's head off? Unfortunately for you it all went wrong didn't it, because you were discovered by fans at the ground committing the act, I'm right aren't I? Go on, why don't you just admit it?" Michael refrained from replying and looked directly into DSI Marsh's eyes.

"I've already told you, sunshine, don't try staring me down. Open that file and look at that photograph."

Michael averted his gaze under duress and pulled the file towards him, and then proceeded to open the file. Inside the folder was a picture of Michael's mother with her decapitated head lying beside her body. Michael's reaction was one of revulsion; Michael swiftly pushed the folder away from him.

"Why are you showing me this? This is my mother and I don't appreciate you showing me pictures of my dead mother."

DSI Marsh pushed the file back towards Michael.

"I know who it is, son and when you discovered the man killing her, you and your friend in the hospital chased after him to the football ground, and it's there where you ran him through with this sword." DSI Marsh lifted a bundled refuse sack from under the desk and unveiled the sword which had been lodged inside the stomach of the man at the stadium.

"What? I can't believe you're saying this, you know that is just a made up story, I have already explained that the man at the stadium killed himself and I discovered my mother dead when I returned from the hospital, where incidentally, I was with my friend Bill who will tell you the same story as me, if you bother to ask him." Michael looked up at the DSI and then quickly looked away to avoid being berated again.

"Don't get cocky with me, boy, do you think we haven't tried to speak with your friend? Unfortunately we can't. Most people who come in contact with you either end up dead or incapacitated and he looks like he's heading that way."

Michael looked towards the door in the office in the hope that he might be able to leave.

"I know what you're trying to do, you're trying to get me to confess to this, well I'm not, I've told you the truth and that's it, anyway I'm sure I should have a lawyer present before you interrogate me."

The DSI was becoming increasingly frustrated by Michael's obstinate attitude; Michael once again looked towards the door.

"Laddy, don't be looking towards the door, because you're not going anywhere until you tell me exactly what happened."

Michael quickly stood up from his seat and turned his head towards the DSI.

"Jesus, you just don't listen do you, I didn't kill the man, and while you have me sat in here, there's a person who murdered my mother running around this town completely free; but you're too incompetent to understand that."

The DSI moved to push Michael back into his seat, but as he neared Michael's shoulder with his hand Michael thrust his arm up and grabbed the DSI's wrist. Before the DSI could pull away, Michael twisted his arm over with a hand lock on his forearm, he then yanked the DSI's body forward with his tightly gripped wrist and forced his face down into the office table in front of him. Michael without thinking instantly lifted his elbow in the air and was about to strike down on the DSI's face.

"Do it!" the DSI shouted. "Go on do it and I will add assaulting a police officer to the list of charges that I'm going to stick on you and then it will be even longer that you're banged up."

Michael paused, contemplated his next move, and instead of getting himself into more trouble, he refrained from striking the DSI... A cold draft sucked into the room at that very moment, as the door to the office burst open with a window shaking bang as it clattered against the cabinet behind it.

"Okay, Michael you can release DSI Marsh now." Two men dressed in black suits were standing at the door with the sergeant alongside them. The DSI thrashed his arm to one side pushing Michael's arm away from his to avoid embarrassment. He jumped to his feet straightening his clothes in the process, and turned to confront the people standing in the doorway.

"Who the fuck are you two?"

The two men walked through the door and stood to one side of the room.

"Get him out of here, Sergeant."

"Yes, sir, come on, Bob, you have to come with me now." The sergeant swung the door wide open, allowing the DSI passage out of the room.

"I'm not going anywhere, this is my case and I'm here to do my job, which is to lock this piece of shit up for murdering someone in my town. Besides, I don't even know who you two are and... and... what authority do you have in this matter?" The DSI stood resolute with his arms folded.

"I'm Agent Carson and this is Agent James, we are from MI6 and we have authority over you in this matter. With regard to your job, you will be lucky if they allow you to walk the beat after this; we have sat outside listening to you interrogating this suspect with methods that were out of date in the fifties, let alone the seventies. I suggest you go out there, clear your desk and make your way home before I have you arrested for gross misconduct."

The DSI dropped his arms by his side and directed a long glaring look towards Michael; Michael looked him straight in the eyes without flinching. The DSI walked slowly towards the door, before he exited the room, he stopped near the opening and glared at the sergeant.

"You two-faced bastard, you fitted me up didn't you?"

The sergeant was shaking his head.

"No, Marsh, you fitted yourself up, there is no place in our police for a copper like you." The sergeant followed the DSI out of the door, closing it behind him.

"Hello, Michael, pleased to meet you, I'm Agent Alan Carson and this is Agent Roger James and we are from MI6."

Michael looked across the table at both men.

"Look I didn't do it, I've already ex…"

"Don't worry, Michael, we know you didn't do it," Agent Carson consoled Michael. "We know it was in self-defence what happened at Roker Park."

Michael wore a bemused and tired expression on his face.

"What's MI6?"

"We are a secret intelligence service looking after interests of the British Government in other countries, our aim is to…"

"I'm really sorry to interrupt, but did you say you knew what happened at Roker Park? The thing is I'm really weary of all this, everyone is thinking I killed the man at the stadium, and they're thinking I killed my mam too."

Agent Carson moved across the room to stand in front of Michael. "Relax, Michael, we know you're telling the truth, you have no need to worry about that right now, DSI Marsh will not be coming back." Agent Carson sat in the seat the DSI had vacated and Agent James pulled up another chair and they both faced Michael across the desk.

"We need to come clean with you, Michael," Agent Carson said as he looked straight into Michael's eyes.

"We are here to ask for your help."

Michael's countenance changed from one of bemusement to one of shock.

"You want my help?"

Agent Carson and Agent James answered assuredly, "Yes we do."

"What help could I possibly give you? Look at me, I'm a wreck and besides, help with what?" Michael held his hands out in a gesture of his inability to help anyone; nonetheless the two agents observed that Michael's hands were perfectly still.

Agent Carson spoke out.

"That's exactly my point, I feel completely vindicated by my decision to ask for your help." Michael looked at Agent James and then stared at his own hands out in front of him. Agent James pointed towards Michael.

"You have just gone through a traumatic police interview to say the least and your hands are held out in front of you without the slightest movement, not one minute shake: it's that calmness under pressure at such a young age that I admire about you," Agent James explained.

Michael sat back on his chair and started shaking his head.

"I'm sorry, Officer... erm Agent, okay what do I call you?"

The agent stuck his hand straight out in front of him and offered to shake Michael's hand, Michael obliged.

"You can call me Roger." Agent James then directed Michael towards Agent Carson, at which point Agent Carson also shook Michael's hand.

"And you can call me Alan, pleased to meet you, Michael."

Michael cagily replied,

"Nice to meet you too, now would someone care to explain what's going on here?"

Agent Carson stood up from his chair.

"I'll get us all a cuppa while you help Michael understand why we are here."

"Okay, cheers, Alan," Agent James replied.

When Agent Carson left the room, Agent James pulled his chair in closer and produced a dossier which he placed on the table in front of Michael.

"Michael, I have the unenviable task of showing you some things in this dossier that are going to shock you, so I want you to prepare yourself for that."

Michael leaned forward towards the table.

"Have you any idea what I've been through in the last few months? I've lost my father, my mother and..."

Agent James cut Michael's response short.

"I know all that, Michael. I know everything that's happened to you; and why do I know? Because it's my job to know, all will become clear very soon."

Michael slumped back into his chair and prepared to listen. The agent opened up the file and placed four photographs on the table. The first photograph was of May Lin, the second photograph was of Michael's father, the third photograph was of Kobyashi and the fourth photograph was of Ashikaga. The agent pointed at the photographs of Ashikaga and Kobyashi.

"This man to the left here is Ashikaga Yoshimitsu, he is the leader of a notorious group of Yakuza running illegal casinos in Tokyo, Amsterdam and London and is wanted by police in all three countries for murder, embezzlement, fraud; you name it, and he is up to it. This man here to the right is his henchman, this is a man called Kobyashi, a nasty piece of work and he is wanted for murder too."

Michael pulled the photograph of Ashikaga towards him.

"So that's what he looks like then, the man that tried to have me killed and succeeded in running me out of Japan?"

Agent James did not comment, pointing towards the other two photographs, he looked directly into Michael's eyes and spoke very slowly,

"Michael, your father was an exceptional man, and as an employee of MI6, he was one of our best operatives, he is a huge loss to our agency."

Michael uncomfortably adjusted his position on his seat, he was staring at Agent James with a look of disbelief, he opened his mouth to speak, but his words were not forthcoming.

Michael stood up from his chair and walked towards the window with the look of a man with no concept of where he was. He put his hands in his pockets, then leaned against the window and stared into the sky with the side of his face squashed against the window pane.

"I'm sorry about this, young man, but because of recent developments we needed to inform you."

Michael did not move from the window and continued to stare outside. The agent flicked through information in the dossier and continued with his description of his father.

"He was also mentioned in dispatches on a number of occasions, in one particular incident he…"

Michael spoke without looking at the agent.

"You said you wanted my help, what use can I be, how can I possibly help you?"

The agent picked up the picture of May Lin and walked over towards the window where Michael was standing, he placed the picture of May Lin on the window sill in front of him. Michael looked down at the picture of May Lin, but his mind was still thinking about his father. A double decker bus was driving past the window and made an emergency stop to avoid running a dog over, when the horn blasted from the bus the sound reminded Michael of the ships blasting their fog horns while negotiating misty conditions up the mouth of the River Wear: that very sound always reminded him of training near the river banks with his father. The horn sounded once more, the ear piercing blast concentrated his thoughts and brought his mind back to the room and the photograph on the window sill.

"You can help us get May Lin back," the agent nervously suggested.

Michael rolled his head away from the window and turned it to face Agent James. "Get May Lin back from where? I don't understand, what do you mean?"

"May Lin also works for us."

Michael started laughing.

"What's so funny?" Agent James asked.

"If I didn't laugh I think I would cry. My father would go out to work and come back from work; I have been to his office out there in Japan. He has entertained work colleagues at parties; I have even stayed at some of his work colleagues' houses. When did he ever find time to work for a secret intelligence service?"

Michael picked up the photograph of May Lin and carried it across the room, he flung it on the table alongside the other photographs.

"And this woman… this woman." Michael's bottom lip began to wobble, "I don't know what to say about this woman, I feel betrayed, deceived, used."

The agent moved to comfort Michael.

"In difficult circumstances, Michael, our people have to do what they think is best at that moment in time to protect themselves and to protect other operatives in the field, these decisions are sometimes made in minutes, with very little time to think them through, and May Lin was not exempt from that. However, I can categorically reassure you that May Lin had no intention of hurting you."

"How much do you actually know, Agent James? What do you know about May Lin and my father?"

"We know everything, Michael, that's why we believe you can help us get May Lin out, but more importantly we think you can help us nail Ashikaga."

Michael composed himself.

"Why can't you just go in there and sort him out, take the police in and arrest him?" Agent James picked up the dossier and brought Michael over to look at it.

"Because we don't have any evidence that we can make stick, Ashikaga always seems to evade us. Anytime we feel we are getting close, he seems to know our next move; nonetheless, you may be able to change that. The police are corrupt in the city which Ashikaga controls, that's probably why he always knows when we're coming." The agent once again pointed at Michael. "Fortunately, we know Ashikaga has summoned you to him."

Michael started shaking his head.

"Now you have lost me, what do you mean he has summoned me? I have had no contact with Ashikaga."

Agent James cracked a beaming smile across his weathered and bearded face.

"Not directly, but we know that May Lin phoned you at your mother's house suggesting that you meet her. If you do return to Japan and meet her, this could be our way to obtain evidence to put Ashikaga and Kobyashi away."

Michael walked away from the window and positioned himself behind the seat at the table in the centre of the room; he glared at Agent James before speaking.

"Hold on, hold on, I must be missing something here, or am I just stupid? What has May Lin asking me to come and visit her in Japan got to do with getting evidence to put this man Ashikaga and his henchman Kobyashi away?"

The agent checked his watch and gazed at the door to the office.

"When Alan returns we will explain everything."

Michael walked towards the desk where the dossier was lying, he picked up the picture of May Lin and looked towards the agent. Michael paused before speaking.

"He's got her hasn't he?"

The agent looked into Michael's eyes, and without saying a word, he nodded his head slowly.

Michael dropped his head into his hands, sat down on the chair and remained perfectly still.

Agent Carson returned to the room with the tea, he placed his and the other agent's tea on the table and proceeded to deposit the other cup of tea on the table next to Michael.

"I presume you already have told him by the look on his face, Roger?" Agent Carson asked.

"I didn't need to, he worked it out."

Michael lifted his head from his hands; a silence fell upon the room as both agents looked at each other and in turn looked at Michael. Agent Carson pulled a seat from under the table and swung it round to face Michael before sitting down. The sound of voices carried from the offices next door as Michael carried on looking at May Lin's picture.

"What do I need to do to get him?"

Agent Carson pulled his chair closer and placed his hand on Michael's shoulder.

"Listen, we're not forcing you to do this, especially as you have just turned sixteen, so it wouldn't surprise us if you said no."

Michael raised one eyebrow, portraying a questioning look.

"Please don't patronise me, you know what I'm capable of, or you wouldn't be asking me."

Agent James walked forward whilst expressing a concerned look.

"Yes, Michael we do know what you're capable of, but this man is an evil bastard, so don't think you're going in there for a fight, this is about getting the evidence to put him away and getting you and May Lin out..."

Agent Carson interrupted,

"If we can get enough evidence to send Ashikaga down, we will crack this corrupt Yakuza group wide open and who knows what other rats will leave the sinking ship on its way down? That said, we need to minimise the danger to your and May Lin's lives, therefore we need to plan meticulously."

Michael stood up from his chair like he was standing to attention; he clenched his fists in anticipation.

"Right, when do we start?"

Agent James now moved towards Michael, he placed his hand on his shoulder in an attempt to diffuse the situation.

"Hey listen, leave the initial planning to us and then we will bring you back when we have an executable plan. In the meantime you need to attend your mother's funeral and maybe spend some time with your girlfriend Rachel."

Agent Carson called out an instruction from the far side of the room.

"You should try to see your mate Bill in hospital too."

Michael replied to the agent's request,

"I would like to, but I doubt I would make it past his mother."

"Leave that with myself and Roger, we will see what we can do, and by the way, happy sixteenth birthday for Friday."

Michael was taken home in a car by a policeman from the station. The policeman was instructed to watch the house by Agent Carson, and immediately positioned himself outside while Michael went inside.

Michael thought about his next few days ahead, which would start with the funeral of his mother in two days' time.

CHAPTER 27

The following day arrived, and Michael was awoken by a knock at the door. The sun was piercing through a gap in his bedroom's poorly fitting curtains; the pounding knock echoed through the house again, and Michael's first thought was that this was a policeman waking him to inform him of a development at the hospital relating to his friend Bill. When Michael approached the door, the silhouette was that of a female rather than a male, and it certainly wasn't the police. The smell of a cherry scented shampoo slithered its way through the draft in the door and wafted its message under Michael's nose. Michael prised the blind apart that was fastened to the inside of the door and sneaked a quick peek through the window. Rachel was standing there in a full tracksuit and a pair of training shoes. Michael quickly unlocked the door.

"Rachel, what are you doing here?"

Rachel made a jogging on the spot gesture and then waved her arm in a 'come on' to Michael.

"I thought we would have a jog up to Penshaw monument for a bit of fresh air and maybe you can show me some of your sword techniques or your martial art moves?"

Michael was cheered by Rachel's forthright attitude and accepted her invitation with an accommodating thumbs up. He watched as she reciprocated with an alluring smile, which suggested to Michael that she wanted him to hurry up.

"You better come in until I get ready."

Michael and Rachel left the house and headed out of town towards the Penshaw monument; Michael grabbed his katana before leaving.

On arrival at Penshaw monument they both took a moment to soak up the view and to catch their breath following their run together. The bright yellow sun was intermittently piercing its way through the cotton wool cumulus clouds that were speckling the blue sky. The monument was emblazoned with the rays of the sun, until slowly wandering clouds cast a shape-shifting shadow across the columns that stood proud at the highest point of the hill. The monument looked so out of place, as if left behind by a retreating Roman garrison who were too busy to build anything else and decided to move on to other things. The view across the Wear Valley inspired Michael to draw his katana from his scabbard and perform his fighting moves. Rachel looked on with excitement.

"Try not to cut yourself."

Michael ignored the comment and continued to flash the blade through the air with lightning speed and power, his moves were fast and controlled.

"Funny, I'll do my best," Michael replied.

Each time Michael executed a move it was accompanied by the sharp sound the blade made as it cut through the air, each move in his repertoire was performed with an imaginary opponent attacking him from different angles. Thrusting, slicing, jabbing, and deflecting. Each consecutive move became faster and more aggressive. He was beginning to sweat profusely, but had no intention of stopping. On and on and on he trained, pushing harder and harder. Rachel was not expecting this kind of single-minded determination from Michael while he was practising his technique.

"Are you going to take a break and sit over here with me, Michael?"

Michael did not reply, and continued with his strict training regime. He was driving the sword to one side, then the other, pulling it back, swirling it around his head, carving it to the front and thrusting it to the rear. He was stretching Rachel's patience, so she walked forward from the monument directly towards him; standing two feet in front of him she looked straight into his face.

"Michael, please stop, you're scaring me."

Michael did not respond again and continued to practice. She detected an anger building in him that disturbed her, so much so that she was ready to walk away and leave Michael alone. She gave it one more shot and screamed at him.

"Michael please stop!" Rachel watched as he swung his sword around his shoulder for the final time and slowly brought it down to his side; he looked over to her and appeared to come away from his trance-like stare to his normal look. He re-housed his blade in the scabbard and dropped to the ground on his knees, completely exhausted. Rachel ran towards him.

"What happened to you there? You never stopped for almost twenty or thirty minutes, look at you, you're completely exhausted."

Michael was panting to catch his breath.

"Sorry, Rachel, I need to train hard today, it's the only way of improving my technique, besides, it clears my head of all the crap that is swilling its way around in there."

Rachel's retort was succinct, because Michael's reply confused her.

"It's the only way for improving your technique, what does that mean?"

"Nothing, Rachel, please just forget it and let's sit down like you suggested and enjoy the view."

Rachel was compliant, although she did feel somewhat excluded from Michael's deepest thoughts; she sat at the base of the monument looking away from him. He sat down beside her and placed his arm around her. She moved away from his arm and continued staring into the distance.

"There's something you're not telling me, Michael, I'm not stupid, what is it?"

Michael did not look at Rachel when he replied.

"It's nothing really."

"Michael, I've just said I'm not stupid, now stop trying to deceive me and tell me what's wrong."

"All I can say, is that it's something I need to do in honour of my father, you… you… you need to trust me and believe that what I'm doing is necessary to help someone who once helped me and my father."

Michael held Rachel's hand.

"And if I could tell you more, then I would."

"Is it something to do with the covenant that we looked at a few days ago?"

"I can't say… really I can't."

"You don't trust me do you, Michael?"

Michael picked up his sword and walked towards a bench where he sat down facing away from the monument. He looked over the Wear Valley and towards the River Wear. The sun was now slowly losing its heat as the day drifted towards dusk. Michael looked upwards and watched the gulls flying back to the coast from inland: each group of gulls etched a v formation into the sky as they passed overhead; all the birds were heading the same way with their effortless return flight to the coast.

"Why are you watching the birds like that, Michael?" Rachel curiously enquired as she followed Michael to where he was sitting.

"There are things you miss about the area you were brought up in which makes it such a special place to return to. Just seeing the birds flying over Penshaw monument like this, brings it all back… And by the way, it's not that I don't trust you at all, it's about keeping people who I care about safe, that might sound hard to believe, but it's true."

Rachel moved close to Michael and he carefully moved his katana to one side, and as he did this, the dusky orange sun glinted on the shiny edge of the blade and flashed the light across Rachel's face, illuminating her skin in a way that enhanced her youthful innocence.

"You're going away aren't you, Michael?" Rachel asked.

Michael placed his katana on the floor and wrapped his arms around Rachel's waist, pulling her towards him.

"You must not reveal this to anyone, promise me that will you?"

Rachel turned away from Michael and walked towards the middle of the monument, He followed her until he was standing close behind her, he could hear her crying.

"I promise I… I… I won't say anything: I know this is going to sound silly, but I'm going to say it anyway, I really care for you, Michael and I'm going to…"

Michael held Rachel's hand and turned her to face him, tears were trickling down her cheeks. He cut her off in mid-conversation.

"Don't say it, Rachel, please, just let me hold you." Michael kissed Rachel and hugged her once again.

"I need to get you back home, it's getting dark, and your father will have that crazy dog out looking for me if I don't return with you soon."

Rachel smiled and giggled while trying to stop her tears from dripping into her mouth, she grasped Michael's hand.

"I might let Zimba grab you so you can't leave."

Michael also smiled.

"Don't take this the wrong way, but my previous experience of your dog does not make me feel comfortable about where he would grab me."

Rachel stopped smiling, and her look changed to one of consternation.

"Please take care wherever it is you're going, you will be coming back, won't you?"

Michael walked over to his katana and flicked it up from the ground with his foot, catching it with one hand and holding Rachel's hand with the other; he replied in a nonchalant manner.

"Yeah of course I will be." Michael hoped because of the manner of his reply, he sounded convincing enough, but knew deep inside that it may not happen.

CHAPTER 28

Michael was awoken from his deep sleep by the letterbox rattling in the door, and the post thudding onto the mat. He stirred from his bed and wandered down the stairs of his mother's house. He carried the post through to the kitchen placing it on the dining table while he boiled the kettle and placed some bread in the toaster. With his tea and toast in front of him, he pulled the mail towards him, and there peeking out from between the other letters was a crisp white envelope with a wild bird stamp stuck in the corner, with the word 'Japan' written in red across the middle of it. Michael grabbed a bread knife from the drawer and prised the letter open, a number of pound notes dropped out onto the table. Michael continued to pull out the remaining money which had a letter wrapped around it. He straightened out the crisp folds in the letter and began to read.

'Dear Michael,

It was great speaking with you on the phone and I am so pleased you can come back to Japan. Just your appearance will fill me with joy and will also give my mother great hope as she is very unwell.

It would also be good if you could bring the document that you retrieved from your father's dojo as we discussed: I think you are already aware of the importance and value of this document and I truly feel that this document could provide my mother and I with enough money to allow my mother to receive the treatment she so desperately needs to help her make a full recovery. My contact number is on the separate paper enclosed; please ring when you get your tickets at the airport next week.

I am so looking forward to seeing you. Yours always.

May Lin. X'

Michael knew that the time had arrived to meet up with the two agents to assess their plan, and inform them of the letter and the money he had received from Japan, but first he had the ordeal of attending his mother's funeral.

Michael pulled on his black jacket and ran down the stairs to meet up with his aunt and uncle who were waiting outside his house in a car alongside the funeral procession. Michael walked past the hearse and gave a melancholy look towards the coffin; it was a poignant moment seeing the word 'MA' made from yellow flowers through the hearse window. It was a sunny, but very cold day, appropriately cold to match how Michael was feeling inside over the loss of his mother. Michael made his way to the car where he joined his aunt and uncle.

"Did you bring the wreath for me, Uncle Patrick?"

"I've sorted it, Michael; your uncle was too busy down the betting shop."

"Thanks, Aunt Lena and thanks for helping to organise all this."

Michael's aunt gently placed her hand over Michael's hand as it was rested on his knee.

"I'm sorry for your loss, love, yah know where we are if yah need us."

Michael was squashed alongside his uncle in the back of the funeral car, who sat with his enormous frame barely fitting inside the back seat of the shiny black *Austin Princess*.

"Was it your idea to get the wreath with the word 'Ma' on it, Aunt Lena?" Michael asked with a feeling of ambivalence.

"No, Michael, your Uncle Patrick said that yah called her ma instead of mam."

Michael turned to look at his uncle in disbelief.

"No I didn't, I never called her ma."

Aunt Lena dug Uncle Patrick in the ribs with her elbow.

"What on earth did yah do that for? I thought it was odd and a little bit coincidental that yah call your own mother ma, being Irish and all, yah stupid sod."

Michael watched as Aunt Lena doled out a filthy look to his Uncle Patrick: Michael was finding it hard not to burst into laughter; it certainly was a good way of alleviating the stress of his mother's funeral. Aunt Lena slapped Uncle Patrick on his thigh this time and gave him a curious stare.

"Now I know where yah got that money for the betting shop, it was the money for the 'M' wasn't it, yah bloody Irish shite, instead of paying for 'mam' yah paid for 'ma' and gambled the rest of the money on a horse."

Uncle Patrick by now was cringing in the middle seat of the car, wondering when the next elbow would land itself in his ribs. Michael meanwhile was laughing to himself to the delight of his uncle.

"The pair of yah are as bad as each other, yah have no bloody respect."

"I just thought I would put a bet on for Michael to see if I could win him some money to cheer him up."

Aunt Lena turned and looked at Uncle Patrick with an indignant scowl.

"I wish I had a pound for every time yah have said those very words to me, yah bloody liar."

Michael was still laughing.

"Come on you two, we're here now, let's just forget it. Oh... and thanks for cheering me up."

"We're not meant to cheer yah up, it's the day of yah mother's funeral."

"I know that, but I would much rather be smiling than have a face of doom and gloom."

"Bless yah, son, that's a good attitude to have after all you've been through." Aunt Lena immediately turned her attention to Uncle Patrick, and her amenable smile quickly turned to an angry scowl.

"Yah never cease to amaze me, Patrick Finnan, here we are at the lad's ma's funer... Look, you've got me bloody well saying it now, we're at his mam's funeral and yah lower the tone for a quick laugh, well I'm not laughing and neither should yee be."

Michael leaned forward and looked across at Aunt Lena who was now crying. Aunt Lena spoke with sadness in her voice.

"Your mam wasn't a bad woman, Michael, she didn't deserve this, yes she lost her way with Trevor somewhat, but she... she." Michael's aunt could not speak further and bowed her head, continuing to cry.

"I know she didn't, Aunt Lena and the people who did it will pay."

Aunt Lena looked across at Michael curious to find out more.

"Have the police mentioned something, Michael?"

Michael opened the door to the car as they arrived outside the cemetery.

"Kind of."

"Well what does that mean, they either have or they haven't?"

Michael helped his aunt and uncle out of the car.

"I can't really say anything, I've been told not to reveal anything to anyone for their own safety."

Aunt Lena began waving her index finger at Michael.

"You're just like your dad yah are, always secretive, no the wonder our Shirley and your dad split up, she couldn't work him out."

Uncle Patrick moved towards Aunt Lena in an attempt to stop her saying anymore.

"Dat's enough, Lena; we're here for da funeral not to cast aspersions on Michael and his father." Uncle Patrick put his hand on Michael's shoulder and enquired about what the police had been saying to him. Michael remained tight-lipped.

Michael put his arm around his Aunt Lena who by now was sobbing uncontrollably as they both walked up to the chapel of rest.

"You've had so much hardship for someone so young, Michael; losing both your parents the way yah did must have taken its toll on yah."

Michael continued walking without commenting and never changed his stoical expression all the way to the chapel. The day had turned from a cold sunny day into a dank and misty one, with all the mourners now making their way to the chapel with thick overcoats, hats and head scarves on. The mourners were expecting a sombre day due to the circumstances of Michael's mam's death, and this was accentuated by the bleak weather. Thirty people were huddled inside a very bijou chapel of rest. The reverend began the service and the room fell silent. Each different section of the sermon was met with the sounds of sniffling and sobbing, and the normally tranquil room began to breathe with the sounds of sorrow. The soporific effect created by the slowly undulating noise levels of the crying, was beginning to contribute to low concentration levels within the chapel. This was soon transformed with the clash of the entrance door against the thick stone walls inside the building. The sound echoed around the cold stone chapel and everyone turned their head towards the entrance. A man's silhouette appeared in the arched doorway and a slurring voice rang out from where he stood.

"Anybody wondered why the son hasn't been arrested, when the mother gets found with her head cut off by a Samurai sword? Who always trains with a sword? Ask yerself the question, who?" Standing in the doorway was a drenched and completely inebriated Trevor, his face was dark from the overgrown greasy beard that smothered his chin, he was wearing a National

Coal Board donkey jacket with the collar up and his long straggly hair lurched across his shoulders creating damp patches on his coat from the rain trickling through his out of control locks. His boots were caked in mud which conjured the impression he had walked across open fields to get to the chapel. Everyone in the congregation turned to discover who was speaking the words that managed to instil a nervous silence across the whole room.

"Yah all heard me, it was him who did it, me and Shirley were happy until he reappeared." Trevor staggered to one side and used the large wooden church door to break his fall before he crashed into it, only holding himself up by the bronze door knob. Michael rose from his seat near his aunt and uncle and was readying himself to walk to the rear of the chapel to confront Trevor, but as he did so his uncle alighted from his seat and stepped in front of Michael.

"Sit down, son, I will deal with dis, I won't have any member of my family shown any disrespect, especially not on da day of his mother's funeral." Michael's uncle walked slowly towards the end of the pew where all the close family were sitting. At this point the reverend had continued with proceedings, but Michael's aunt relayed a message to Michael's uncle over the top of the reverend's words,

"Please be calm, Patrick, please don't start any trouble inside the chapel on this supposedly special day."

Patrick answered with great assurance,

"Der will be no trouble in da church, Lena, yah have my word on dat, we just can't have dat kind of disruption can we?"

Michael looked over at his uncle and his uncle winked at him.

"He's a peaceful man your uncle is, he's good at negotiating in situations like this, yah need to be more like that yerself, Michael and not be as reliant on your fists and feet."

Michael slowly nodded his head in considered acceptance of what his Aunt Lena had said. No sooner had the thought of his change of approach in these circumstances entered his mind, than it was flushed straight out the other side by the sound of a dull thud reverberating through the now closed doors at the entrance to the chapel. Michael glanced back to the chapel doors to get an understanding of what the noise was. His uncle sauntered into the chapel and closed the doors behind him before making his way back to the seat next to Michael. By now the reverend was close to finishing the sermon.

"Thank yah for helping with Trevor, Patrick; and for preventing any violence in the chapel of rest," Aunt Lena congratulated Uncle Patrick.

Michael by now was most intrigued.

"How did you deal with him, Uncle Patrick? How did you manage to have no trouble in the chapel and no use of your fists and feet?"

Uncle Patrick leaned forward towards Michael and out of earshot of Aunt Lena, he whispered in Michael's ear,

"I took him outside and nutted him."

Michael once again found himself struggling to contain his laughter.

Aunt Lena whispered under her breath,

"Yah need to talk to Michael and help him understand how talking is better than fighting in these kind of situations."

Uncle Patrick's eyes rolled to the back of his head and he turned to Michael and smiled.

Michael showed his approval by patting on Uncle Patrick's back and as a way of placating his aunt.

Finally the proceedings were at an end and all the people who were there to pay their respects were informed by the reverend that everyone was invited back to Lena and Patrick's house for the wake; Michael of course had other things on his mind.

CHAPTER 29

Uncle Patrick and Aunt Lena were inviting everyone who had attended the funeral into their home as they stood in the porch at the front of their house.

"Please do come in, we have food and drink through in the dining room, please help yerself and we shall join yah in a few minutes."

Michael was standing by Uncle Patrick's side greeting everyone who entered the house with a handshake for the men and a kiss and a hug for the women.

"You didn't have to bother with all this, Aunt Lena; you have really done more than enough with the organising of the funeral," Michael said.

Aunt Lena became all tearful and overcome with emotion again.

"Your mother would have loved a do like this, Michael, she was a good sort, she just liked the simple things in life... Are yah okay, Michael? Yah seem to be miles away."

"Sorry, Aunt Lena, I just have a lot on my mind."

One of the arriving guests placed an arm around Aunt Lena's shoulder to console her.

"Come on, Lena, yah should come through with us and leave Patrick and Michael to greet everyone."

Michael nodded his head in agreement.

"That's a good idea, Aunt Lena, please go through and have something to eat and drink with the other mourners." Michael guided her through allowing her to mingle with her friends. Michael continued to greet the arriving guests who were there to pay their respects. Car after car arrived with mourners, each one carrying cards and flowers; most of the people Michael had not seen before. Patrick explained to Michael that these were people who would often sit with Trevor and Shirley at the working men's club; or they were women who would sit with Michael's mam at the bingo.

The cars carrying the mourners continued to arrive in their droves, each one bringing more flowers and cards.

"Dis is Jennifer and Councillor Alex James," Patrick observed. An immaculately polished white *Jaguar XJ6* arrived and parked on the other side of the street. Alex and Jennifer got out and made their way towards the front of Aunt Lena's house where Michael and Patrick were waiting to greet them. Alex was dressed in a black suit – as was expected of all the gentlemen mourners that day – his suit was made from silk. His wife on the other hand with her bleached blonde hair and dark sunglasses, wore a leopard skin fake fur coat with a black roll neck jumper, a tight white skirt and white knee length patent leather boots. Michael and Uncle Patrick looked at each other, and then gave a long lingering stare towards Jennifer as she made her way to the house. Jennifer had a look about her that made men stare uncontrollably, with her pretty face, blonde hair and Marilyn Monroe figure. Being married to a councillor meant she was elevated to a status that for a town like Sunderland, made her as close as you could get to being a celebrity. As they made their way across the road, a *Ford Cortina* taxi pulled up in front of them. Michael and Uncle Patrick completely ignored the arriving car and continued to follow Jennifer's every move as she walked around the car and onwards towards the house. What they didn't notice was the man in the long black mac and cloth cap with a large bunch of flowers that climbed out of the *Ford Cortina* taxi.

Uncle Patrick greeted Alex and Jennifer in a somewhat sycophantic way.

"Very pleased yah could make it, Councillor, yee and Jennifer will certainly brighten da afternoon with your presence."

Michael turned to look at Uncle Patrick in disbelief.

"I'm sorry to hear of yah loss, Michael," Jennifer said sincerely.

Alex offered his hand to Michael.

"Me too, Michael, I hear you're helping the police with their enquiries, please do not hesitate to ask if I can assist in any way, and I mean that."

Michael shook Alex's hand in appreciation of the gesture.

"Thank you for that, Alex."

Alex and Jennifer entered the house and Michael watched as his Uncle Patrick followed Jennifer's wiggling bottom with his glaring eyes, not in the slightest bit perturbed that Michael was watching him. Michael turned away shaking his head in amazement, only to find himself looking straight at a man ten yards in front of him, walking towards him with a bunch of flowers. Michael observed something strange, unlike the other mourners he was carrying the flowers in front of his face instead of down at his side as he approached; as Michael continued his inquisitive look, he subsequently discovered he was also wearing white training shoes, not really normal etiquette at a funeral: Michael knew there was something very unusual about this man as he approached.

"Excuse me are you here for the funer...?" Before Michael could complete his question, the man in front of him dropped the flowers and ran at full speed towards him and his Uncle Patrick whilst hastily unbuttoning his coat at the top. Whilst observing this, Michael's mind instantaneously flashed back to the men who attacked him at Roker Park and he recollected the black mac from his assailants that day. The man in front of him was now six yards away and was reaching inside his coat; he pulled out a katana and was now running towards Michael with the katana down by his side, his eyes betraying his desire to inflict maximum carnage on those who stood in his way.

"Move, Patrick!" Michael yelled at his Uncle Patrick and pushed him into the doorway of the house.

Uncle Patrick tumbled into the door leading into the living room and the door gave way, busting open the mortice latch in the process. He was catapulted into the living room which was full of mourners standing together drinking and eating.

"What da hell did yah do dat for, Michael?" Uncle Patrick screamed.

Michael did not reply, he was preoccupied with a katana hurtling towards his side and was moving through the doorway in the same direction as his uncle to avoid it slashing straight across his stomach. The noise that followed was not the sound of a katana slitting open a stomach – which was the noise Michael was expecting – but the sound of an almighty crash. The sound resembled a lump hammer pounding against an enormous kettle drum. The katana missed Michael's torso and clattered into the cast iron drainpipe running down the wall outside the door.

The impact stopped the attacker for a split second and threw him off balance. Michael seized the opportunity to kick out at the attacker while he was wrong footed, his side edge kick thrust into the attacker's ribs spinning him backwards.

"Quickly move away from the door," Michael shouted as he forced his way into the hallway. Michael made his way inside and through the door to the living room; he turned to the people in the room, gesturing instructions for them to leave via the back door.

"What is it, Michael, why have yah pushed Uncle Patrick over?" Aunt Lena wondered.

Michael started to reply to Aunt Lena while grabbing the handle on the door to the living room.

"Just get everyone out before..."

The door handle came off in his hand and before he could look down at it the door burst open. The attacker was standing in the doorway grasping the handle of his katana with both hands, he was pointing the katana up towards the ceiling in an aggressive manner which made everyone in the room panic. The screams from the women in the room were ear piercingly loud, glasses were breaking on the floor sending a ripple of crashes around the room, this created a sound like porcelain dominos collapsing on a terracotta tiled floor. The screams continued while people panicked and scrambled for a way out. The attacker looked directly at Michael and ignored the fleeing bystanders; his evil grimace towards Michael sent a message to him: he was here to kill him or he would die trying. The attacker slowly moved the katana from vertical to horizontal and pointed it straight at Michael, oblivious to the fear he had promulgated throughout the room. He slowly moved forward keeping his eyes trained on Michael. He flicked the katana over with a twist of his wrist then flicked it over again, this action was portraying a message to Michael that he was a formidable opponent.

"Please don't harm anyone in here, this is not their quarrel, please just let them pass," Michael pleaded with him.

The attacker either had no intention of listening to Michael or he could not understand English. Michael held his hands out with his palms up indicating that he was unarmed, but the attacker kept moving closer and still pointed the katana towards him. By now the screaming was beginning to fade as more and more people were escaping through the back door. Michael moved away from the attacker until his back was against the wall, all the while keeping his eyes fixed on his opponent. He was waiting for something to give him that edge, a split second hesitation, or a lapse in concentration to gain an advantage. And without it, against a man with a katana, he could be finished.

Michael's edge came from an unlikely source. Uncle Patrick, who was crouched down behind the table near to the fireplace, swung a poker from the hearth of the fire straight down onto one of the attacker's arms holding the katana. His arms buckled under the force of the blow and the katana dropped from his hands towards the ground. Without hesitation Michael rushed forward to grab the katana on the ground. Michael's fingers gripped around the katana handle, but before he could grasp it tight enough to pick it up, one of the final fleeing mourners - who was running towards the back door of the house - kicked it out of his hand. It spun across the living room floor and under the table, below the area where the food was displayed. The attacker watched the katana hurtle across the room and quickly dived after it. Michael dived for the katana too and both of them endeavoured to clutch onto the katana handle to gain an advantage. Michael lifted up onto his knees while still grappling over the katana and his back crunched into the side of the table spilling food and drink all over the tiled floor. Again he noticed his attacker was off balance at this point, while kneeling in front of him; desperately trying to regain control of the katana, his attacker wobbled backwards, presenting an opportunity for Michael to side swipe his elbow into his attacker's face. The attacker felt the full brunt of Michael's forearm and tumbled backwards, releasing the katana. As Michael's attacker fell, his head collided with the edge of the mantelpiece and bounced towards the feet of Uncle Patrick. This time his uncle finished him, he held the poker with two hands above his head and brought it to bear on the attacker's skull, knocking him out cold.

Michael slumped to the floor; he was lying flat out on his back relieved that the attacker was dealt with. Uncle Patrick also flopped to the ground leaning against the side of the hearth, completely exhausted. Uncle Patrick looked over towards Michael whilst still panting from exhaustion.

"Jesus and here's me thinking I would die from smoking too many cigarettes."

Michael smirked.

"That might still be the case."

"Well thanks for dat, Michael, cheery sort yee aren't yah, after helping prevent yah being run through by a Soomarai sword wielding madman, dis is da appreciation I get."

"It's called a Samurai sword or katana." Michael walked over to the fireside and placed his fingers on his attacker's carotid artery.

"He's still alive that's for sure, you will need to help me lift him into Aunt Lena's *Ford Escort* outside, so I can take him to the police station."

Uncle Patrick stood with a bemused look on his face.

"Why don't yah just ring da police and they will come and pick him up?"

Michael shook his head.

"No. Agent Carson and Agent James the two intelligence officers will want to speak with this gentleman before the police get anywhere near him."

Uncle Patrick was ever so slightly disturbed by that comment.

"Yah don't want me to come to da police station, do yah? Dat's not a great idea for someone like me, Michael, me and da police don't see eye to eye."

Michael shook his head.

"Uncle Patrick, we're not going there to play dominos, we're going there to present them with my mother's murderer."

Uncle Patrick gave a very sheepish look.

"Could yah not take your Aunt Lena? She's good with da police; after all it is her car, I'll shout her for yah."

Michael was aghast.

"What? Are you serious?"

Aunt Lena walked in to the room following the call by Uncle Patrick.

"What the hell was all that about and who's that madman on the floor?"

Uncle Patrick began walking outside clutching a packet of cigarettes and a lighter. "Michael thinks dis is da nutter who killed your sister."

"Is that right, Michael?"

"I'm not sure, Aunt Lena, I guess there's a good chance though, seen as he has just tried to kill us with a katana. I need to get him into a car and get him to the agents who are working at the local police station, however it appears that your husband has done a bunk, so will you take me in yours?"

Aunt Lena turned towards the back door and watched Uncle Patrick walking outside.

"What's wrong with Patrick helping yah? Anyhow, why are yah not just phoning the police?"

Michael gritted his teeth.

"I've just explained that to Uncle Patrick, but just so you know, the local police will just delay things, I need answers quick. Can we just bloody well get him in your car outside, please?" Michael was becoming fraught and berated his Aunt Lena once again.

"And with regard to Uncle Patrick helping me, he made some lame excuse that he and the police don't get on."

Aunt Lena's look of bewilderment said everything.

"Well that's what he said," Michael exclaimed.

"Patrick's never been in trouble with the police, well at least not that I know of."

Michael reached under the unconscious man's shoulders and started to drag him out of the house and towards the car parked outside.

"Look, I don't have the time to discuss this, I'm making sure I get him to the police station before he wakes up, so the agents can glean as much information from him as possible; will you help me or not?"

Aunt Lena picked up his legs and helped Michael carry the attacker outside.

"Yes, yes I'll help yah."

Michael and Aunt Lena carried him outside and past the congregated mourners standing near to the house, everyone was huddled together consoling each other, the disapproving stares were directed towards Michael. He resolutely faced forward without giving them the satisfaction of eye contact, but a demeaning comment was hurled anyhow.

"It's yee and yah father's fault, all this trouble yah have brought on our community."

Michael was not distracted by the comment and made it to Aunt Lena's car without looking towards the crowd. With the help from her he bundled the man into the car, she climbed into the driver's seat and pulled the car keys from her jacket pocket.

"Don't let them bother yah, Michael, they're making their own assumptions with no evidence to back it up."

"I'm close to believing it myself, this whole thing is a mess, my father dead, my mother decapitated in her own home, my friend in hospital and now a mad Samurai who is clearly here to kill me creating havoc at my mother's funeral."

Michael gazed back at the mourners who were walking back inside the house.

"They must think my family is a disgrace."

"Michael, listen, there's one thing I have learned in my time in this town, never worry about what opinion other people have of yah, whether that's good or bad, because what's important is your opinion of yerself, as long as yah believe that you're doing your best to be a good person to others, that's all that matters."

Michael tried his best to smile as he turned to look at Aunt Lena.

"Thanks for that, Aunt Lena that means a lot to me."

Aunt Lena started the car.

"Now let's get this guy to the police station before he wakes up." Aunt Lena sped off down the street leaving a puff of smoke from the car's tyres.

CHAPTER 30

"This is Agent Carson and I'm Agent James, we are from MI6, do you know where you are?"

Nishimoto did not respond and began to glance around the room with a look of bewilderment. His hands were cuffed and he was placed upright in a chair at the desk in the interrogation room of the police station. He was clearly disorientated and would or could not speak.

"You are in a local police station in Sunderland in England; do you know why you are here?" Agent James asked. Again there was no reply.

"We need an interpreter; I think this guy does not speak English," Agent Carson said.

"Michael can speak Japanese, why don't we ask him in here, we're getting nowhere with this as it is?"

Agent James left the room and returned with Michael. Agent Carson informed the suspect through Michael's interpretation that Michael would be helping to translate what he was saying and that with good co-operation in relation to events occurring there and in Japan, he could help reduce his sentence in an English prison. Michael moved forward to sit opposite Nishimoto and spoke with him in Japanese. He asked if there were any more of Ashikaga's men in England. His question was met with silence; he then proceeded to ask him what he knew about the covenant. Again his question was met with silence. Michael then lunged forward and grabbed Nishimoto by the throat and dragged him over the desk. He shouted over and over again in Japanese,

"Why did you kill my mother? Why did you chop off her head? Why? Why?"

The two startled agents pulled Michael and Nishimoto apart and pushed them down into their respective seats.

"Michael, you must refrain from attacking the suspect, please calm down and help us to get the information we need to get at Ashikaga."

Michael looked into Nishimoto's eyes with a look of anger tinged with frustration. Agent Carson pulled up a chair and sat alongside Michael.

"Did you tell him about reducing his sentence if he helps us?"

Michael's eyes said it all.

"Okay, I need you to get that across to him; tell him that, and then ask him if he knows how many men are guarding Ashikaga Yoshimitsu?"

Michael duly obliged. There was no response from Nishimoto again. Agent James stood up to leave the room.

"This is getting us nowhere, leave him in the cells overnight and we will try interrogating him once more in the morning, and if that fails, we will just have to carry on with the original plan regardless."

Michael and Agent Carson also stood up to leave the room; Agent James was shouting for the duty officer to bring his cell keys. At that moment Nishimoto slowly turned his head to face Michael and Agent Carson, before speaking in clear English.

"When we arrived at your mother's house, the man who had been arguing with your mother then proceeded to fight with her. We had nothing to do with her death, our only instruction was to retrieve the covenant from you, no matter what that took; we are honourable men and we would not kill an innocent woman."

"You can speak English, why did you not speak before?" Agent Carson enquired.

"You were asking me questions I couldn't possibly answer without betraying all that is sacred to me."

Agent Carson walked to the back of the room and picked up a cassette recorder. Michael once again sat down in front of Nishimoto.

"Do you know who killed my mother?"

"No," Nishimoto replied.

"Please try and remember who you saw and please describe him to me if you can," Michael asked hopefully.

Nishimoto started shaking his head once more.

"We could barely see the face; we could only make out a silhouette."

"Michael, we understand your grief over what happened to your mother, but we must concentrate on Ashikaga and what information we can glean to help us get to him," Agent James explained.

Agent Carson continued preparing his cassette recorder.

"Let him continue, Agent James, while I find what I'm looking for, you never know Michael may find some interesting information that will assist the local police."

Michael pulled his chair closer to Nishimoto, at which point Nishimoto nervously flinched.

"I'm sorry for grabbing you earlier; I was frustrated with your silence. Please just think back to the night and see if you can remember anything that could help."

Nishimoto shuffled nervously in his chair, and then leaned back away from Michael's reach, placing his cuffed hands over his face with his eyes closed. His hands then flopped to his lap and his eyes opened.

"I can remember what your mother was screaming, but I have no idea if this will be of any use to you."

Michael leaned forward.

"Please tell me what you heard."

"She was screaming, 'no, Paddy, no, Paddy'. We by this time had already checked your room over and could not find you or the covenant, so at that point we left."

Michael turned his head towards the two agents on the other side of the room, his eyes were glazing over, Michael calmly turned his head towards the exit door and was staring at the handle. The two agents could predict what was coming next. Agent Carson immediately ran towards the door and grabbed the handle and Agent James lunged towards Michael and grabbed the back of his shoulders; at the very same time Michael reared up like a bolting horse and thrust his huge torso towards the exit, dragging Agent James behind him like he was a rag doll being yanked along by a rabid dog. Agent Carson threw himself in front of the door with his chest puffed out and his arms spread past the architrave of the door. Michael surged towards where Agent Carson was standing, oblivious to the fact that Agent James was clinging to his shoulders like a lion clutching on to the back of a raging bull elephant during a hunt. Michael reached out for Agent Carson and grabbed his body, throwing him away from the door. He grabbed the handle of the door, but as he pulled it,

Agent James thrust his boot square onto the door slamming it shut. Agent James yelled at Michael in desperation, knowing that he was pumped with adrenalin and neither he nor Agent Carson could stop Michael if he really wanted to get out and find Paddy.

"Michael, please listen to me, let the police deal with this, we need you to help us catch Ashikaga. For us to help May Lin and avenge your father's death, we need you here with us formulating a plan, not running after someone who potentially could be innocent."

Michael had both hands on the door handle ready to pull the door open and leave.

"Why my family? Why? I have no one left, no one."

Agent James removed his boot from the door.

"We know, Michael and we understand that, but more people will suffer grief like your own if we don't bring Ashikaga and his empire down, and they won't be restricted to Japan, his crime empire will stretch all over the world, including here if we don't stop him."

"I can't take him on." Michael pointed at Nishimoto.

"Look at the type of man he has working for him; they obey everything he asks."

"You can get close to him, Michael, you have something he desperately wants, that covenant; and I also believe he reveres you too, these things will allow us to get you in there and... and..." Agent James altered his train of thought and pointed to Nishimoto.

"Get Nishimoto into a cell, glean as much information from him as we can, then you, Agent Carson and I can conclude this plan. Come on, Michael, sit down, and leave the police to sort out the issues over your mother's death. Believe me if Paddy does have something to do with it, they will find out."

Agent Carson lifted Nishimoto out of his chair by the arm and escorted him to the cells. Michael flopped into the chair and looked across at Agent James exhaling a heavy sigh.

"Okay, I'm all ears, what do you want me to do?"

CHAPTER 31

May Lin was woken by the sunlight piercing its way through the windows that beamed the rays of morning into the room, the window frames were all rotten in the room where she was being held and none of the windows had blinds or curtains fitted. Because there were so many gaps in the window frames, numerous ants and cockroaches had made their way into the room and were creeping and crawling all around her bare feet. The gaps also allowed the sound of the birds singing outside in the trees to be clearly heard each morning, and this sound lifted her spirits each day. To stop her from succumbing to suicidal thoughts she executed a ritual every morning: using the top she was wearing, she cleaned her teeth by wrapping it around her index finger and rubbing it inside her mouth, following this she would fulfil an exercise routine beginning with press ups, continuing with different reps of workout exercises, and finishing with sit ups. Following each session she would rub her cupped hands on the cold windows to collect the condensation, she would use each carefully collected scoop to wash herself and try to freshen herself up before finally running her nails through her hair for around thirty minutes each morning in an attempt to keep her hair tidy. This ritual helped distract her from the reality of being imprisoned in a room with no contact with the outside world, apart from a daily meal and drink hastily pushed around a quickly opened and closed door.

Today, that ritual did not occur, the door was not opened with the same haste, quite the contrary. It slowly swung open and juddered to a halt against the wall. A bright ceiling light was swinging from behind the person standing in the doorway, with an action that resembled a swinging lantern on the captain's deck of a pirate ship. The glare from the room outside cast a shadow from behind the person that swayed on the floor of the room where May Lin was crouched. The footsteps of the man echoed in the corridor as he made his way into the room where she was imprisoned. She had endured many assaults by the guards and had occasionally needed to fight them off, receiving ruthless beatings as a consequence. She braced herself for the yelled instruction to stand up and the accompanying back handed slap across her face. The shout was on cue, but the contact from the slap did not follow it, instead she heard an aggressive admonishment conveyed to the guard.

"Enough! Touch her again and I will be the one dealing out a beating to you."

May Lin lifted her head from her cowering posture and observed Kobyashi standing over a wincing guard, the guard's hand was primed to strike her. Kobyashi was gripping him tightly by the throat with one of his hands, and clasping the wrist of the guard's left arm with his other hand. He threw him with great force against the wall of the corridor, like a child discarding an abandoned doll. His body crumpled in a heap onto the floor. Kobyashi turned his attention to the other guard at which point he stared deep into his eyes until the guard averted his gaze down towards the floor.

"Get a glass of water and bring it in for her to drink," Kobyashi growled.

"Yes, Kobyashi san, at once." The guard disappeared out of the room to bring back a drink for May Lin.

Kobyashi turned his thickset neck and was looking directly towards May Lin. She feared the worst, she, more than anyone, knew what Kobyashi was capable of, as she was often first on the scene following one of his punishment beatings during her work with the police.

"Can you stand up?" Kobyashi asked May Lin.

May Lin looked up towards Kobyashi's giant stature and lifted herself from the ground. As far as the guards were aware, she was weak and unable to do much, and she wanted to continue the deception. As she attempted to stand she feigned an injury and fell back towards the floor. She was surprised to feel a strong grip grasp the side of her arm and lift her upright. Kobyashi's enormous hand hoisted her up and positioned her facing him.

"Are you alright? Wait while I get you a seat."

May Lin was completely bewildered by Kobyashi's reaction; he was showing compassion to her. He pulled a chair across and made her sit down in front of him. The guard returned with the glass of water and handed it to May Lin.

"Leave us, both of you," Kobyashi instructed the guards. Kobyashi leaned forward and helped May Lin sip the water by lifting the glass up to her mouth. While helping her drink from the glass with one hand, he lifted his other hand up towards her face and touched her bruised cheek. He slowly ran his finger down the side of her face to a healing scab on her chin where her face had been grazed. May Lin could feel her heart thumping inside her rib cage and her breathing intensifying, she was trying desperately not to shake, in fear of showing weakness to Kobyashi. She continued to sip the water with his face inches away from hers. She started to feel her eyes filling with tears, she was trying her hardest not to blink, but could not prevent it. As her eyes finally gave in to the involuntary action, her blink sent a trickle of tears meandering down her face. Kobyashi observed the tear droplets falling towards the base of her rosy cheeks and as they continued downward, they amassed on her chin. At the very moment the tears fell from underneath her chin, Kobyashi thrust his hand forward at lightning speed. May Lin flinched at the same time as she took a sharp intake of breath, fearing what was coming next. Kobyashi caught the tear drops.

"You asked the boy to ring you on this number when he reached the airport at Heathrow; you need to be out of here to allow you to answer his call."

May Lin nodded in agreement, Kobyashi wrapped his huge arm around her tiny back, lifting her off the chair, he carried her into the hallway and out towards Ashikaga's office. He reached across to her face with his hand and picked her head up by cupping her chin in his shovel sized palm.

"Don't allow your head to droop when you are in front of Ashikaga, he will see this as a sign of weakness and he will exploit it."

Ashikaga sat in his leather office chair behind his desk, his two Japanese Akita dogs were sitting to attention near his legs at the side of the desk. Kobyashi pushed the door open with his shoulder and carried May Lin into Ashikaga's office. On entering the room the pair of dogs flared their lips, revealing two sets of ivory white razor sharp teeth which resembled icicles hanging from the inside of a dark watery cave. Their low resonating growls instantly sent ripples of fear rumbling across the room. May Lin started shaking, but remembered Kobyashi's words and endeavoured to keep her head up.

"Here she is, my favourite employee, or should I say, former employee. These two dogs have more loyalty than you; the licentious lady that is May - cheap trash - Lin, not even good enough to feed to my dogs. Bring her in front of me, Kobyashi."

"Yes, Ashikaga san." Kobyashi lifted her towards Ashikaga's desk.

"In a few hours from now, your schoolboy lover will be on a flight from Heathrow to Narita Airport to meet his true love, even as I say the words it makes me feel nauseous. He will bring with him the covenant that your other lover, Doug Harris..." Ashikaga started walking around the room, but all the while his gaze was fixed on May Lin. "Oh yes I know alright, I know all about what you have been up to behind my back...

Your other lover, Doug Harris, stole from me and when his stupid boy turns up to meet his supposed true love, I will have what is rightfully mine, and then I will take great pleasure in watching the two of you die a slow death, a pleasure not afforded to my son, who the pair of you butchered."

May Lin tried desperately to explain,

"It was in self-defence, Michael had no intention..."

"Silence! I don't remember telling you to speak. You are only alive because you are integral to the plan that helps me lure that boy back to Japan, he will return the covenant that belongs to me, and then you and he can be together."

May Lin was transfixed on Ashikaga's eyes, not daring to look away for fear of reprisal. Ashikaga pointed towards the edge of the large desk in the corner.

"Put her near the phone in that chair; we will wait for her lover boy to call. Bring me your blade, Kobyashi."

CHAPTER 32

The rattle of an alarm bell in the distance jolted Michael from a deep sleep, and his eyelids peeled open from his tired eyes, revealing long iron bars straight in front of him that were casting a shadow on the walls. Only at that point did it dawn on him that he was asleep in a cell in the police station. He could hear music in the distance, 'Papa was a rolling stone' by The Temptations was playing in the room outside the cell. It was all becoming clear now; the two agents had given Michael a blanket and a pillow and locked him in the police cell overnight for his own safety. As he approached the cell door, he discovered that it was now unlocked, and as he pushed it open the door made an old heavy metal creak and alerted his presence to Agents Carson and James in the next room.

"About time, we needed to set the fire alarm off to wake you, tea and toast are on the go in five if you want to get a quick scrub up first; it's five now and we leave at five thirty to head off to Heathrow, so you need to get your shit together," Agent Carson urged Michael.

"I think I should try sleeping in a cell more often, I slept like a log."

Agent James was shaking his head.

"No that's not something I would recommend; do you need to go over the plan again, Michael, before we leave?"

"No, I can remember every detail."

"Good."

Michael walked past the other cells in the station, taking a look in every one.

"I don't see Patrick Finnan in any of these cells; I thought the local police were going to take care of it?"

Agent Carson picked up two slices of toast and walked across to where Michael was standing; he took a huge bite out of one slice of toast and then a huge bite from the other, filling his cheeks with bread like a hibernating hamster. Agent James was singing along to The Temptations song while packing a rucksack at the back of the room. Agent Carson tried to reassure Michael.

"Listen; don't worry about all that, it will be taken care of by…"

"I'm not worried by it, but if I don't hear that they have caught someone for all this soon, I will deal with it myself."

Agent Carson put his hand on Michael's shoulder in the hope of placating him.

"You really don't want to be doing that, Michael, or the law will be after you too."

Michael pushed Agent Carson's hand away from his shoulder.

"Don't fucking patronise me, Agent Carson, do you think I don't know that? It kind of doesn't really bother me right now." Michael could not stop thinking of the horrible sanguinary death his mother experienced. All this was intensified by the fact that he now knew that it was his Uncle Patrick who had committed the atrocity.

"My mother lived a destitute life after my father left, and in death she was spared no decency by her killer, if I meet her killer and for that matter anyone who killed my now departed parents, I will show the same mercy to them as they did to my family; and if that means I go to prison for that, then so be it."

Agent James walked over towards Michael with a cup of tea and a drooping slice of toast with jam on it; he offered up the tea and toast as a calming gesture. Michael accepted the offering and sat at the table in front of the agents, looking both of them in the eyes.

"My mother really lost her way when my father and I left for Japan, and it now appears that all the people who she tried to build her life around just shit on her, that was bad enough on its own, but to then chop her fucking head off and leave her the way they did, soaking in her own blood: I'm sorry, but I just can't get that image out of my mind. I will never rest until I know that the bastard responsible for that is brought to justice."

"Michael, everything is being done to apprehend him, that's what we are being told, I can only reiterate what I said before; you will prevent this kind of thing from happening again by your actions against Ashikaga in Japan, I can't say any more than that."

Michael sat drinking his tea and eating the toast he was given, while finishing the final touches of his packing for his flight. Agent James looked across the room towards him and raised his thumb up in the air. Michael slowly lifted his arm with a very heavy heart and a melancholy look and repeated the gesture: he was now totally prepared in his mind for his trip back to Japan.

The sound of a horn echoed along the hall of the police station; Agents James and Carson were pleased to be finally leaving the station where they had spent the last few nights roughing it on the floor. For Michael, he was more pleased to stay at the station, than back at his mam's house, all that had transpired there had become just too much for him to bear.

"That's our ride, everyone, let's roll." Agent James doled out the instruction.

Michael picked up his bag and followed the agents towards the exit, as he stepped outside the station, dawn was just beginning to creep its way up the shaded streets and illuminate all of the cars and terraced houses into view. Michael paused and glanced along all the familiar streets. He was once again leaving the place where he was born to head back to Japan. There was stillness and silence along every road, but that was short-lived when a whirring sound in the distance began to inscribe its noise on the atmosphere near to the station. The sound became louder and louder and made Michael stop in his tracks to discover what it was. The sound intensified and by now was attracting the attention of Agents James and Carson. Out of the darkness the sound increased more and more. A milk float came whizzing up to the station from one of the side streets, closer and closer until it screeched to a halt immediately beneath the station windows near the exit. Agents James and Carson dropped their bags and jumped down the steps pulling two pistols out from inside their jackets. Michael instantly leapt behind a wall with his case grasped in his hand. The man on the milk float leaned over behind the driver's seat on the vehicle - oblivious to the pandemonium he had created - and was pulling some kind of object out from behind him; he was turning towards Michael and the two agents. Michael was now watching from behind the wall which was adjacent to the steps. Agents James and Carson were now two feet away from the vehicle and ready to engage the man in the driver's seat. The man turned around holding two pint bottles of milk, when he noticed the two agents standing in front of him with their guns pointing at him; he instantly dropped the milk bottles. The explosive crash echoed around the streets and immediately initiated a roll of house lights being turned on in the bedrooms of the houses.

"Jesus fuckin' Christ, yah scared the fucking life out of me, if yah want a pint of milk yah can take one, there's no need to pull a fucking gun on me." The milkman turned around again and grabbed another two pints of milk, this time jumping down from the float and delivering them to the steps of the station. He then walked back down the steps from the station while glaring at the two agents and jumped back into his driver seat.

"You two owe me fifty pence for two bottles of milk."

Michael climbed over the wall, at which point Agent Carson paid the milkman a pound and asked for another two pints of milk. The milkman obliged and then drove off shaking his head as he did so.

Agents James and Carson turned to look at Michael, their ensuing laughter was echoing in the crisp atmosphere of the very early morning.

"How were we to know he was just a milkman?" Agent James asked.

Michael walked down the steps and picked a pint of milk out of Agent Carson's hand.

"Maybe the fact that he was driving a milk float full of bottles of milk and he was dressed like a milkman?"

Agent James was still laughing.

"Now don't be facetious, young schoolboy."

Agent James jolted Michael with a reality check by mentioning the word 'school'.

"My God, I forgot about school, my teachers, what will they say about all this?"

Agent James continued laughing.

"We are heading off to foil the plans of one of the biggest gangsters in Asia and you are worried about school?"

By now Agents James and Carson were being shouted at by people who were disturbed from their sleep in the surrounding houses, this was as a result of the agents' incessant laughter: Michael was feeling great about joining in.

Agent James placed his arm around Michael's shoulder,

"Listen, Michael, if we succeed with this operation, you won't need to worry about school anymore; you will be working for us."

Now Michael began laughing again, but immediately stopped when he realised that Agent James was deadly serious.

CHAPTER 33

Michael and the two MI6 agents arrived at Heathrow with plenty of time to organise their phone call to May Lin. Agent Carson collected their tickets and Agent James entered an office with Michael, this office was often commandeered by MI6 while working at the airport. Inside the office to meet them was Agent McDermott, he was Agent James and Carson's superior; a former captain in the Scots Guards of twenty-two years, he worked his way through the ranks with many commendations along the way. Agent McDermott's work ethic was all about knowing your enemy and ensuring that you have the advantage of good intelligence and a committed team when faced with an opponent who wants to do you harm.

Agent McDermott was of average height with a muscular stocky build; his strong Glaswegian accent was grained into his voice from growing up in the Gorbals, where he frequently visited family since leaving the army. It was whilst living in the Gorbals that he received a scar on his right cheek from an encounter with one of the razor gangs that tormented the estate. Now in his early forties and sporting a short back and side's haircut, the jet black waves of his Latino-like hair did not betray his age. His knowledge of covert operations and intelligence gathering made him ideally suited to working towards the capture and extraction of Ashikaga from the worldwide corruption ring he was embroiled in. Dressed in a tweed jacket, immaculately pressed slacks and a navy roll-neck jumper, he wore his now civilian clothes like a uniform; finished off with a pair of gleaming black spit and polished shoes.

On Michael's entrance to the office and following Agent James's formal introduction, Agent McDermott sat still in his chair at the office desk without saying a word. He proceeded to rise from being seated and slowly walked over towards where Michael was standing, he walked around him as a way of inspecting him, just how a drill sergeant would do while inspecting his troops when on parade. Each time he looked Michael up and down, he still did not speak. Michael stood perfectly still, mirroring how he would stand when in the lines at his martial arts training.

"I hear you've just turned sixteen is that correct?"

"Yes, Agent McDermott," Michael compliantly replied.

"Don't you think you're a tad young to be involved in something as dangerous as this?"

Michael was confused by the question, particularly as it was MI6 who involved him in the first instance. Firstly with May Lin and then with Agents James and Carson. Michael mulled over the question, not replying immediately.

"Well, come on lad, what's your answer?"

Michael believed that this question was designed to determine what his attitude was like. Was he a resilient character? And what kind of mind set did he have? He answered with brevity and clarity.

"I am young, but I am mature enough to know that I hold the key to capturing Ashikaga, a Japanese Yakuza who is now exporting his violence and racketeering to our shores, following years of practising this in his own country. He has also imprisoned your agent May Lin in an attempt to regain the covenant that I have in my possession. We can't just arrest him, because we have no evidence of any wrongdoing on his behalf, this is mainly due to the corruption in the Japanese police. He has a strict code that he abides by that prevents guns being used within his enclave - although I am convinced he ordered someone to kill me with a gun while I was travelling with May Lin in a car - with this exception, this is the reason all the people who protect him are excellent swordsmen.

I have an opportunity to get close to him, yes, because I have the much sought after covenant that gives the holder vast influential powers in Japan, but also because he wants to kill me to avenge his son's death."

Agent McDermott paused before speaking, while looking at Agents James and Carson as he did so.

"You have certainly gathered good intelligence on this man and you explained it very clearly, but you still haven't answered my question."

Michael turned to Agent James with a perplexed look. Agent James looked back and nodded his head, urging Michael to answer the question.

"No I don't think I'm too young, my mother and father are both dead…"

"That's all I wanted to hear," Captain McDermott shouted tersely.

"James and Carson vouch for you; I just wanted to hear it from you. Come and sit down. James, ask Carson to join us; I want to know that your plan is watertight before you leave for Japan. Oh and by the way, Michael, Ashikaga was not trying to kill you with the gun attack at the lights, he was trying to kill the driver of the car, of which he succeeded."

CHAPTER 34

"One word that makes him suspicious and I will slit your throat. Pick it up and let him know how pleased you are that he phoned," Ashikaga instructed May Lin.

"Hello, Michael, it's great to hear your voice again, I'm so pleased you phoned."

"It's great to hear your voice too, how is your mother?" Michael asked.

May Lin replied quickly to this question confirming her mother to still be poorly and then immediately asked about the tickets for the flight to Japan. Ashikaga pushed the blade tight against her neck worrying that she could make Michael suspicious by brushing aside the conversation about her mother. Michael quickly asked a question.

"Does that mean she is going to recover?"

Ashikaga once again forced the blade against May Lin's neck and shook his head from side to side in a defiant gesture.

"I don't think she will, Michael, unless we can pay for her to have more treatment."

Michael made a point of emphasising that he had the covenant in his possession.

"This covenant is valuable as we know, so when we meet up we can investigate where would be the best place to sell it and use the money to help your mother." Michael was playing his part and trying not to arouse suspicion.

Captain McDermott was also listening in on the conversation and encouraging Michael to ask as many questions as possible. This would enable the agents to glean as much information as they could. Michael continued asking questions about how May Lin was doing and repeatedly telling her how much he missed her in order to continue the deception.

Ashikaga was now growing impatient and whispered instructions into May Lin's ear telling her to arrange the meeting. May Lin quickly relayed the instruction to Michael.

"It would be good once you arrive in Tokyo if you could make your way to the Meiji shrine in Yoyogi Park, Michael. I will meet you there and we will make our way to my mother's which is only ten minutes away. If we say two in the afternoon and that will give you enough time to disembark from the plane and make your way there. How does that sound to you, Michael?"

Michael looked across the room awaiting acknowledgement from Captain McDermott. He wrote on a piece of paper in front of Michael to ask her where exactly at the shrine.

"Where do you want me to meet you at the shrine?"

She too was being instructed to inform correctly.

"Meet me at the steps where people start their prayers."

Michael agreed to her instructions and was receiving nods of acknowledgment from the agents in the room for the way he executed his phone call, when May Lin nervously said her goodbyes and the phone went dead. This meeting place was not the ideal place to conduct an operation against Ashikaga due to it being in an open place, but the agents all knew that they needed to go along with the plan in order to allay suspicion with Ashikaga. Their challenge now was to surreptitiously find cover at the Meiji shrine and do it before Ashikaga arrived.

Michael and the three agents quickly gathered their belongings and equipment and left the office to head to the check in desk. They immediately boarded their flight and headed for Japan.

CHAPTER 35

Inspector Bando informed his colleagues in the police department that he was not feeling well and that he would be heading home early. He collected his belongings and made his way to the car park outside the police station. Instead of pulling out of the car park and turning right to head off home as he normally would, he turned left instead and started making his way towards the airport, but before he did so he pulled into a layby and made a call from a nearby pay phone to the Koan Keisatsu. The back-up needed for this operation required more qualified personnel than he had available to him at his local police station, and the National Police Authority as it was known by MI6, was the organisation to provide it. Inspector Bando relayed the message to the NPA about the progress of the operation and asked the team there to await his signal before executing their plan for the arrest of Ashikaga.

The months of planning for this operation were about to be tested against one of the most devious criminal minds in Japan and Inspector Bando was being relied upon as the lynchpin between the British MI6 agents and the Japanese NPA. Ashikaga had managed to evade prosecution on many occasions in the past, and to prevent that occurring again each finite detail required meticulous attention to ensure success. Inspector Bando concluded his conversation with the senior officer at the NPA and headed off to the airport.

The flight from Heathrow was just landing as Inspector Bando arrived at the airport terminal. He made his way to the arrivals and waited for the three agents and Michael to clear airport security.

Michael and the three agents disembarked the plane and made their way through the baggage reclaim and onwards to meet up with Inspector Bando. Inspector Bando watched as Michael and the three agents approached after a quick passage through customs. Michael's facial expression quickly changed from one of calm and collected, to one of shock and disbelief.

"Michael, I believe you have met Inspector Bando before?" Captain McDermott introduced Michael to the inspector.

"What the hell is he doing here? He sold me out the last time I had dealings with him, why is he here? I don't trust him," Michael vehemently protested immediately, while pointing his finger in Inspector Bando's face.

Captain McDermott walked across to where Inspector Bando was standing and shook hands with the inspector; they both embraced in a way that certainly confirmed Captain McDermott's trust in him. Michael was shocked with the captain's actions and stepped away when Inspector Bando offered him his hand to shake. Michael gave Inspector Bando a steely look and confronted the inspector.

"You were there that evening when I was attacked by Ashikaga's son."

Inspector Bando began to shake his head.

"I think you're mistaken, son, all that evening I was at the station. Don't question me, son, I'm on your side and the side of MI6 and the NPA. We have been after Ashikaga for years and finally with your help and May Lin's help, we are going to get close enough to obtain the evidence to put him away for good."

Michael was still not convinced and continued to stare at the inspector.

"I don't like this, Captain McDermott, I don't like it one bit."

"Relax, Michael, we know Inspector Bando as well as we know May Lin, they are first class agents who know exactly how to play their parts, so leave it, okay?"

Michael pulled away from the group while everyone got reacquainted; he looked stupid after questioning Inspector Bando when he could clearly see how much Captain McDermott and the inspector knew and trusted one and other. He began to doubt his own judgement and moved even further away from the group to avoid embarrassing himself further.

Agent James noticed Michael standing alone and away from the rest of the team; he walked over to talk with him.

"Let's go, Michael." Agent James put his arm around Michael's shoulder and guided him towards the exit of the airport.

"Because of your size and maturity, we forget how young you actually are, and that often means that you are naive in some of these situations. Grab your gear and let's get ourselves prepared for this afternoon; it's important we know our plan and we stick to it."

Michael walked out with Agent James under some duress as they followed Inspector Bando. Michael remained well behind Inspector Bando as all four of them made their way out of arrivals and towards the airport car park. They arrived at a white long wheelbase *Land Rover* parked across the road from the airport exit. The *Land Rover* had a V8 engine and wider than normal tyres, it also had blacked out windows which Captain McDermott insisted on. It was the type of vehicle the team were comfortable about using during these operations because of their reliability and suitability for carrying them and their kit, the organisation of which took place back in London before they left for Japan. Captain McDermott and his team loaded all their gear into the back of the *Land Rover* and climbed inside. Michael placed his holdall in the rear of the vehicle, all the while avoiding any eye contact with Inspector Bando. He climbed in the back and was making his way to the rear seats of the vehicle, he was sitting down close to where all the equipment was stored when Captain McDermott stopped him.

"Michael, would you sit up front in the passenger seat alongside Inspector Bando who is driving, those rear seats where you're about to sit are needed by Agents James and Carson."

Michael directed an indignant look towards Captain McDermott and could not understand why the captain had insisted he sit there. Michael duly obliged with his request nevertheless, and climbed into the passenger seat. Michael turned his head left towards the side window and did not look in the direction of the inspector who was already sat at the wheel with the engine idling.

"I know you have your doubts about me, Michael, but I can assure you that I am here to help you and May Lin and most of all to help with bringing Ashikaga down. Nonetheless, I do not underestimate what you and May Lin are sacrificing to secure evidence and how this will enable his prosecution and hopefully put him away for life."

Michael remained silent and sat staring out of the window. He preferred to remain quiet to keep the peace.

Agents James and Carson were now deep in discussion in the rear seats of the vehicle; they sat at the back, allowing them to clean their weapons in preparation for the operation. Michael watched through the rear mirror of the car as they assembled and disassembled their weapons and meticulously cleaned them over and over again. He continued to watch the activity in the rear of the vehicle as Captain McDermott approached. Michael noticed Inspector Bando watching Captain McDermott getting into the back. Michael observed how nervous he was, constantly gripping the gear stick with his fist, grasping and releasing, the way a bird of prey would with its talons when choking its kill. Sweat was forming on his brow and his chest heaved quicker as his breathing rate increased.

"What is it, Inspector? Why so nervous?" asked Michael.

"I always get nervous at the beginning of an operation," the inspector replied in a bellicose manner.

"I hope that aggressive attitude is directed towards Ashikaga's men and not us."

"I am here to see that we remove Ashikaga and that is what I am focused on."

"Is that the same way as you intended to have me removed at the ryokan?"

Inspector Bando quickly reached across and grabbed Michael's chest with both hands and pulled him towards the driver's side of the vehicle.

"I have had enough of your false accusations and derogatory remarks, you need to understand…"

Before the inspector could finish his words, Michael removed both of his hands from his chest with two upwardly directed elbows and was already transforming the inspector's grip into a hold of his own on either side of the inspector's shoulders. As quick as the inspector had grabbed him Michael landed his head square onto the inspector's nose propelling him backwards with only the driver's side window preventing him from being expelled from the vehicle.

"For fuck's sake will you two stop it? We are about to embark on an operation where everyone needs to be on their mettle and you two are at each other's throats. We are leaving in one minute, but that won't happen until you two put this behind you," Captain McDermott shouted.

"He's broken my fucking nose, the ugly shit."

"You're lucky that's all I broke," Michael snidely replied.

Captain McDermott yelled again,

"Enough! That's enough, drive on, Inspector please. Michael keep quiet and stay out of Inspector Bando's space.

"Await my signal, Inspector, when I tap you on the shoulder I need you to pull off the road to allow us to do our final weapons check."

The inspector started the vehicle and they set off to the meeting point at the Meiji shrine.

Michael turned to his left side and stared out of the window again, he continued to stay that way for the rest of the journey as they made their way to their destination. The car was now moving at pace through the centre of Tokyo and getting closer to the rendezvous point at the shrine. The dark overcast clouds which could be seen through the windscreen at the front of the car were growing ever closer and were threatening heavy rain, undeterred, the team continued to make progress towards their destination. A solitary splash of rain landed in the middle of the screen, prompting Michael to turn round, another huge raindrop cascaded onto the windscreen, then another drop and another, until the dark grey sky completely engulfed the car. The noise of the downpour was similar to that of a mistuned radio that is mistakenly switched on while it is still turned to full on the volume button. The noise made any discussion taking place within the car barely audible to those trying to listen.

Captain McDermott waved his hand at Inspector Bando to attract his attention, he did this because speaking to anyone in the front of the vehicle was futile while the rain storm continued. He gestured to the inspector to pull over at the next layby. At the top of his voice he shouted his command.

"This is the point for the final check, everyone check their weapons and monitoring equipment!"

Michael sat watching as Agents James and Carson again gave their equipment the once over; he also observed Captain McDermott lifting his 9mm pistol and checking it too. Michael turned from observing what was happening behind him and looked to the front to observe Inspector Bando making his final preparations. He was very nervous sitting next to Inspector Bando while the inspector carried a loaded gun. He watched intensely, not looking away from Inspector Bando for one moment. The inspector continued to grip his gun ever so tightly and point the weapon towards the foot well of the car with a face of determined concentration. Each time he checked his equipment Michael watched, and each time the inspector glanced across at Michael, Michael remained transfixed on the inspector. Inspector Bando turned to face him.

"If you are watching me because you don't trust me then..."

His words were stopped by the clump of bloody flesh that was expelled through his open mouth and straight out of a punctured hole in the windscreen;

the spray of blood was vast within the car and covered the whole of Michael's face.

"Shit! We're being shot at, get out of the car," Michael shouted, and immediately tried to open the passenger side door. He was prevented from doing so by a man's shoulder charging the door from outside and trapping him in the car. Michael turned behind him shouting at Captain McDermott,

"We're under attack, what are…" Michael was shocked at what he witnessed as he turned to shout for help from Captain McDermott. The captain was firing multiple rounds into the bodies of Agents James and Carson while they sat helpless and unarmed behind him.

Within seconds Captain McDermott had blown the back of Inspector Bando's head off and dispersed the insides of his skull all around the front of the vehicle; he had then turned around and emptied a full magazine of bullets into Agents James and Carson, killing them instantly. Michael was completely disorientated and shocked by the vicious and brutal attack, and was expecting to be dealt the same fate at any moment. A loud clunking sound preceded the driver's side door being yanked open on the car, a man reached inside, grabbed Inspector Bando's body, pulled it out from the seat and threw it down on the roadside, where it splashed into running rainwater which was gushing along the kerbside. The rainwater washed under the car and carried the dark red bouquet of blood from the inspector's head all the way down the street, the river of blood resembled the blood running from a slaughtered animal in an abattoir. Two more men jumped into the *Land Rover* at the back and pulled the two dead agents from the vehicle, disposing of them in the same disrespectful fashion. The three men then entered the vehicle. The man in the front asked Michael a question.

"Are you Michael Harris?"

"Yes, why?" Michael tentatively replied while still in shock.

"Because I am taking you to the Meiji shrine, someone there wants to see you."

The man passed a briefcase to Captain McDermott; he asked for the document in his possession and then asked him to leave the vehicle immediately. Captain McDermott received the briefcase, checked the contents and handed over the covenant before turning to exit the car. An air of eerie silence fell on the inside of the vehicle as the captain opened the door in preparation to exit. Michael stared at the captain with a look that would fry a man's skin.

"If I ever get out of this, I will track you down, wherever you are and I will show you the same mercy you showed these men." Michael spoke with a venomous hatred in his voice.

"Ha, you won't be getting out of this, son, not when Ashikaga gets his hands on you. You and May Lin will be fed to his dogs. This money will help me disappear to a tropical island where I will live the rest of my years in luxury, and while you are being chopped up by Ashikaga's sword, I will be in first class on a plane, dreaming about the moment I am sitting on a deck chair with my feet swinging in a turquoise coloured sea, I will not give you a thought while I sip a glass of Bollinger in the sun, not a thought."

Captain McDermott pulled on the handle of the car door; he placed his other hand on Michael's shoulder and turned to exit the car.

"Bad luck, schoolboy, give my regards to May Lin." The car door crashed shut and Captain McDermott was gone.

CHAPTER 36

"Ashikaga has instructed me to make sure that you wear this." Kobyashi threw a red and black kimono on the floor of the room where May Lin lay tightly curled up in a ball.

May Lin knew before she lifted her head that she would see Kobyashi standing over her, his after shave was so distinct and pungent that it announced his presence before he arrived in a room. Always immaculately attired, he stood with his grey silk jacket swung over his shoulder and his flared suit trousers tightly clinging to his thighs and fanning out over his shiny black shoes. His white open necked shirt was folded back at the cuffs revealing his huge forearms, which he used to allow May Lin to pull herself up. He dragged a wooden chair into the room from the corridor, and pointed to it as an instruction for May Lin to sit on it.

"You two, outside."

Kobyashi flicked his thumb over his shoulder and the two guards scampered out of the door. He reached inside his pocket and pulled out a key, he opened a door to a bathroom in the adjacent room. He pointed to the bathroom.

"In there and get cleaned up."

May Lin stood up from the chair and walked towards the kimono on the floor.

"Leave that there, you will get dressed in here when you are clean."

May Lin did not answer back and continued with her subjugate actions as a way of placating Kobyashi. She knew that provocation could result in a painful experience for her.

"Do I get a towel to dry with?"

Kobyashi looked in the bathroom and then out into the corridor.

"It appears not."

Rather than trying to defy Kobyashi, May Lin made her way into the bathroom and then turned around to close the door.

"Leave it open," Kobyashi instructed. "We wouldn't want you disappearing would we?"

Once in the bathroom she started to undress; she turned to face the open door and expected to see Kobyashi watching her, but to her surprise he was gone.

May Lin finished cleaning herself, picked up her dirty clothes, clutching them in front of her and made her way out of the bathroom into the room where she had been held captive, and there sat on the chair was Kobyashi holding a towel.

"Give me those old clothes and I will get rid of them; get dried." Kobyashi handed May Lin the towel and exchanged it for her old clothes. As she reached out for the towel he trailed his eyes up and down her svelte naked body.

"Why do you look at me like you desire me, yet you treat me so badly?"

May Lin had no sooner uttered the words when she wished she had not spoken, she feared a reprisal. She was astonished at his response.

"Have I treated you badly?"

"I have been locked up in this room for weeks, I have been beaten and fed scraps and…" Kobyashi quickly reminded May Lin that he was in charge and not to forget her place.

"If I had treated you badly, you would not be alive, Ashikaga has dealt out the punishment to you, and Ashikaga has kept you alive as a way of getting at the boy, your treatment is Ashikaga's doing, I merely follow his instructions."

"But why? You are a man of honour, why…"

"Silence! That's enough, put the dress on now." Kobyashi stopped May Lin from mentioning anything else that might shroud his judgement, and made it clear that no more questioning of his actions was allowed.

She continued putting on the kimono, he continued to watch.

"Why have you fastened it with the right side over the left?" Kobyashi enquired..

She paused before answering and gazed a sorrowful look into his eyes.

"Because I know that Ashikaga will be intending to bury me in this dress, that's why he asked you to insist I wore it, for burial the kimono is folded with the right side…"

"I know what it means, I'm not a fool, turn around."

Kobyashi was disturbed by May Lin's candour in the description of the wearing of the kimono and preferred not to be looking her in the eyes following that description.

"Since you have insisted that I turn away, would you please fasten the Obi to my back and then I am ready for Ashikaga?" She stood with her back to Kobyashi, quietly waiting for him to approach. The first she knew of him standing behind her was when his hands gently rested on her curved waist. He gently tugged the kimono down at the sides to ensure it sat neatly around her hips. The kimono fitted her perfectly and despite not having make-up on, May Lin still looked alluring and innocently attractive. He lifted her hair out from inside her kimono near her neck and straightened it with his hands; he then proceeded to carefully fasten her Obi at the rear of her kimono. The outfit looked like it had been specially made for her, with every inch of it hugging every curve of her petite figure. Kobyashi gripped firmly on her hips and turned her around to face him: he could not stop staring at her in the kimono. The reputation of this tough Yakuza was melting away with the presence of her aura peeling back the layers of his tough outer shell.

"You can stop all this, Kobyashi if you really..."

"Quiet. Who gave you permission to speak?" Kobyashi soon allayed any hope May Lin had of breaking in to his softer insides through potential chinks in his armour. And just to confirm where his loyalties lay, he pulled her to one side and sat her on the chair in the centre of the room, telling her to remain seated until he entered the room once more.

Kobyashi swiftly returned with a box in his hands which he handed to May Lin. Inside the box was the make-up essential for putting the finishing touches to any kimono outfit. He instructed her to take the make-up into the bathroom to use, and he would return to collect her shortly. The guards returned to the room on his departure and watched May Lin prepare herself for the fate that awaited her.

Once she was finished in the bathroom, she made her way back to the room and took her seat on the chair; she sat facing the door. Her appearance was accentuated by her upright posture and resembled a porcelain doll in a toy shop window. She sat patiently waiting for Kobyashi to return. Sadly, she was awaiting execution by her tyrannical captor and not to be purchased for a play thing by a passing child.

She sat quietly and forlorn with only the guards at her side to witness her isolation, isolation she had become accustomed to all the while she was being held by Ashikaga. The solitude was foreboding, but dressing in attire to ready oneself for death was breaking her resolve. A tear meandered its way from her tear duct, seeking its way down her cheek and through the white make-up on her face, cutting a channel as it descended, readying itself to drop onto her kimono. As it fell to her thigh, the brightly coloured kimono was impregnated with a white blemish the same way a descending asteroid would pound out a crater in a desert. Just as the teardrop made contact with the fabric, Kobyashi returned.

"Guard, bring me a handkerchief," Kobyashi instructed.

The guard scuttled away to the bathroom, returning with a white handkerchief. Kobyashi meticulously wiped the stain from May Lin's kimono and carefully wiped the area on her face to leave no trace of a tear. His warped sense of honour would not accept her any other way than perfect.

"You are ready to present to Ashikaga, stand up and follow me." Kobyashi turned about and prepared to walk towards the exit. Before he did so, May Lin moved her hand and placed it inside the palm of Kobyashi's hand, squeezing it tight. He turned to look down at his side; he was too surprised to speak, seeing her tiny hand clutching his was a shock. Her hand was trembling. He looked directly into her eyes before composing himself to speak.

"Uphold your honour and dignity and your mind will overcome the fear."

She was instantly lifted by his words, not only because they were words of encouragement, but because they were words making a warped connection from him to her.

"Follow me and keep your head bowed when we enter his room."

She nodded in acknowledgement and followed him into the corridor towards Ashikaga's room. His office door was wide open, and as Kobyashi and May Lin neared the door, the sound of choristers resonated from the room and along the corridor. It was the music of Samuel Barber and Adagio for strings for the choral arrangement of Agnus Dei: Ashikaga was playing the music in his room. The chorister voices were ringing out eerily from the room the way they would in a cathedral during an evening mass.

Kobyashi and May Lin made their way inside and were now standing two feet in front of Ashikaga's desk. Ashikaga was facing out towards the window.

"I can smell that the whore has arrived," Ashikaga said while continuing to stare out the window. His two dogs were sat to his front anticipating their next instruction; neither of them moved when Kobyashi and May Lin entered the room. The dogs' eyes did not deviate from their intense stare towards Ashikaga. Kobyashi gestured towards May Lin to kneel and look down to the floor. For a few minutes the room thronged with the sounds of the choristers' voices. Ashikaga spoke with a malicious tone while still continuing to gaze out over his garden.

"We are taking you to the Meiji shrine in Tokyo, where two of my best men will present your murdering boy to me, but before we do, I will finish listening to this fine piece of music."

On finishing his words Ashikaga turned towards May Lin to gauge her reaction. Her head was still sloped forward without movement.

"Oh, and don't build your hopes up that the knights in shining armour are coming to rescue you. Inspector Bando and his MI6 accomplices are dead and your trusted Captain McDermott is now on his way to the Bahamas to dip his feet in the cool blue ocean, courtesy of the very generous Japanese Yakuza."

May Lin's head raised slowly from her bowed position; her face was revealed to Ashikaga. Her eyes were wide open with shock and her shaking hands were clasped together. Ashikaga watched as she started shaking uncontrollably throughout her body: Ashikaga's words hit a nerve with her and he knew it. He looked down at her concealing a sneering grin.

"You didn't for one minute think you could get one over me did you? A mere whore like you, deceive a Shogun like me?" Ashikaga scowled smugly.

He promptly moved closer to May Lin to gauge her reaction. He placed his face inches from hers, before speaking again.

"Apparently Inspector Bando's brains are still wedged in the hole in the windscreen, the hole that was made by the bullet fired through his deceitful skull."

May Lin looked straight into Ashikaga's eyes, her eyes filled with rage. She surreptitiously raised herself up from the ground, preparing herself to lunge at him, but before she moved an inch, his dogs lurched forward, placing themselves between her and their master.

"Did you learn nothing while you were supposedly working for me? It seems you have forgotten how utterly devoted these two dogs are to their master. Something you could never achieve with your deceit and your duplicitous ways. One more threatening move from you and they will rip that kimono from your body before you can blink."

May Lin slumped back to the ground completely dejected and feeling ridiculed by the whole affair.

"Back to your corner." Ashikaga instructed his dogs to return to their corner on the other side of the room, which they promptly obeyed.

"Bring the car to the front, Kobyashi, and we will head off to the shrine to meet up with Hamaguchi and Yoshiro. Ask the others to follow, but to wait outside the shrine; sit her in the back with you and keep a close eye on her."

"Yes, Ashikaga san."

Kobyashi lifted May Lin to her feet and proceeded to walk her out of the room.

May Lin looked back towards Ashikaga and shouted,

"There will be back up coming, eventually they will get you, you can't evade capture forever."

Kobyashi continued to remove her from the room and Ashikaga continued to listen to his music, completely ignoring the comments made by May Lin. All that concerned him now was how long it would take for his car to arrive and how long it would be before he could avenge the murder of his son.

CHAPTER 37

When Hamaguchi and Yoshiro arrived at the Meiji shrine with Michael it was still raining profusely and the sky remained black with water laden rain clouds. Hamaguchi and Yoshiro pulled Michael from the *Land Rover* and escorted him up the path leading to the entrance to the shrine. The trees that lined the pathway were bending with the force of the wind and scattering their gathered rainwater in clumps upon the path, the dispersal was more like the jettisoned water from the spout of a hosepipe than a down pouring of rain. Due to the excessive amounts of rainwater the pathway was becoming flooded in patches on the route to the centre of the shrine: Michael was wet through to his skin as his *Adidas* tracksuit top was no defence against the deluge and his training shoes were taking in water from the flooded path. Hamaguchi and Yoshiro were wearing suits and were closing their jackets to prevent the water penetrating their shirts underneath. Michael watched how they became distracted by the rain and wind as it blew into their faces, unfortunately for Michael, they weren't distracted enough to take their eyes off him and they regularly grasped their swords to prod Michael in the back as a reminder to him to keep moving, or discover how sharp their blades truly were. Michael continued to follow the path through a tunnel of trees that lined the access to the main area of the shrine.

"Is this where I am meeting Ashikaga Yoshimitsu?" Michael tentatively asked.

Neither Hamaguchi nor Yoshiro answered Michael's question.

Under the watchful eyes of Ashikaga's henchmen, Michael climbed the steps to the main praying area of the shrine and entered the main hall. Inside the hall was a grand wooden roof structure with huge exposed beams spanning from side to side within the walls; these beams supported an enormous vaulted ceiling with windows wrapped inside within a circle that stretched from the bottom to the apex of the vaulted ceiling itself. Hanging from the centre of the ceiling was a huge silk flag. On the flag was written the word 'Muromachi', and the numbers 1333 to 1568. Following this was Ashikaga Yoshimitsu's name with a seal matching Michael's once possessed covenant below it. Under this seal was written a statement. *The Daimyo has a right to conquer and control all that he covets with such force required that is deemed necessary to maintain his birthright as described in the historical covenant.* Michael walked closer to the flag, it was only at that point that he realised that his captors had disappeared; he was left on his own within the huge, chillingly cold and silent hall. The only sounds he could hear were that of the rain thrashing its way around on the roof outside and the howling wind whistling its way under the front entrance doors. He observed the primitively glazed windows struggling to prevent the rainwater from cascading down the inner walls of the shrine as the storm continued to bombard the building. In the centre of the hall on the old weathered mahogany floorboards were two chalk lines three feet long, these were drawn at a distance of around twelve feet apart; Michael recognised these marks as the starting points for two opponents in a fight.

A voice echoed from the rear of the hall.

"Take your place, boy."

Michael looked across the hall in the direction of the voice to observe a tall man with slicked back hair making his entrance into the hall. He was instructing Michael to stand on the chalk line. Michael observed his entrance with great trepidation, not really certain who it was. He was dressed in the full Samurai regalia, a black silk kimono with a dark blue hakama over the top. Michael continued to look across the hall to the door where this man had appeared; as the man moved closer, Michael recognised the message he was attempting to portray with his outfit. He suspected that he was trying to represent the seven virtues of the Bushido with his adorned attire and the calligraphy inscribed upon it. Michael assumed it was his way of immediately trying to intimidate him with his foreboding presence. He carried two swords, a wakizashi and a katana, both enclosed in their saya, one fastened to his side and one carried in his hand and held rigidly at arm's length in front of him. Barefooted, he slowly headed in Michael's direction. Michael watched as he walked from the entrance at the other side of the hall all the way across the floor towards Michael's position. Michael shouted across the hall in his direction.

"I suppose you are Ashikaga Yoshimitsu are you?"

"Well well well, you aren't that stupid after all; and here's me thinking that you must be a halfwit to travel all the way back to Japan with a botched up rescue plan and a priceless covenant that belongs to me in your possession."

Michael immediately felt threatened by Ashikaga's presence and unnerved that he was ridiculing him. Michael grew nervous of his intentions and the thought of standing so close to him, particularly after hearing from May Lin how brutal Ashikaga and his Yakuza could be. Each slow step brought him increasingly closer to Michael. As he approached, Michael could see that he was tall, but found himself still looking down at him. His slim build helped accentuate his height and with his hair being fastened behind his head he appeared taller than he actually was. As he continued to approach, Michael could easily see his eyes and the rage that burned inside them. The hand that was grasping the katana remained at the handle end of it and began to twist the katana so that the blade and the saya it was contained in were facing towards the ground. At the moment Ashikaga arrived at the chalk line opposite the place where Michael was standing, he raised his arm holding the katana from below his waist and hurtled the katana straight towards Michael's face.

Michael just noticed the katana flailing towards him as it left Ashikaga's hand; this allowed him just enough time to thrust out his hand and catch it midway up the saya. The impact of the katana pounding into his hand was sufficient to knock him off balance and send him stumbling backwards. After regaining his composure he stepped forward and found himself standing directly over the white chalk line. Ashikaga completed his last few steps and was also now standing directly over the other chalk line. Michael could see Ashikaga's wakizashi was still fastened to his side. On taking a closer look he observed that the wakizashi handle had a white dragon carved along the side in what resembled polished alabaster, this seemed to be intertwined with gold that intricately wrapped its way around the weapon in such a way as to provide grip on the handle. The saya also displayed the white dragons all the way to the end with the same gold edging which glistened in the light each time the wakizashi twisted at Ashikaga's side.

Michael was now standing twelve feet away from Ashikaga Yoshimitsu; the father of the son whom Michael had killed at the ryokan all those weeks before.

The only noise to be heard in this grand hall was the wind and rain whistling and howling outside. Ashikaga stood silent and stared at Michael. He waited patiently expecting an attack to come from Ashikaga at any moment. Still he waited, and Ashikaga did not move, if this was meant to unnerve Michael, it was working. Michael was gripping the handle of the katana tighter and tighter readying himself to fight. His thoughts were focused on unsheathing the katana and clashing blades with his opponent, the thought of injury or death were the furthest from his mind as he resolutely stood firm; and still Ashikaga just stood completely still, continuing to stare into Michael's eyes. Michael was suddenly drawn to the movement of Ashikaga's hands near to his wakizashi, Michael's muscles tensed in his wrist and forearm in preparation for moving his katana swiftly to meet an attack, but again this was not necessary as Ashikaga's hands appeared to move upward and away from his wakizashi. Ashikaga slowly raised his hands and clapped twice, leaving an echoing noise rebounding off all four walls of the hall. Michael was now not only surprised with Ashikaga's actions, but completely bewildered. With a distant creaking of an opening door, all became clear, from the far side of the hall appeared two figures. A man and a woman began walking towards Ashikaga and Michael's position.

"I have a surprise for you, boy, someone who has betrayed me is going to join us and witness me kill you the same way she witnessed you kill my son."

Michael looked across the hall and immediately recognised the silhouette.

"May Lin," Michael called out.

"That's correct, boy, the duplicitous whore that is May Lin. The scheming bitch who tried to infiltrate my people and bring your MI6 and the Japanese police to bear on me. But she forgot one very important fact, anyone can be bought if you have enough money, and I do. Your Captain McDermott is the perfect example of that." Michael's face showed the disgust of this betrayal.

"Yes that's right, Michael; your colleagues were killed for filthy Yakuza money."

Michael looked away from May Lin and turned to stare at Ashikaga.

"My father, my instructor and my friends were not killed for money. You massacred them."

Ashikaga's face twisted with a bitter distaste for Michael's words.

"They stole something that belonged to my family and I had every right to use whatever force deemed necessary to take it back."

"You ambushed them, they didn't stand a chance."

"Listen, boy, I do not need to justify my actions to you or anyone else, and now I have the covenant in my possession, I am the most powerful Shogun in Japan and what's more, all the Yakuza clans are under my control, no one can stand in my way."

"You're not a Shogun, you're nothing but a murdering gangster."

Ashikaga turned to look at May Lin and then turned to stare at Michael with an expression of defiance creased across his face.

"You have a filthy mouth, boy and I'm going to take great pleasure in shutting it up, and your complicit whore is going to sit here and watch me do it."

Kobyashi walked May Lin over to where Ashikaga and Michael were facing each other. Michael observed how beautiful May Lin looked in the kimono she was wearing. He quickly tried to connect with her by smiling, but May Lin just lowered her head looking very much dejected, she feared the inevitable.

She was instructed to kneel down on the floor and not to move by a stoic looking Kobyashi. She looked up at Michael with sorrow in her eyes. Before Michael could say a word, she turned to Ashikaga.

"Please spare Michael, take my life, but please spare his, he has done nothing wrong and he is only a boy."

Ashikaga turned towards May Lin and shouted,

"Only a boy! He murdered my son, and for that he will die. Fortunately for him, he is having the chance of an honourable death, which is more than he allowed my son."

"Your son was going to kill me, I just defended myself," Michael protested.

"Silence, I have heard enough. You have a katana, make ready." Ashikaga instructed Michael to prepare himself.

Ashikaga drew his wakizashi from its saya and grasped it with two hands in front of him, pointing it towards Michael. Michael looked across at May Lin, who kneeled with her back straight and her head perfectly still; she was doing as Kobyashi requested and holding her head high and keeping her dignity. This inspired Michael and he quickly drew his katana and prepared to fight Ashikaga.

Michael's eyes were transfixed on Ashikaga's as he awaited his move. He observed Ashikaga's toes tightening their grip on the floor, Michael anticipated an attack and Ashikaga did not disappoint, he dropped his blade to his right side and lunged forward towards Michael, swiftly lifting the wakizashi above his own head and thrusting it downwards towards Michael's head. As Michael blocked this attack with the edge of his blade, Ashikaga immediately swung the blade to the side and pulled his wakizashi in towards the side of Michael's stomach. Michael dropped his body backwards leaving himself off balance and just managed to block this attack with the outer edge of his katana, this prevented the blade from slicing into his abdomen. Just as he did so, Ashikaga's foot clattered into the side of Michael's head as he landed a roundhouse kick, propelling him downwards to the floor with a ringing in his ear. Michael managed to hold onto his katana as he collided with the hard wooden floor, but noticed how disorientated he was when he climbed to his feet. Without respite Ashikaga jumped forward wielding his wakizashi once again, this time the side swipe of the blade was heading towards Michael's neck, with Michael unsure of his footing he did not try to block this attack, but instead avoided the blade by ducking down out of the way, surprising Ashikaga in the process. Michael now found himself closer to Ashikaga than he expected and with Ashikaga over committed and off balance he was able to sweep his katana upwards underneath Ashikaga's right arm cutting him from the ribs up to his chest. Ashikaga exhaled a puff of air and stepped away from Michael, shocked that this boy had actually cut him. He seethed with anger after noticing the blood trickling down his arm and onto his wakizashi handle. Michael stiffened his grip on his katana and prepared for an onslaught from Ashikaga, and once again Ashikaga did not disappoint. His flailing wakizashi flashed and swooped, up and down towards Michael, side to side, downward, and upward; the attack was unrelenting, and all Michael could do was try to defend with any means possible. He was being pushed further and further back under such an intense attack from Ashikaga, and finally his defence faltered, he could not bring his katana around quick enough to stop Ashikaga's assault towards his head and in desperation he defended himself with his arm. Ashikaga drove his blade down hard, slicing it deep into Michael's forearm. Not content with wounding him once, Ashikaga took advantage of Michael's lack of concentration and pulled back his wakizashi in preparation for another attack. This time his wakizashi was swung round from Ashikaga's right side straight across Michael's abdomen, cutting the tip of the blade into his flesh. Blood instantly seeped through his top and dripped down onto the wooden floor beneath him. Michael placed his hand over his stomach and the blood slowly oozed through his fingers, and he fell to his knees. Ashikaga walked towards Michael, he removed the katana from his hand and flung it to the ground.

"People who betray me do not get the opportunity to die an honourable death like this; I remove their heads from their shoulders. You will now watch me do just that with May Lin before I finish with you."

Michael tried lifting his head to speak, but was close to passing out, he was losing copious amounts of blood.

"Bring May Lin to me," Ashikaga instructed Kobyashi.

May Lin was directed to walk to where Ashikaga was standing.

"Kneel down in front of me," Ashikaga instructed May Lin.

She dropped her head in preparation for what was to come as Michael cried out,

"Please don't do this."

"Be quiet, boy, I will get to you next."

Ashikaga raised his wakizashi above May Lin's head, and his blade flashed as the reflection from the outside light glanced the blade like a bolt of lightning. He dropped the blade down towards her neck. Michael closed his eyes in an attempt to block out the image of her being decapitated. He awaited the sound of flesh and bones being chopped as the blade sliced into her neck, knowing that he would be next, but to his surprise he heard the distinctive sound of steel clashing with steel. Michael opened his eyes and looked over towards Ashikaga. Standing right next to Ashikaga and May Lin was Kobyashi. He was gripping the handle of a katana and holding it in-between May Lin's neck and Ashikaga's extended wakizashi. Ashikaga thrust his head to his side glaring at Kobyashi.

"You imbecile, what do you think you are doing? Remove your blade at once."

Kobyashi was steadfast with his defiant stare towards Ashikaga.

"No, enough is enough; this is not the way of the Samurai, you dishonour us."

Ashikaga's aggressive glaring look turned to one of complete astonishment.

"How dare you defy me? I said remove your blade, I don't care about the honour of the Samurai, this is the way of the Yakuza."

Ashikaga's words brought the nearest thing to silence upon the hall, it seemed to last an eternity. In his dazed state, Michael noticed that the wind and rain had stopped and the distant sound of the rainwater dripping from the leaking window at the far side of the hall was all that could be heard. The dripping conjured up the sound of a clock and seemed to be ticking every second towards a crescendo, echoing its countdown around the hall and waiting for Kobyashi's response. Kobyashi was purposeful in his defiance and in the time it took from one drip of water to the next, he turned Ashikaga's wakizashi over and away from May Lin's head, forcing it in the direction of the floor.

"I said no and I mean no."

Ashikaga hurled his wakizashi up from the ground and flipped Kobyashi's katana over to its side, this allowed him to wield his blade towards Kobyashi's neck. This audacious move was an attempt to catch him unawares, but Kobyashi was a match for Ashikaga with a katana, and was already moving away from the attack and preparing his own. He dropped his body below Ashikaga's blade and spun around, thrusting his leg out backwards to sweep Ashikaga off his feet. The attack sent Ashikaga spinning into the air, but before he fell to the ground, Kobyashi released his katana in a rear sweep, slicing his blade across Ashikaga's stomach, producing a deafening sound like a cracked whip. The sound punctured the air around the hall. As Ashikaga landed on the floor, the collision created an expulsion of pain induced groaning normally associated with one of Ashikaga's unfortunate victims. Predictably, Ashikaga was a hardened campaigner and rolled out from his landing towards Kobyashi, still clutching his wakizashi. As he rose to his feet - his regalia stained with blood - he thrust his blade forward and pierced through Kobyashi's clothing into his chest, just missing his heart. As Ashikaga withdrew his blade from deep within his sternum, Kobyashi howled with the pain and staggered backwards disorientated by the resultant shock. Sensing his weakness, Ashikaga lifted his wakizashi above his head and raced forward in an attempt to drive his blade down between his collar bone and his neck. Kobyashi lifted his katana in an attempt to stop him, but Ashikaga was too quick and was beginning to drop his wakizashi onto his target before Kobyashi could defend himself. Once again the blade flashed a sparkling reflection of the penetrating sunlight as it cut through the air. Kobyashi feared the worst: just as he expected Ashikaga's wakizashi to slice through him, Ashikaga froze completely still. Kobyashi's attention was drawn to Ashikaga's stomach; a blade was protruding from the centre of his abdomen. Dark red blood slowly trailed its way to the apex of the blade, dripped off the end and splashed onto the wooden floor. Ashikaga exhaled a screech of breath and dropped to his knees. Standing behind him – grasping tightly with two hands to the handle of a katana – was May Lin, immaculately dressed in the formal attire Ashikaga had requested her to wear, the sunlight beaming down upon her white face. She was shaking, but continued to grip the katana tightly. Kobyashi looked towards her.

"Let go of the katana, May Lin."

She was entrenched in her action and remained grasping the handle of the katana. Kobyashi spoke louder.

"Please, May Lin, let go of the katana, it's over, he's... he's dead, Ashikaga is dead."

She released her grip, the katana handle whipped forward and came to a halt in an upright position as it followed the passage of Ashikaga's body towards the wooden floor. The katana handle and blade swayed from side to side as it remained lodged in Ashikaga's back while his body was face down against the ground. May Lin let out a cry of relief as she watched Ashikaga's body slowly release a pool of glistening blood onto the dusty mahogany floor. A groan from Kobyashi focused her mind on what was happening around her. She rushed to help him.

"How bad is your injury?" May Lin enquired.

"My wound is bad, but I'll live, don't worry about me, see to the boy." Kobyashi got to his feet, but grimaced as he did so.

"You're badly hurt aren't you?" Kobyashi grasped hold of May Lin's hand.

"Listen, I'm on my feet now, we need to see to the boy, I fear he may be worse off than I."

May Lin quickly turned around and ran over to Michael who was still lying on his side and appeared to have lost a lot of blood.

"Michael, can you hear me? Wake up, wake up, Michael."

Michael's eyes opened.

"I'm awake, I'm awake, what is it? What's happened?"

May Lin pulled Michael's clothing to one side revealing the cut in Michael's stomach.

"You passed out; you have lost a lot of blood, we need to see to your wound."

Michael looked at May Lin who was emboldened with a new spirit following Ashikaga's death.

"I was closing my eyes to stop the sun from blinding me, really, I'm okay."

May Lin refused to accept Michael's explanation and proceeded to tear strips from the kimono she was wearing to create bandages she could wrap around Michael's stomach.

"Keep your hand pressed firmly on this." May Lin directed Michael's hand towards the makeshift bandage. She fastened one after another together and wrapped them around Michael's stomach, covering the wound.

Michael pointed behind May Lin and shouted,

"Look out, behind you."

May Lin turned, only to discover it was Kobyashi coming to help.

"It's okay, it's Kobyashi, he is… he is… he's our friend."

Michael rubbed his eyes in disbelief.

"What? He was with Ashikaga."

"Yes, but he helped us by confronting and defeating Ashikaga."

"When?" Michael asked.

"I think you must be a little delirious, Michael, it's just happened in front of you, right now."

Michael watched May Lin finish tightening the bandage around his stomach, he clenched his hand around May Lin's arm and began to pull himself up.

"I think you should stay lying on the floor, Michael, we need to get you help."

Kobyashi stood to the side of Michael and held his other arm helping him to his feet.

"Let him get to his feet, he shows great courage and dignity, don't take that away from him."

Michael flinched from his other injuries as he got to his feet, but was determined not to let that stop him.

"I'm walking out of here the same way as I walked in, with my head held high."

Michael walked towards the exit heading past the prostrate Ashikaga as he did so. As he passed alongside his body he turned his head towards him with a look of disdain.

"Gi, yukki, jin, rei, makota, meiyo and chuugi, not much use to you now are they, Mr Yoshimitsu."

May Lin turned to Kobyashi with a jaded look on her face.

"What was all that about?"

Kobyashi spoke while pushing one of May Lin's bandages into his wound on his chest to slow the bleeding.

"Michael has recited the seven virtues of Bushido, in what I presume is his way of dishonouring and mocking what Ashikaga stood for."

"I can't say I blame him," May Lin replied.

Kobyashi pointed towards Michael heading towards the exit.

"I need him to stop where he is, before he heads outside I need to speak with Hamaguchi and Yoshiro and the rest of Ashikaga's men."

May Lin shouted for Michael to stop his march towards the door, to which he reluctantly obliged; this allowed Kobyashi to get to the exit to speak with Ashikaga's men prior to Michael leaving.

May Lin guided the still delirious Michael away from the exit and towards an old wooden bench pushed up against a drinking fountain inside the hall.

"Sit here, Michael while Kobyashi speaks with Ashikaga's men, he will get us safe passage away from here and we can get your injury looked at in hospital."

May Lin sat Michael down and carried a ladle of water to him from the fountain. He gave a terse reply to her suggestion.

"Look I'm fine, I don't need the hospital, I just want to walk out of here and make arrangements to get back to England."

May Lin held up her hands in acceptance of Michael's desires, but still believed he was not being rational in his decision making.

"That's fine, Michael, I understand." She placed her arm around his shoulder and helped him sip the water.

"You are a strong character who has been through…" May Lin watched as Michael dropped his head into his hands and hunched his body forward on the bench.

"What is it, Michael?"

"What is it?" Michael asked in disbelief.

"It's my shit life… First of all my father, the only person who knew me, is massacred along with my karate instructor and all my friends. I then inadvertently kill the son of a Yakuza while trying to defend you and I from being sliced in half, that psychotic Yakuza then sends his clan to retrieve a piece of fucking paper of dubious value and in the process almost kills a new friend of mine in the new life I try to start in England. But it doesn't end there; I then discover that I have a crazed Irish uncle who is a compulsive gambler who murders my mother. I'm then persuaded to help a captain in MI6 to infiltrate the very Yakuza that killed my father, only to discover that he is a double dealing bastard who has been bought off and is willing to wipe out his own men for a pot of money. Not to mention the fact that I lose my virginity to a woman who was actually shagging my father and apparently while he was still married to my mother. Other than that I suppose I'm fine really, bar a six-inch slash in my stomach and a gash in my arm."

Michael turned to await May Lin's response with a questioning look on his face. May Lin turned her head away from Michael trying to compose herself before answering.

"I'm not proud of what happened with your father, Michael, but if it's any consolation I loved…"

Michael lifted his arm in the air,

"Woah… I don't want to hear, I just want to head back to Sunderland to rebuild my life, but before I do I want to pay my respects to my father at his grave, so if you tell me where he is buried, that's where I'm heading."

Michael took a long drink of water from the ladle and then raised himself from the bench at the very moment that Kobyashi entered the hall with Hamaguchi and Yoshiro. They remained at the exit while Kobyashi spoke with May Lin and Michael.

"You have safe passage out of the shrine." Kobyashi put his hand on Michael's shoulder.

"If anyone asks, you killed Ashikaga Yoshimitsu and passed the covenant to me. The authority of the covenant will allow me to inherit all his business interests and any existing deals with other parties will be honoured."

Michael lifted Kobyashi's arm off his shoulder and let it drop by his side.

"So you are just going to step straight into his gangster shoes and carry on as if nothing happened?" Michael enquired in disbelief.

Kobyashi spoke with reticence in his tone.

"I will be more honourable than Ashikaga and bring about change that means as a Shogun I can co-operate with the police and the authorities and not create as much conflict."

Michael began to walk towards the exit shaking his head.

"Well I'm glad I won't be about to see it, I've witnessed your Yakuza co-operation first hand at Tokugawa's dojo, and quite frankly it stinks."

Kobyashi turned to May Lin to see her reaction to Michael's comments before preparing his response, but May Lin just shook her head at Kobyashi willing him not to reply.

Michael continued his walk towards the exit on his own.

"Your father is buried at the Shinjuku cemetery, Michael," May Lin shouted.

"Are we keeping in touch, Michael?"

Michael arrived at the exit and walked between Hamaguchi and Yoshiro, he pulled the door open, but before he walked through he turned to look at May Lin and replied,

"I need to visit a few people when I leave Japan, starting with a Patrick Finnan, so I think keeping in touch isn't going to be my immediate priority, but who knows?"

THE END

Lightning Source UK Ltd.
Milton Keynes UK
UKHW04f0816240818

327708UK00009B/58/P

9 781912 601233